"Do you mind if I ask you a favor?" Sarah said impulsively. "May I bring over a steak for you to grill for me?"

Sam shook his head, appearing as if he was trying hard not to laugh. "How do you know I'm up to your fine standards?" he teased.

She eyed the steaks he was putting onto a plate. "Because I know quality when I see it."

He barked out a laugh.

"And I was so determined not to like you." He shook his head as he set the plate down and sank into an Adirondack chair beside her. He laughed again.

"Excellent," she said cheerfully. "Let me go get the steak I bought." She rose. "I can bring over a salad for you and Lucy to share with me."

"Already taken care of. Plus, grilled corn on the cob will be coming later. But tell me." He leveled his gaze at her, suddenly serious. "Why should I even do this? All you seem to do is insult people, and frankly, I'm not up for that when it comes to my family."

"But...I apologized to you," Sarah said.

"Oh, boy!" He gave her a mock cheer.

"Look, I never apologize, Sam! Apologies admit weakness. So this is a first in the history of the world for me—be flattered."

"You're quite self-centered." Sam paused and grinned at her wickedly. "And I never insult people—be flattered."

Were they *flirting*?

Dear Reader,

Welcome to *Summer by the Sea*, a new Wallis Point, New Hampshire, story set in the fictional seaside town first described in *The Long Way Home* and continued with *The Secret Between Them* and *The Undercover Affair*.

Sarah Buckley is a driven type A tech entrepreneur who is at first enraged to be banished to a rustic beach cottage for a quiet summer sabbatical.

All Sarah wants is to return home to her busy Silicon Valley company, where she can continue her quest to conquer the tech world. First, though, she needs to prove that she's learned to relax and "become more Zen" in her relations with others.

So, is her beach neighbor Sam Logan, a laid-back lifeguard without any apparent life goals—and his genius eleven-year-old daughter, whose future he and Sarah conflict over—the person to teach her?

A summer by the sea can work wonders and heal any wounded hearts. I hope you enjoy Sarah and Sam's spark-filled romance!

All the best,

Cathryn Parry

CATHRYN PARRY

—

Summer by the Sea

HARLEQUIN® SUPERROMANCE®

Recycling programs
for this product may
not exist in your area.

ISBN-13: 978-1-335-44915-3

Summer by the Sea

Copyright © 2018 by Cathryn Parry

Printed in U.S.A.

HARLEQUIN®
www.Harlequin.com

Cathryn Parry is the author of ten Harlequin Superromances. Her books have received such honors as the Booksellers' Best Award, HOLT Medallion Awards of Merit and several Readers' Choice Award nominations. She lives in Massachusetts with her husband and their entertaining cat, Otis. Please see Cathryn's website, cathrynparry.com, for information about upcoming releases and to sign up for her reader newsletter.

Books by Cathryn Parry

HARLEQUIN SUPERROMANCE

The Undercover Affair
The Good Mom
The Secret Between Them
Secret Garden
Scotland for Christmas
The Sweetest Hours
Out of His League
The Long Way Home
Something to Prove

Other titles by this author available in ebook format.

For Megan Long. Every book that you edit you make better. Thank you for being a blessing in my life!

Acknowledgment

A special thank-you to Cape Cod lifeguard Sarah P. for answering my questions and teaching me about torps, rip currents and—in an unplanned encounter—how to treat a jellyfish sting.

CHAPTER ONE

SAM LOGAN'S SUMMER plans were turned upside-down in a single phone call.

Twenty-four hours later, his eleven-year-old daughter, Lucy, stood in his tiny bachelor kitchen, surrounded by her suitcase, her iPad, and a ragged and well-loved stuffed bear that he hadn't even known she still slept with.

Sam stared at it—and her—in shock. Seeing that teddy bear made him realize he really had no idea what was going on with his daughter. He felt completely inadequate to the task of being Lucy's full-time dad.

Ironic, considering Sam worked with kids her age every day. He taught environmental science to middle school students. Sam was known as a laid-back teacher. A guy who could handle whatever came his way without getting his feathers ruffled or ruffling feathers. It was his great strength, his inner Zen.

But the panic rose from deep in his chest and clutched at his throat, affecting his ability to breathe. This must be what swimmers felt like when they were caught up in a giant, sucking rip current.

Sam had never been caught in a rip current himself. As a professional lifeguard at Wallis Point beach in summer, he knew the signs and avoided the trap. A few times per season, he rescued people caught in the grip. He even taught the younger guards—college-aged men and women—to notice the signs so they could warn others, too.

Avoidance of danger had always been key in Sam's world.

Sam wiped sweaty palms on the back of his shorts. Lucy was here, sitting at his kitchen table, pushing her light brown hair from her eyes and staring at her luggage, probably as uncomfortable as he was. Her mother had decided to head to Alaska for the summer to work as a singer on a cruise ship, so Sam was now responsible for her. For ten long weeks. Alone. During lifeguard season.

Shaky, he wondered what he should do with her—feed her lunch, maybe? Usually she came to his house for two Saturday afternoons per month—had ever since she was a toddler—and before they left for whatever fun activity he'd planned that day, Lucy always sat and ate a peanut butter sandwich and drank an orange soda. That was their tradition.

So he opened his refrigerator door. No orange sodas. Instead, one whole shelf was filled with a batch of craft brew he'd made earlier in the week. He bent and felt past the beer bottles, finding two cold cans in the back of the fridge. "Luce," he said, straightening, "I'm out of orange soda. Would you like a ginger ale?"

His daughter regarded him stoically. "Yes, please. I'll make my own sandwich."

"Okay. Good." Feeling a little more hopeful, Sam popped the two cans open then passed her one. Without any drama, she stood, got a plate, bread, peanut butter and knife and began making lunch for herself.

He should calm down. He and Lucy would be fine—they could figure out this new arrangement as they went. He saw her often enough to know the basics of caring for her according to the rules Colleen had insisted upon since Lucy was a baby.

Sam had been blindsided when she'd been born. Though he and Colleen hadn't been together anymore and Sam had been a young father—just twenty-one at the time—he had coped. He would have preferred to see Lucy more often, but the lawyers had told him what was best for the three of them, and Sam had rolled with it. He would roll with it now.

He seated himself across from Lucy and took

a long drink of the almost medicinal-tasting ginger ale. Even if he had no idea what he was going to do with her for the next ten weeks—and he couldn't take Lucy to a movie or a museum or a theme park or even his brother's house near Boston every day, like he usually did when he had her—he wasn't going to freak out. Neither was he going to put the burden on Lucy. The situation wasn't her fault. Sam didn't want to be like his own parents and force inappropriate decisions on her the way they had with him and his brother when they were kids negotiating a difficult divorce.

Be Zen. Be detached. Stay cool.

That's what Sam had learned young. Dealing with other people's kids in the public school system reinforced the lesson for him daily. It was best to keep calm under pressure. Have non-emotional and non-threatening conversations. Use humor whenever possible.

Sam gave Lucy his easiest smile. "It's all good, Luce. There are worse places we could be stuck together for the summer, right?"

She gazed up at him with her serious brown eyes. "Maybe," she replied calmly. Then she went back to cutting her sandwich precisely in half with a serrated bread knife.

The most grown-up kid I've ever known, Sam's brother had once said. Sam had been proud of it at the time. But now he glanced at Lucy's teddy bear leaning forlornly against her adult-looking black luggage, and he wondered if there was more to her stoic behavior than was apparent on the surface.

Too bad he couldn't just let her be a free-range kid like he and his brother had been during their carefree, predivorce summers on the beach. But nowadays, the powers that be frowned on unsupervised kids, especially in a high-traffic tourist town. Even at eleven years old, Lucy needed somebody to watch her and be responsible for her. He worked as a lifeguard full time. What was he supposed to do?

Sam gazed over Lucy's head and out the window toward the seashore where he'd spent most of his life working and playing during the short-but-sweet New England summers. He loved his summers here. He would never live anywhere else. He liked waking up to the smell of salt water outside his bedroom window and the sounds of rolling waves and cawing seabirds. Beyond a long expanse of sand was the deep blue Atlantic Ocean, and all he had to do was stare at that horizon whenever he needed to find peace.

"Do you remember when you were little, and you used to sit up on the lifeguard chair with me?" Chair ten, right outside his window. It wasn't set out for the season yet, but it would be soon. "You used to love spending time on the beach."

Lucy stopped chewing and stared at him. "I can't sit on the beach with you while you're working, Sam."

Sam. That about killed him. He smiled anyway. "Yeah, I know. And I know this isn't what you had planned for your summer vacation, either, but don't worry, we'll figure it out and make it work for us."

He took another long drink from his ginger ale can. "Are there any day camps you might be interested in for the summer?" He figured he should ask—maybe she had something in mind that he didn't know about. As a local teacher, maybe he could use his connections to get her a last-minute slot. "Wallis Point has a swimming program and a sailing academy. Then there's always tennis lessons—"

"No, thank you, Sam."

He winced and glanced back at the beach. His friend Duke drove by on one of the two open-roof all-terrain vehicles that the Wallis Point lifeguards employed. During the school year, Duke was vice principal of the high school in town. In summer, Sam often drove with Duke on patrol. Today, though, was the day after classes had let out for the summer, and if not for Lucy,

Sam would have been flying out of Logan Airport for his yearly backpacking vacation before he started his lifeguard job. This year, trekking through Scotland for a week.

"I like the library," Lucy suddenly said.

Sam turned around. "The library, in summer?"

"Yes, please."

She really was a serious student. If he was honest with himself, he was worried about that. Lucy was eleven years old, and she didn't have fun easily. It occurred to him that she was a throwback to his own mother. That was the only conclusion Sam could come up with.

Lucy finished the last bite of her sandwich, so Sam reached for his sunglasses. He gave her another bright smile. "Okay, Luce. How about we take a walk on the beach and discuss this some more?"

"No, thank you. I'm going to see Cassandra," she said simply, and stood. Lucy never asked permission. She just did whatever the inner force inside her told her to do.

"Okay, sure," he said reasonably. Cassandra was Sam's next-door neighbor. Seventy-something and eccentric, she was a bona fide working artist—an internationally famous children's book illustrator. Lately, Lucy had taken to ending their Saturday visits with a stint at Cassandra's cottage. Sam hadn't interrupted them. The relationship was good for Lucy, he thought. Lucy seemed to love visiting Cassandra, and that was what mattered to him. Besides, a couple of hours every two weeks hadn't seemed as if it would be a burdensome interruption for his neighbor.

He leaned back, watching Lucy clear away her lunch dishes and load them neatly into his dishwasher. Lucy just did things like that. She was independent and capable, but there was no getting around it. *Somebody* needed to be here for her full time, and that somebody needed to be him.

And wasn't this his opportunity to get closer to her, scary as that seemed?

He slipped on his sunglasses and stood. He might ruffle feathers for what he was about to say, but... "I'll walk over with you. I need to see Cassandra, too."

Lucy looked him straight in the eyes and nodded. "Okay."

"Just so you know, if it's all right with Cassandra that you hang out with her a little more often than usual this summer, then it's cool with me."

"Good." Lucy seemed more animated and hopeful than she'd been when she first arrived. "Last time I saw her, Cassandra said she would be home today."

"Great." Sam opened the glass slider that led

to the porch. "Before we go over there, though, could I ask you something?"

Lucy slipped her hands into her jacket pockets as if bracing herself.

"We need to figure out something for, ah…" He didn't want to say "childcare," but that was the only word he could think of, so he swallowed his reticence. "Someone to take care of you. I, ah…" He took a breath. He'd never wanted to face this. And it pained him to say so, but he'd made a monumental decision. He was going to sacrifice something for her, his only child, that he'd never thought he could ever sacrifice for anybody. He needed to resign his lifeguard job. There really wasn't any other way out of it.

"Sam, I want Cassandra to watch me this summer."

He blinked in surprise. "Do you really think it's fair to ask Cassandra to do that?"

"We already discussed it, she and I." Lucy set her chin.

How was that possible? "Cassandra doesn't have a phone," he pointed out.

Lucy used the toe of her sneaker to outline the edge of his breakfast bar in the kitchen. "We talked about it the last time I was here."

He willed himself to breathe easily, in and out. He would not care. Would not get upset.

"You were here almost a week ago." Four days

before Colleen had called him. "We didn't know then that your mother was going to go off to Alaska for the summer." He'd tried to keep the sarcasm out of his voice, he really had.

"Mom knew she was going," Lucy said in a small voice.

"She told you?" he asked softly.

"No." Lucy shook her head vehemently. "I heard her on the phone with the cruise ship people."

"By accident?"

Lucy moved her wispy bangs to one side. "I listened on the extension because I thought it was a call from my teacher."

Okay, should he be concerned? With his students, he only rarely called their homes. Usually because there was a problem with the child. "Why do you think your teacher would be calling your mom?"

"That's not important," Lucy said.

Yeah, it was. And he was going to lose his patience if he wasn't careful. "Okay. We'll go see Cassandra," he said simply.

He grabbed his windbreaker from a hook and put on a ball cap. They stepped through the sliding door onto his deck overlooking the beach. In mid-June, it was windy and cool. Cassandra's cottage was only about twenty yards away, but despite the nearness, they didn't talk often. They usually just waved when they saw each other. Most days, he caught glimpses of her working on her paintings. A bit of a bohemian, the lady often dressed in Indonesian batik and straw hats. She smoked imported cigarettes that smelled like clove and cinnamon spices, and she seemed more detached and easygoing than even he was. Every now and then she stopped by Sam's house parties in summer, and nothing seemed to faze her. Yet she didn't seem irresponsible. She taught art classes to teens regularly at the local library, and she was a popular teacher.

Lucy adored her.

She always had. The first time Lucy had toddled over to greet Cassandra, she'd been three, and Cassandra had given her an ice pop and let her play with her paint brushes. His serious, stoic daughter had been hooked on the woman ever since.

They walked through the beach sand together, he and Lucy. When she was little, he'd held her hand, but now that she was older, they didn't do that.

When they got to Cassandra's door, Lucy gave a small, hesitant knock on the glass.

Cassandra answered immediately. She radiated "earth mother" authority, her billowing, colorful pants as bright as her smile. Reading glasses sat atop her head of white-gray hair, and in her right hand was a cane—solid metal of some type and vividly purple.

"Come in, come in." She opened the door wider, smiling broadly at his daughter. "Welcome, Lucy." Then Cassandra looked directly into Sam's eyes. "You've brought your father with you this time. That's good."

Sam nodded to his neighbor. "Good to see you, Cassandra. I don't mention it often enough, but thanks for everything you've done to help Lucy over the years."

"I enjoy her company very much."

He glanced over to find that Lucy had taken up a perch in a vintage, lime-colored beanbag chair. A small black-and-white tuxedo cat wandered over to investigate her on silent cat feet. Lucy scooped him up into her lap and pressed him to her cheek.

Yet again, Sam was taken aback. Lucy had never been cuddly with him. Other than the worn teddy bear he'd been surprised to see in her luggage, he hadn't realized she had this side to her.

Cassandra shuffled over to her kitchen and bustled with a plastic grocery bag on the counter. The front half of the cottage was one big room—a combination art studio/library/kitchenette and seating area. A stereo on one of the shelves played a jazz song from the thirties or forties, sung by a woman with an emotional, raspy voice. Sam felt unsettled by the unfamiliar environment and the strange new revelations his daughter had given him.

Cassandra brought over a snack for Lucy.

"Blueberry cake!" Lucy said, excited.

Sam remained standing, not sure what to say.

"Cassandra gave me *The Witch of Blackbird Pond* to read," Lucy told him, her tone serious again. As she contemplated him, that studious look came over her and she turned silent once more.

He instinctively touched the doorjamb. "What's *The Witch of Blackbird Pond*?" he asked Cassandra.

Cassandra smiled at Lucy. "Shall you explain the story to your dad, or should I?"

"It's an old story," Lucy said, settling the plate on a table beside her. "It's a novel about a teen who has to travel to a new place in the 1600s, and it isn't anything like what she's used to, and she gets upset because she doesn't fit in. So she runs away and meets a kindly Quaker lady who lives by herself on a pond, and she takes her in and feeds her blueberry cake and lets her play with a kitten every time she comes to visit."

He just stared at Lucy. "So you're saying you're upset when you come to see me, and that every time you visit Cassandra's you eat blueberry cake and play with a kitten?"

She rolled her eyes. "No. It's not literal, Sam."

But there had to be some truth to it. And Cassandra appeared to be watching him closely. He wasn't sure he liked the scrutiny.

It bothered him that his neighbor seemed to know more about his daughter than he did.

But he shook the feeling off. Decided to get right to it. Giving Cassandra his charming smile, the one that usually got him places with women, he said, "Lucy's mom is going to be away for the summer. It looks like she's going to be staying with me for a couple months."

"Yes, I heard that from Lucy last week," Cassandra said noncommittally. "You must be very excited."

The back of his neck tightened. He'd momentarily forgotten that his neighbor had known about the change of plans before he had.

But he kept smiling. Folding his arms, he said quietly to Cassandra, "I *am* excited that she's here. In fact, I'm resigning as a lifeguard supervisor in order to spend as much time as possible with Lucy."

As he said it, he knew it was the right thing. Years ago, he'd never expected he would one day have the privilege of living with his only child. Maybe this summer was a gift to him.

But evidently, Lucy didn't think so. Her face drooped as if he'd dropped a depressing bit of news on her. He felt his own sadness in the hollow of his breastbone.

Outside, the new lifeguard recruits were being drilled. Wind sprints.

Cassandra took her cane and thumped her way across the room. Picked up a paintbrush from a jar on the table. Based on the chemicals and rags spread on a piece of newspaper, she appeared to have been cleaning her painting implements when he and Lucy interrupted her.

Lucy was gazing down at the cat in her lap, stroking his black fur, saying nothing.

It hit Sam, all at once, that while he'd thought he and Lucy were doing okay together all this time, they really weren't. Lucy was as remote and detached from him as anybody he'd ever known.

He'd lived this way for years. On the surface, he welcomed his daughter to his home two Saturdays a month. They did something interesting and fun together—a movie, a trip to a marine wildlife reserve or a museum, a visit to his brother's house where she played with her two cousins' electronic toys to her heart's content.

But always she ended the visit at Cassandra's cottage. He'd considered Cassandra a warm grandmother figure to Lucy, filling a role that was missing in Lucy's life, but it was becoming clear to him that Cassandra had been more to her than he'd realized.

Cassandra connected with Lucy. He didn't.

He was a piece that didn't fit in Lucy's story. And he didn't want that to be true any longer.

He glanced back at Cassandra and caught her studying him. She relinquished the brushes and slowly made her way back toward him. *Thump, thump, thump.*

"Isn't this usually the week that you take a backpacking vacation?" Cassandra asked him softly. "School got out yesterday."

"It did." He tried to keep the bitterness from his voice. "And I cancelled the trip yesterday."

"Because Lucy needs you." Cassandra said it as a statement and not a question, and he gave her a short nod. He wasn't even attempting the charming smile anymore.

"Where were you going this year?" Cassandra's voice was very low, meant as a conversation between two adults, with Lucy left out of it.

He frowned. "To Scotland. Hiking."

"Ah, with the Scottish lassies." She exhaled.

The older woman couldn't know. Nobody did. It was his own personal secret. The day after school let out, every year, Sam chose a different place in the world to escape to, alone. Someplace interesting to him. And there, wherever "there" was, he nearly always met a woman, though they never exchanged last names. For a week they would get closer, and it was intimate, yet anonymous. That vacation lasted him for a year. For the other three hundred and forty-odd days, he lived his life separate, detached, not really opening himself to anybody. Not even, he realized now, his own daughter.

"This is a small town," he said to Cassandra, falling back on his old excuse. "A bad idea for a single male teacher to…" *To date, and therefore to provide gossip for the mill*, he was going to say. But he didn't want to get into it in front of Lucy.

"Hmm." Cassandra left it at that. "Your job is very important to you," she finally said.

He shrugged. Honestly, teaching was interesting and it was a paycheck. That was about it.

Cassandra glanced sharply at him as if reading his mind. "I meant being a lifeguard."

He blinked. It was true, he looked forward to his lifeguard job all year. He liked the keeping-people-safe aspect of it. He liked sitting in his chair, looking out over the ocean and feeling calm and at peace with the world.

"Well, yes, it's a good job. But my daughter is more important to me. I'll take care of her, Cassandra, you don't have to worry about her being here all the time while you have work to do."

"Please, Dad!" Lucy interrupted. "I don't want you to quit your lifeguard job to take care of me!"

She'd called him Dad, not Sam.

He felt himself grinning like a fool.

"Cassandra says you're really good at what you do." Lucy continued. "She says you're the only lifeguard trainer she's ever seen who teaches the lifeguards how to meditate to stay calm. And you show them the best way to return lost children to their parents. And…to defuse tense situations."

That was the most Lucy had said to him in a long time, and Cassandra smiled sheepishly at him. "Your lifeguard station is right in the line of sight of my workspace. I've been listening to you lead morning training sessions for years."

Cassandra had obviously been talking him up to his daughter, and he appreciated that. "Thank you, Cassandra," he said quietly.

She folded her hands and slid a sideways look at him. "I wonder if you could do a favor for me this summer."

"Oh?" He felt his smile tightening.

"It's nothing to worry about," Cassandra hastened to explain. "I have a young houseguest coming here from the West Coast, on sabbatical from her demanding job. She's looking for someone to tutor her in meditation. I wonder if you could teach her some techniques?"

He almost burst out laughing. He would just bet this "young houseguest" was single, a sweet young thing, and Cassandra was attempting to fix him up. He was thirty-two and unattached, and his fellow teachers tended to do that to him, too. Cassandra he couldn't get mad at because she was Lucy's friend. Plus, he could see the irony in her request.

Cassandra noted his amused expression and tsk-tsked him. "You know how important meditation is, Sam. Sarah asked me to find her a class, and I thought of you. I never saw anyone teach neophytes at work like that until you came along. The other lifeguard supervisors scream at the recruits and blow their whistles. *Run, swim, practice mouth-to-mouth resuscitation.*"

"Mouth-to-mouth resuscitation is quite important," he teased.

"Staying calm and responding appropriately to stressful situations is more important." She nodded at him.

He agreed with her, but that wasn't the point. "How old is your houseguest?" he asked.

Cassandra didn't bat an eye. "Sarah is in her thirties, like you, and she's quite pretty. She returns to California after Labor Day."

So here was this summer's anonymous yet intimate fling—was that what she was implying?

"No, Cassandra. Sorry." Honestly, the morning's uncomfortable realizations about him and Lucy not having an emotional connection were making him not want to have his yearly fling. It seemed pathetic now. Maybe he'd only thought he'd been connecting with these women, just as he'd thought he'd been connecting with Lucy during their twice-monthly Saturday outings. Lucy had made him see that it hadn't been true, at all.

"Please, Dad, help her!" Lucy's voice was a shriek. He nearly jumped, it surprised him so much.

"Luce, I'm going to be busy with you. You and I can hang out and do stuff together. We can go to the library and read books together all day, if that's what you want." He would miss his job, and money would be tight, but at least the time spent together would bring them closer.

"But, Dad, you don't understand…" Lucy got up and shrugged out of her backpack. She riffled through a stack of books and papers and pulled out a magazine.

Business Roundup. He stared at her, confused. This was an adult publication, and not something he or her mother read, that was for sure.

He couldn't quite picture bohemian Cassandra reading it, either.

Lucy flipped the pages open to an article she'd marked with a yellow sticky note and showed the pages to him. One featured a huge, glossy picture of a severe, unsmiling woman.

He blinked and looked up at his daughter.

"This is Sarah Buckley," Lucy said. "Haven't you heard of her?"

Should he have? He shrugged and held up his hands.

"She's one of the most important women in Silicon Valley," his eleven-year-old informed him.

He studied the picture again. Sarah Buckley wore a black suit jacket with a white shirt and had dark chin-length hair. Her fighting gaze made her look like she battled and scrapped for what was hers and never gave up trying.

"I didn't know you were interested in business," he said to Lucy.

"She's a woman of substance. That's what it says. Read the article."

He took the magazine from her and flipped through the piece. It was five pages long. When he heard his daughter loved the library, frankly, he'd thought she meant the young adult section. Cassandra had all kinds of artsy friends who wrote literature for kids and teens, but seriously...*business* magazines?

"Sarah Buckley talks about setting life goals and making daily progress and moving above the limitations of your background." Lucy set her chin as she spoke, and in that moment, there was no question, she absolutely reminded Sam of the driven woman profiled in the piece.

He moved away from the magazine with the photograph of the intense Silicon Valley executive that Lucy so admired. He strode over to a couch across the room and sank deeply into the cushions. The whole day so far had been staggering to him. What other parts of herself had Lucy kept hidden from him? He had such a gap to bridge with her that it felt overwhelming.

Lucy settled back in the chair, rereading the article about the woman she obviously idolized. Cassandra wore a thoughtful expression that Sam couldn't place.

"She's my niece," Cassandra said quietly. "My deceased sister's only daughter. She's in trouble with her job and she's coming here to destress for the summer."

"Sarah Buckley is your niece?" He stood up and glanced over Lucy's shoulder at the photograph again. He saw no family resemblance to Cassandra.

A movement out the window caught his attention. On the beach, a crew on a town dump truck was delivering freshly painted lifeguard stands to each of the assigned stations.

A pang went through him. As much as he wanted to improve his relationship with Lucy this summer, the reminders of what he was giving up for that made Sam think again of all the good things he loved about his job that he would miss once he tendered his resignation. He would miss the early morning swims with the lifeguard teams, being calmed by and at peace in the vast, powerful ocean, his refuge since he'd been able to walk. Being one with the ocean was a feeling he couldn't easily describe, a home to him. It was his peace and his anchor. He'd hoped Lucy would feel this way too, but she didn't.

Not everybody loved the ocean, he reminded himself. Lots of people couldn't swim or didn't know how to manage the powerful rip currents that could drown even strong swimmers in seconds if they didn't know how to read and navigate the tide's unique signals. Sam loved the rescue teams, the camaraderie of the other lifeguards, his older bosses and the younger men and women, still in college, that he trained and mentored. He loved helping lost kids find their families and he loved diffusing tensions between beachgoers who'd sat too long in hot summer traffic.

He was good at it. He would do it year-round if the wages were good enough and he lived in a region of the country that supported it. Because of Lucy, he had stayed in Wallis Point, a town close to her home. It had now become his permanent home, too.

"Dad, you shouldn't quit your lifeguard job," Lucy pleaded again. "*Please* let me stay with Cassandra."

She must have been watching him stare wistfully at the beach. The magazine was slack in her lap, and her serious brown eyes seemed sorry for him.

"She'll be in good hands here," Cassandra added softly.

"What about your work?" he asked Cassandra.

She resumed washing her brushes. "Don't worry about me. I always take care of myself." She glanced up at Sam with an expression he couldn't quite read. "I've never told anyone this, but I do have regrets from Sarah's childhood."

Both he and Lucy had given her their full attention. They waited for her next words with rapt curiosity.

"Her parents both died when Sarah was twelve." Cassandra paused to scrub at an especially tough stain on one of her brushes.

"I know this story." Lucy jumped in eagerly.

"Sarah talks about it in the article. She said that facing tragedy and then a difficult home life in her younger years helped hone her focus and showed her the importance of hard work in creating her own destiny." She read from the magazine. "'Because only in creating one's own destiny can one ever be free.'" She put the magazine down. "She won a full scholarship to study engineering at university, where she started developing her own patents and inventions. She started her own company, and now I think she's really rich. Nobody can push her around anymore."

Sam stared at his daughter, confused on all kinds of levels. Money was what was important to Lucy? He hadn't had an inkling that she placed so high a value on wealth. He certainly hadn't passed that onto her. Business and power had never been important drivers to him. He was more of a helper, and he liked to live simply. Humbly. Sarah Buckley's world just wasn't his kind of place.

Cassandra shuffled over, bringing the platter of blueberry cake with her. She plunked it down before him. "Some refreshment, Sam?" she asked drily.

"That is just like what Hannah the witch gave to Nathaniel, too!" Lucy exclaimed. "Dad, you can be Nat!"

Cassandra raised an eyebrow at him.

"Let me guess," he said, realizing he would have to get used to living with Lucy on her terms and not just spending two afternoons per month on a fun, distracting outing he'd dreamed up. "I'm living in *The Witch of Blackbird Pond*?"

"Nathaniel was Kit's love interest. They both needed blueberry cake and kittens to find their happily ever after," Cassandra explained.

"They get married in the end," Lucy piped up. "Neither of them see it coming. But it's true love and a happy ending."

"Mm-hmm. Right."

"Cynical about love, are you?" Cassandra asked him with a smile.

He laughed. "I'm not cynical about anything." Actually, he was amazed that Lucy was talking so much, and about things she never talked about with him. With Sam she was always so serious and polite. This afternoon's conversation was a revelation, even if much of it was disturbing to him. A reminder of how much he'd let himself off the hook as a parent.

He shook his head. It was bewildering, sometimes, that he was even a father to a daughter.

With a sigh, Cassandra sat beside him on the couch, patting his knee with her hand as she did so.

"Lucy will be safe and happy here, Sam. Let

me watch her during the days for you—this is what she wants. And my cottage is close by—you can glance back at it any time of day from the beach, and here she'll be. Except when we're at the library, of course. And, yes, I do have an ulterior motive in wanting to keep Lucy around for the summer. It plays to my own guilt."

"I don't understand."

"As I was saying before, I wasn't there for Sarah when she needed me," she said in a low voice. "After her parents were killed in an automobile accident."

"So, where were you?"

Cassandra glanced at Lucy, who now had two cats on her lap. The second was a huge guy who looked part Maine Coon, with big bushy ears and a thick black coat. He blinked his green eyes slowly and purred while Lucy petted him.

"That's Simmonds," Cassandra said. "The smaller male in the tuxedo fur is Becker." She turned back to Sam. "Let's you and I step outside for a minute. Lucy will be fine with my two boys to keep her company."

He nodded and rose with Cassandra. Lucy barely noticed, so busy was she talking to Becker, who actually seemed to be "talking" back.

"Becker rules the roost," Cassandra said, as she crossed her small porch and sat in a blue metal seat. Sam sat across from her on an Adirondack chair. "He'll be out here squawking in an instant if anything happens with Lucy. Have I ever told you the story about Becker waking me up when the kitchen was filled with smoke? A wire shorted and I didn't hear the smoke alarm, I'm such a heavy sleeper."

Sam smiled politely. He wasn't a cat person himself.

"Ah, well." Cassandra settled back and closed her eyes. The breeze stirred her gray hair and she sighed. "About Sarah. She was left alone after her parents died, and I wasn't aware that she didn't have anybody else except me to rely on until months later. I was in Naples, you see." Her mouth twisted. "And back then…" She lifted her hands and shrugged. "The authorities in the States didn't know where I was. They tried after the funeral, but couldn't locate me in time."

"What happened to Sarah?"

"She was put into a foster home. Maybe two." Oh. Hell.

That made Lucy's situation look like a walk in a park. "Are you okay with your relationship now?" he asked.

Cassandra leaned forward on her cane and stretched out her legs in front of her. The legs of her batiked pants billowed like flags in the breeze.

"It's certainly affected her and how she feels

toward me, I can't deny that. I'm not sure she ever forgave me for my initial choice to skip the funeral. The truth was, I couldn't bear to face it. And by the time I realized what had happened to her and flew back to the States to fetch her, she'd managed to win herself a scholarship to an exclusive boarding school in California and was building her own life for herself. I didn't stop trying to make it up to her, but..." Cassandra paused. "I had my own problems at the time," she admitted. "There...was a reason I was in Naples to begin with."

"And what was that?"

She waved her hand. "It's not important now. The important thing is that Sarah reached out to me and she's coming here to relax on her sabbatical." She gazed out to sea. "I'm hoping the slower pace can help her."

A summer by the sea could do a lot to help heal people. He'd seen it himself.

"When is the last time you saw your niece?"

"In person?" Cassandra turned her face to the sun. "It must be since she graduated from college."

"That long?"

"She's usually quite busy with her job, Sam." Cassandra crossed her legs. "My thought is that Sarah and Lucy can each be good influences for one another. I confess—I was the one who told

Lucy about Sarah. A young girl needs female role models. And for Sarah, getting out of her own head and teaching Lucy what she's learned would distract her from the stress of work she's dealing with."

"I thought your goal this summer was to improve your relationship with Sarah."

"It is. If she and Lucy click, it could help us all quite a bit. I want to create a good environment for both of them."

He still felt skeptical. Was this really the best thing for Lucy?

"I had my choices to make, Sam," Cassandra said softly. "I did the best I knew how." She placed her hand on her cane and leaned closer to him. "So, will you help me? Will you bring my niece into a class or two with your lifeguards? Encourage her to take Lucy to the library now and then? They could talk about their common interests. Topics that you and I don't have the passion for or knowledge of but that they seem to share."

When Cassandra put it like that, it didn't seem so harmful. A relaxed childcare and niece-helping arrangement that just might make sense for everyone.

Most important, it was what Lucy wanted.

"Well, okay. Sure. As for the meditation lessons, we'll play it by ear once your niece gets here—that's the best that I can do."

Cassandra nodded, obviously relieved. "Sarah is coming at the end of next week. Sam, I can start watching Lucy for you immediately if you'd like. I would enjoy taking her to the library as she pleases. I don't have any contracted commitments for the next month at least, so this would fill my time and give me great pleasure."

Having Cassandra provide childcare for Lucy while he worked *would* help Sam with his finances. And he did love his job.

Plus, he would still see Lucy in the mornings and evenings, at lunch time and around his shifts…

"Fine. I'm off work already this week, and I don't start lifeguarding until Monday morning. I'll walk Lucy over to your cottage then. You can bring your niece over to my lifeguard station when she arrives, and I'll talk to her about the classes."

Cassandra gave him a relieved smile. "That sounds lovely."

The wind was kicking up again; they should go back inside soon. "So…we're set with our plan for summer? Lucy rejoins her mother on Labor Day weekend. Or is there a problem with your schedule for the month of August?"

Cassandra hesitated. "No, not a problem, but…"

He waited.

"My gentleman friend in Naples…we've kept in touch all these years, and there is a possibility he might visit for a week in August. We haven't decided on that yet. It depends how well things are going with Sarah and me."

"Is this gentleman friend the same reason you were in Naples when Sarah's parents died?"

"It was." A sad expression crossed Cassandra's face. "But before he commits to visiting, I'm waiting to see how Sarah feels about it." Cassandra looked quickly at Sam as if to reassure him. "If he does come, I'll have him stay at the Grand Beachfront Hotel while he's here. My cottage is so small."

Sam couldn't help asking, "Was it a love affair that kept you from Sarah?"

"It was." Cassandra turned her face to the wind, and he'd never seen a woman so grief stricken. "I told you I had regrets, Sam." She swallowed.

"Yes," he said, thinking of his regrets with Lucy. He and Cassandra both had relationships to mend.

They sat companionably, side by side. With her faraway look, Cassandra seemed to be revisiting memories. He turned his own face to the sun. It warmed him even though the wind was brisk, and the rolling ridge in the beach blocked the worst of the gusts. It struck him that maybe this summer could work out well, after all, and be beneficial to all of them.

"We'll keep Claudio's visit between us," Cassandra suddenly said. "For now. Until Sarah arrives."

"Sure," he agreed. He didn't see how Cassandra's secret could possibly affect him and Lucy.

"Well," Cassandra sat up and patted his knee, then reached for her cane. "Come. Let's go see what your very bright and imaginative daughter is up to now."

Yes. He was curious about that himself.

He stood, opened Cassandra's cottage door for her and held it while she made her way back inside.

"Be patient with my niece when you meet her," were Cassandra's final words on the subject that morning. "She's had a hard life."

Sam just nodded.

A week later, he regretted everything he'd agreed to with Cassandra for his and Lucy's summer.

CHAPTER TWO

One week later

SARAH BUCKLEY KICKED the door of her rental car shut. The friggin' thing. Hours stuck in traffic driving up from the airport on the wrong coast had done nothing to improve her already pissed-off attitude.

She couldn't remember the last time she'd had to drive herself. Her time was simply too valuable. Instead, other people drove her. She sat in the backseat and made calls and tapped out directives aimed at the future sale of her company. Now, it seemed like she was back to square one with that. She was furious—she'd worked too freaking hard for this crap to have happened to her, especially the way it had.

She reached through the open window and yanked her briefcase off the passenger seat. But the top wasn't zipped securely, and the books she'd packed came tumbling onto the sand in her Aunt Cassandra's weed-lined excuse for a driveway.

Textbook after textbook. Sarah was a tech engineer by training—she'd been reading ebooks well before they became mainstream—but these books weren't for quick perusal or for an underling to bullet-point for her—no, these she'd assigned herself to study. Since her college and MBA days, she'd always retained information better when she'd marked it up by hand.

In disgust, she bent over to collect the textbooks. *Meditation. The Art of Zen Business. How to Speak with Millenials.*

Idiocy. Unfortunately, her new financial partner and major investor was into this crap. She resented that she'd been forced to bring him in as her partner, but she'd had to—she needed his capital *and* his good counsel. The sale of her company couldn't happen unless he was pleased with her. To impress him, she'd even hired a crew to install a Zen garden in her San Jose home—they were probably finishing it up today. The aggravation was enough to make her weep. She'd hated to deface her beautiful home, renovated slowly, carefully over the years—she'd started with the small house when she sold her first company, and then had made additions. Now, she had a beautiful custom-designed house with an attached pool, her own gym—and a ridiculous Zen garden, because Richard Lee was into Zen.

With a snort of disgust, she tossed the books

into her Chanel bag, which was now covered with sand in the rustic New Hampshire driveway. With her heels equally sandy, she leaned against the car and surveyed the wreck that was Aunt Cassandra's cottage.

Tiny. And Sarah knew it because she'd been here once before. The cottage had two small bedrooms and a bathroom that was too cramped for a soaking tub. The paint was peeling and the screen door hung half off its hinges. Rambling red roses bloomed prolifically on the rail fence, just as they had in the summer before the worst day of her life, and it was that small, innocent detail that punched her right in the gut.

Her eyes watered. No swear words occurred to her.

Sarah felt twelve years old and all alone in the world again. She'd spent one magical summer in this place, the last summer her parents were alive. They'd driven her up from Connecticut to spend two weeks with her eccentric aunt, a famous children's book illustrator.

She and Cassandra had ridden fun, old-fashioned bicycles with wicker baskets on the handlebars. Down the boardwalk they'd careened, part of a daily expedition to the library to check out whatever books caught their fancy. Cassandra had bought her ice cream cones and gently drawn out Sarah's hopes and dreams for her future.

"You'll be a woman of substance one day," Cassandra had promised her.

That encouragement was the reason Sarah could never completely hate Cassandra for not being there when she'd most needed her.

Sarah found herself sniffling, rubbing her eyes with the heel of her hand as if she were twelve all over again.

Two months after she'd returned from that August visit with Aunt Cassandra, on a sunny autumn afternoon, the principal at her junior high school had stood solemnly at the door of Sarah's English classroom. After she'd followed him into the hallway, he'd spoken the worst words she could have imagined.

Her parents were dead.

All of her grandparents had already died.

Her father's only brother had been off in the army in Germany.

And Cassandra, her mother's sole sister, had been somewhere on the shore of the Mediterranean Sea, inside an artists' colony with her married boyfriend. They most definitely hadn't wanted to be found by the outside world.

Sarah wiped her eyes. At twelve, she'd learned tough lessons about self-preservation, self-reliance, success and grit. The hard, cruel world didn't help the vulnerable. People could be abusive, both emotionally and physically, and strangers didn't take care of the weak.

But soon she would be invulnerable. Just a few more months of putting up with her new partner, Richard Lee, and his games and indignities, and then she could take her company public. That's when the really, really big money would start coming in. Then she could say "screw you" to the Richard Lees of the world, and anyone else for that matter, for the rest of her life.

Slinging the briefcase over her shoulder, she hauled herself to her feet and glanced around. Hadn't Aunt Cassandra heard her yet? Her arrival hadn't exactly been subtle, with the slamming door and textbooks dropped on the driveway. Then again, maybe her aunt's hearing wasn't great. Sarah guessed she would be in her midseventies by now. Sarah had been the only child of parents who had waited until they were in their forties to marry.

Well, Sarah was turning forty herself this summer. And that milestone birthday wasn't improving her mood, either.

Scowling, she tried the handle of the cottage door, but it was locked. Strange. Aunt Cassandra hadn't believed in locked doors when Sarah was twelve, but that was back in a magical, faraway past when the world seemed so much more innocent than it was today.

Sarah went around to the beach-facing side of the cottage, put a hand up to shade her eyes from the sun and peered inside the living-room window.

The furniture was different than she remembered. The paintings on display were also new. But she could see into the open doorways—the two bedrooms and the tiny, rustic bathroom—and it was apparent that no one was home.

Cassandra must have stepped out.

She couldn't have gone far. Her aunt didn't drive, and her mobility was limited.

Sarah dropped her bag and went out to the beach to search for her. On a sunny June weekday afternoon the shore was dotted with people. Couples, families, groups of moms and kids. A lifeguard with a perfect body stood beside his chair. Arms crossed, listening to one of the moms as she spoke to him in an animated fashion.

But no Cassandra.

Frowning, Sarah checked the time on her phone. She was right on schedule. Cassandra *knew* she was coming. Sarah had written the letter to her aunt herself—no email for her free-spirited, unorthodox aunt—and Cassandra, in her flourishing, dramatic script, had confirmed Sarah's visit.

What the hell?

One would think that if her aunt really cared, then she would be more careful. Or could she be doing it again? Could she be cavalierly reburning the bridge that Sarah had let stay burned for all these years before deciding to tentatively rebuild it just last month?

Sarah didn't know because Cassandra wasn't here to ask in person. And it wasn't as if Sarah could simply direct her administrative assistant to zip off a quick text message to her aunt.

Cassandra had no cell phone, no email address—not even a tablet with banking apps. She still wrote paper checks. She relied on the post office to mail pleasant notes written on real stationery. Her lawyer in town handled any communications of urgent importance.

Sarah didn't have an administrative assistant here to deal with a lawyer, anyway. That meant she had to hunt down her technophobic aunt herself, on her aunt's terms.

Gritting her teeth, she took out her phone and pulled up the lawyer's contact number.

"Kimball Law Firm," a young female voice answered.

Sarah gripped her phone and spoke firmly, like she always did, as a woman of substance.

"This is Sarah Buckley. Put Natalie on the line." She swallowed and thought of Richard Lee's admonition to her. "Please," she added.

"Ms. Kimball is in a meeting right now, but I'll take a message."

"Who is this?" Sarah demanded. "What is your name?"

There was a slight pause at the other end. As there should be.

"This is Sophia, Ms. Kimball's assistant," the woman said pleasantly. "Would you like to leave a message for Ms. Kimball?"

"Yes, tell her to get her ass down to Cassandra Shipp's cottage to let me in. Otherwise, my aunt will be looking for a new lawyer to manage her affairs." Anger coursing through her, Sarah clicked the phone off and tossed it onto the sand.

It sat there, winking in the sun.

What the hell was she doing?

Sarah knelt and picked it up, brushing off the beach sand. This phone was her lifeline. With it, she could call Richard Lee and beg him to reconsider her temporary banishment from the company *she* had started.

She wasn't cut out for a "retreat." She didn't want to "put her head on straight," or "think about her actions" as he'd instructed. She was meant to *work*. To get things done and accomplish business miracles.

She put her head in her hands and began to weep again. Honestly, she'd reached rock bottom. She hadn't even wept when her entire staff had resigned en masse.

Just because she'd called them "ungrateful little shits" during their morning motivational talk. Who the hell needed morning motivational talks—aside from Richard Lee, apparently? What were they all—in kindergarten? These were business professionals working in Silicon Valley's most up-and-coming tech firm, for the California Business Bureau's Woman of the Year.

Yet again, she wiped her eyes.

Her phone still remained silent. No one called her back. No one jumped at her command.

This was not her usual life.

Sarah sat cross-legged, imitating the picture on the cover of the meditation textbook she'd marked up for all six hours of her flight. Airy-fairy, none of it made a bit of sense to her, but since she was at rock bottom, she was going to do anything she possibly could to claw her way out of this pit of despondency.

Breathe in, breathe out, she told herself. *Breathe in, breathe out*.

So friggin' idiotic. What was the *point* in counting breaths like a child just learning her numbers?

Still, maybe she shouldn't have called that

lawyer's assistant—she couldn't even remember her name—an ass. Or had she called the lawyer an ass? Sarah couldn't remember. It didn't even matter, to tell the truth, except that if she didn't please Richard, didn't at least try to "calm down," then she would never influence him to bring her company public in the timely manner she wanted.

She needed Richard's goodwill. Richard Lee was respected. A big-time mover and shaker in the Valley, with a track record of bringing companies public and making the founders as well as himself wealthy beyond all belief.

She took a breath and grabbed the phone. Richard would want her to apologize to the lawyer's assistant. But it had been a long time since she'd apologized to anybody.

Her phone suddenly rang, shocking her.

"Hello?" she answered the call tentatively.

"Ms. Buckley?" This was the same young female voice as before. "This is Sophia, Ms. Kimball's assistant again."

"Hello, Sophia. I'm…sorry for using harsh language with you. I apologize."

There, she thought. *Richard would be proud.*

"Um, that's okay. I called Ms. Kimball, and she said she'll be over to Cassandra's cottage in about an hour. She's at a real-estate closing with a client, and as soon as it wraps up, she'll be there."

An hour? "What am I supposed to do until then?" Sarah demanded.

"Well…there's a beach right there, isn't there?"

"I don't care about the beach," Sarah snapped. "I need a shower. And Wi-Fi."

There was silence on the other end.

Damn it. It occurred to Sarah that if Aunt Cassandra didn't have email, then she certainly didn't have Wi-Fi, either.

Sarah held back her scream. The summer was going to be worse than she'd thought. "Fine," she gritted out. "I'll expect her in an hour." She felt hot and sweaty and disgusting from the long plane ride followed by a long drive in a rental that smelled of cleaning fluid and didn't work too well in the air-conditioning department. "Until then, I'll change into my bathing suit at the gas station down the street and then take a long jump in the ocean. That'll freshen me up from my journey."

She was sounding too much like a martyr, so she cleared her throat. "I'm looking forward to meeting my aunt's attorney," she added. After all, as Cassandra's only surviving family member, Sarah would likely be an executor of her aunt's will someday, so she saw the practicality in having a decent relationship with the woman.

You see, Richard, she thought, *I can be nice when I need to.*

"Ms. Shipp brought the *Business Roundup* article you were in to show us," Sophia continued, oblivious to Sarah's irritation. "We're *so* excited you'll be visiting us in Wallis Point this summer. You're a local celebrity."

Wait, what? Cassandra had seen that article? Sarah didn't know which was more surprising, that Cassandra had noticed it or that she'd been proud enough to show it to people.

"Well, it may not be for the whole summer," Sarah said. Indeed, she was hoping Richard could be persuaded to let her come back earlier. Say in a week or two, when she could meditate and radiate Zen with the best of them. Sarah had always been a good student when she'd put her mind to something.

"Hmm," Sophia was saying. "Maybe you could give a talk at the library? I'm a volunteer, and we—"

"No," Sarah interrupted. *Nip that idea right in the bud.* Sarah didn't intend to get *too* comfortable in this beachy backwater. Her time here was an exile—her punishment for forgetting that she'd ceded too much power to Richard, her investor. She needed to focus on sucking up to him again so she could grab her power back.

Besides, she was still wary of her aunt, truth be told. For good reason.

"Sorry," Sophia murmured. "I know you're very busy. We won't disturb your vacation." She cleared her throat. "Excuse me, but I have a call coming in. Rest assured that I'll follow up with Ms. Kimball and keep tabs on how her time is running. She's promised she'll be right out with Cassandra's key as soon as she can. In the meantime, please do enjoy the beach. It's a gorgeous day, and I would kill to be outside with you."

And Sarah would kill to be back in her office in California, but that wasn't likely to happen within the next week or two, at least. Her plan was to master meditation in a lesson or two with Cassandra, and then have her charming and illustrious aunt call up Richard Lee himself. By next Sunday—or the following one, at the latest—Sarah should be back in San Jose. Ready to be calmer with her staff. More communicative. Less angry.

"Very well," she said to Sophia, testing her new communicativeness. "I'll be out on the beach. Please have Ms. Kimball come and find me when she gets here. Thank you. Have a nice day."

I DON'T BELONG HERE, Sarah thought one hour later, gazing at all the serene, pleasant, happy people spread out on beach towels, lounging in sand chairs and meandering along the shoreline with the flowing tide.

Everybody within sight was either coupled up, with children or hanging with a group of friends. Sarah was the lone singleton. And her aloneness, combined with the uncomfortable memories of one perfect August summer, made her want to weep.

Again.

Until Richard had banished her, she couldn't remember the last time she'd cried.

Swallowing, Sarah wrapped her arms around her knees. The beach was just as she remembered it, but smaller, maybe because she was no longer small. The air was cool with a salty sea breeze, different from the breeze in California. The sand was brown and soft like sugar. There used to be sand dunes between her aunt's cottage and the sea, but sometime in the intervening years they'd eroded away, so now her aunt had a clear, direct view of the beach.

The tide was pushing her back—it was coming in fast. Sarah got up and moved her towel above the high-water mark. The waves were large today, larger than she remembered. A long time ago, her aunt had taught her to body surf. She'd taught her to stride into the water vigorously and without fear of the cold. To dive into a wave was preferred. Then, to wait for just the right one, at just the right time, and put her hands over her head and ride the wave face down in to shore.

Once she'd gotten the hang of it, it had been exhilarating. She'd felt such power in being part of nature's force. Sarah felt herself smiling.

She glanced down at the one-piece bathing suit she'd changed into at the gas station down the street. The suit was red. Concealing. She would have no wardrobe malfunctions when she rode those waves again. No one was in the water right now, but Sarah was braver than most people—she'd had to be. She'd quickly learned not to shrink from a little frigid water, from hardship, from a challenge. It wasn't in her nature anymore.

She stretched, shifting her face away from the strong sun. Just then, a lifeguard in orange shorts and no shirt—just a whistle around his neck and a baseball cap on his head—pulled up on a single-rider all-terrain vehicle, about twenty feet in front of her. He lazily got off, sauntering to the tall lifeguard chair. He put his hands on his hips and peered up at the younger lifeguard occupying the seat.

Sarah took off her sunglasses to get a better look. The lifeguard who'd driven up was definitely older than the near boy on the chair. Perhaps he was a supervisor. Still, he was younger than she was, and once again, she remembered with gloom that she would be celebrating her fortieth birthday soon. Hopefully back at home rather than here with Cassandra.

But for now, Sarah didn't mind looking at the man. He had a nice chest, tanned and buff, and she liked the look of his face, too. Intelligent and guarded.

The older lifeguard said something to the younger man that Sarah couldn't hear. She sighed and forced herself to stop looking at them. A small plane flew overhead with a banner: Eat at Billy Joe's. Fried Clams and Pasta. Family-Sized Dinners.

No, thank you, Sarah thought with a shudder. She worked hard to keep herself healthy. It was definitely harder these days than it had been at thirty, never mind *twenty*. And why was she looking at younger-than-her lifeguards without their shirts on, anyway?

That wasn't what this week was for.

Shaking her head, she got up and wiped sand off her bottom. The breeze had stilled, and she was getting hot sitting on the sand. And it wasn't good that she'd neglected her sunscreen. When she got back, she would cover up with the cheap towel she'd bought at the store beside the gas station.

The sand squishing between her toes, Sarah beelined toward the water. She was tired of being angry, upset, inconvenienced, out of sorts and shoved from her environment. For once, she wanted to feel fun again, young again.

Maybe it was being on this beach that had affected her. This was the last place she remembered enjoying herself before it had all turned to muck. The most fun thing she remembered from back then was running into the waves and body-surfing with other kids she'd met at the beach.

Sarah decided to go for a swim. She wouldn't mind that her limbs moved more stiffly, more heavily, than they had when she was a girl. The wind was still in her face and she would brace her body for the shock of the cold New England ocean when she felt it.

SAM WATCHED THE woman as she sprinted for the surf. He didn't make a habit of checking out women while he was on the job, but there was something about this one that drew his eye.

He paused on the driver's seat of the ATV. Duke had asked him to check in with the newer guards. For about half of them, it was their first summer, and Sam, at thirty-two, was an old hand. He was practiced at constantly scanning the water and the beach. He knew when swim-

mers ventured too far out; he would summon
them in with a whistle and a wave.

Very few people were swimming today. In
June, the water was frigid and the air wasn't hot
enough to drive people into the water seeking
relief. Farther up the coast, the surfers would
be wearing wetsuits. Here, at the fringes of the
family beach, still not quite on the main boardwalk section, there was little incentive to wade
in beyond one's ankles.

It was a sleepy, easy day. Great for a lifeguard
new to the job. Not too many kids—it was still
early for family vacations, and school was still
in session in some local towns. Midweek was
prime time for retired couples, groups of moms
with preschoolers and the odd pair of early vacationers relaxing here and there with their books.

When the woman appeared again in his pe-
ripheral vision, he couldn't help turning to watch
her pass. Of everyone on the beach, she stood
out. It was the way she moved. One thing that
had always fascinated Sam was watching the
different people in the grand parade of humanity that passed up and down the shoreline in
summer.

Some people strolled. Some marched. Some
lolled. Some shuffled. Others strutted—the
young, usually. Teens slunk along in too-cool-
for-school groups. Little kids skipped or danced.

Young couples walked hand in hand. His own daughter strode with purpose.

This woman—she *commanded*. It was the only word he could think of, the only action that described her.

He liked that she was confident and powerful. She strode toward that water like she wasn't afraid of it. Like she was going to possess it and make it her own.

He paused, aware that he was smiling. The first lighthearted, happy moment he'd felt all day. His cares lifting, he leaned back and waited to see what she would do when her toes hit the frigid water. Her pale skin suggested she didn't get much sun. The grim set of her jaw told him she was determined to bathe in the sea.

The foamy tide surged toward her. He watched, waiting. With her ankles submerged in the chilly surf, she paused. Where others shivered and hugged themselves, she was stoic. A look crossed her face, a small, sad smile. He wondered why.

She was someone he would like to talk to. Not here. Not now. But if he were across the world, in Scotland, say, hiking on the West Highland Way (as he had planned, but he wasn't going to think of that), he definitely would have found an excuse to catch up with her. To match those powerful, determined steps. To walk beside her and make light conversation.

And later that night, to take her into his bed.

With a sudden set to her jaw, she shocked him by surging forward. With great, long-legged, awkward steps she raced through the cold water as fast as she could. When she was waist deep, she thrust her arms over her head and made a graceful, curving arc. She dove directly into the wall of a large, nearly breaking wave.

It was magnificent.

But she didn't come up right away. Frowning, he stood up straight, on alert.

And then he noticed what he should have noticed, if he'd been concentrating on the water and not on the woman.

The water was dark and swirling—a single lane that led from the beach out to sea. On either side of the lane were tiny ripples of white waves.

The woman had entered straight into that dark tunnel.

"Damn," he said aloud. He jogged to the guard's chair, knocking on it. "Charlie? Radio to chair nine, tell Jeannie McLaren to get over here and join us ASAP. Tell her to bring her rescue equipment."

The young man gaped at him. "Why?"

"Rip current," Sam said grimly, gazing toward the woman. Her head had appeared. Already she was being pulled farther from shore, but she might not have noticed that yet.

"Rip current?" Charlie repeated, shading his eyes and staring at the surf ahead.

"Yeah, we talked about it yesterday. Do you remember what we need to do to save her?"

"Yeah." The kid set his jaw. "Yeah, I'm on it."

"Call chair number nine," Sam instructed again. And then he grabbed a rescue torp and sprinted toward the woman who'd thought she could master the sea.

At first Sarah decided to swim out past the waves to where it was calmer. Swimming seemed easier than she remembered.

How long had it been since she'd swum in the ocean? Funny, but she'd lived in California for over twenty years now, and she'd never once taken a dip in the Pacific.

Catching a glimpse of how far out she'd come, past where the waves were breaking, she paused. Immediately, without her blood pumping as hard, she started to shiver. This water really was freezing, and she couldn't ignore that any longer. She tentatively stretched her legs, but her toes didn't touch bottom. Or maybe she just couldn't feel it.

In any event, as she realized how far out she

was, it was pretty obvious that she must be way over her head.

And the longer she watched the shore, the farther out she appeared to get. The beach was receding by the second, and that wasn't her imagination.

Taking a breath, Sarah started to swim directly to shore. The salt water stung her eyes and her lungs burned with the effort. But when she looked again, she seemed farther out, if that was even possible.

It simply made no sense. She felt like she was in a science fiction movie, lost in a twilight zone. Or on some strange planet where the laws of nature didn't apply.

I'm just out of shape. I need to do something about that. Now I have all sorts of time to remedy it.

Hysterical laughter erupted from her throat. But it did no good; she was being swept farther and farther out as the seconds ticked past.

I might die here, she thought.

Panic bubbled in her chest.

Flailing, she tried harder to swim and make progress. *Stroke, stroke, stroke*, she told herself. *Kick, kick, kick.* Her lungs ached with the effort. She couldn't control her breathing any longer— oh, to be able to count breaths and meditate! Another small, hysterical laugh broke from her mouth, and with that, a snort of seawater went down her throat.

She choked, sputtering. But she couldn't hear herself panicking, because the roar of the ocean filled her ears.

Don't give up, Sarah! Work harder! Fight harder!

She stroked and kicked with all her might.

Until she couldn't anymore.

CHAPTER THREE

SAM'S TEAM OBSERVED from the shore while he swam out as fast as he could to reach the woman caught in the rip current.

He gripped a flotation device—one of the bright red rescue cans that they called torpedo buoys, or torps, because of the shape—and kicked out past the breaking waves on a course parallel to the swimmer he intended to assist.

Sam's adrenaline kicked in. He didn't think he loved anything better than the intensity of making a save.

When he was as far out as she was, Sam turned sharply and swam toward the female swimmer across the narrow rip current, kicking hard, holding the torp in front of him with outstretched arms. Though the woman's dark hair was matted to her head and her blue eyes were huge, he assessed that she wasn't in such distress that she couldn't understand him.

"Grab the handles and I'll pull you to safety," he called to her. When he was close enough, he helped the woman latch onto the flotation device and then guided her out of the lane of the rip current.

Sam had to give her credit; she was breathing heavily but she was alert and hadn't panicked—her skin wasn't clammy and her pupils looked okay. She was a fighter, that was for sure.

"Hang on," he said to the woman. "Just a few more yards. I'll stay with you until you can touch bottom. Then we can walk in to shore together."

"I'm fine," she insisted through clenched, chattering teeth. "I can handle it on my own."

He said nothing in response. They would talk again when they were safely on shore and he'd called in a medical team to assess her.

His feet hit the sandy bottom, and he shifted one hand to the waist of her red bathing suit. Soon they were sloshing through the shallow waves together. He kept his hand on her waist, guiding her in.

"Let go of me," she hissed.

"Your legs might be shaky. You've been through a rip current."

"I had it under control," she muttered. "I don't need you."

"Maybe so," he answered. "We're just being careful. Rip currents can be quite powerful and tough to escape from." He went into science teacher mode. "In this case, they're formed by a depression, or low point, on the ocean floor, which in turn causes a strong surface flow of water running from the beach back to the ocean."

"I know all that," she snapped. "I've had plenty of science classes in my day."

He nodded and remained silent, just walking in with her. Once on shore, she bent over and gave herself a little shake. He could tell she was a bit stunned from her ordeal, but it was obvious she'd be okay.

He motioned to Jeannie McLaren to take out her radio. The new lifeguard looked at him owlishly. She seemed frozen.

"We'll review the procedures again in training tomorrow," he said quietly to McLaren. "But right now, it's customary to call the medical team. They'll check the lady over. Then I'll make a report to the lifeguard captain. Typically, just one person is needed to handle a save like this, but since it's the beginning of the season, I wanted you all to learn and get experience firsthand. As such, all of you will get credit."

Charlie perked up. "Credit?"

"For the save," Sam explained.

The lady he'd rescued shook her head at them. "No one saved me. I'm *fine*. And if you call any EMTs…"

She paused and gazed toward the direction of the cottages. They all did. A woman in a business outfit—skirt and sleeveless blouse—was picking her way across the sand toward them. She carried her shoes in one hand. Across her shoulder bounced a briefcase.

"...then I will sue you," the lady they'd rescued continued, turning back to smile at them triumphantly. "And if I'm not mistaken, *here* is my lawyer."

Sam squinted. The lawyer with the briefcase looked an awful lot like the only lawyer he knew in town, Natalie Kimball. Or had her name changed since she'd married? He couldn't remember. In any event, she wasn't his lawyer because she didn't handle child custody cases.

While he was ruminating over name changes and custody cases, his "distressed swimmer" staggered off toward Natalie. Sam's two lifeguards looked at him expectantly, as if to say, "Now what?" To add to the fun, most of the people who'd been soaking up the sun nearby wandered over, too. Everybody liked a show.

"What did you mean by 'credit for a save'?" Charlie asked him. "Does that get us a cash bonus or something?"

"No, Charlie." Sam sighed. "It just gives you bragging rights at the end-of-summer banquet."

Charlie looked disappointed, but honestly, all lifeguard groups that Sam had ever known set up friendly competitions during the season.

However, Sam didn't need to be explaining all that with an audience of civilians gathering before them.

He slid a gaze back over at the lady. He couldn't hear what she was saying to her lawyer, but could very well guess.

"Okay, good news—our distressed swimmer is obviously feeling better," Sam said to his green staff, wrapping this lesson up so they could disperse the crowd as soon as possible. "The takeaway for the day is that we can't force a person to go for treatment if they don't want to. This is all perfectly normal."

Charlie and Jeannie nodded in unison, along with some of the people in the crowd.

Usually, the medical team with the resulting paperwork would have been here by now—even if just to handle the victim's refusal of treatment—but the season was still young and Sam supposed the recent hires were getting used to Wallis Point lifeguard protocol. In any event, he'd seen new teams being a bit clueless before. Nothing he couldn't handle.

The radio on his all-terrain vehicle squawked. Sam's boss. Sam headed over to answer the call. Probably, Duke had heard about the save. McLaren had radioed it in, and now there would be a report due.

Damn it. Sam still needed to get the victim's information for the save statistics.

He glanced back up at the angry lady staggering away from them. He would have to follow her.

Again, nothing he couldn't handle. In his years as a lifeguard, he'd seen many different types of victim reactions before.

Keep things smooth and easy—that was Sam's motto.

SARAH CONTINUED HER march toward Cassandra's cottage, her aunt's lawyer beside her. She tugged tighter on the beach towel she'd wrapped around her wet bathing suit. The towel smelled strange, and the flimsy material of uncertain provenance felt gross against her skin.

"...and it's *such* a pleasure to meet you," Natalie was saying breathlessly as Sarah strode through the sand. "I don't know if you realize it or not, but Cassandra showed your magazine article to everyone in the office. I love reading about strong female role models. We all think it's wonderful. My daughter, Hannah, is six, and I hope women like you will be an inspiration to her."

"Yeah, well—" Sarah stopped herself from a biting retort and glanced sideways at the lawyer. They were approaching Cassandra's cottage now, near the tired-looking wooden deck without any railings, and the lawyer didn't appear to be sucking up to Sarah or even blowing smoke. Natalie seemed strangely, provincially sincere. Sarah needed to adjust her expectations. She squeezed the towel tighter around herself. "Where is my aunt, anyway? She was supposed to be here to let me in. She knew what time I was set to arrive."

"Yes. She asked me to handle that for her. I'm sorry I got held up so long." Natalie pulled her briefcase from her shoulder. Daintily, she balanced it on the arm of an Adirondack chair as she opened a side pocket. "Here, I have a note from Cassandra explaining the situation to you. And your copy of the house key."

"What situation?" Sarah spit out as she grabbed the letter with one hand and the key with the other. "Why is she always so damned dramatic? You should tell her to get a phone like regular people. Who uses a lawyer or a post office box to communicate with her flesh and blood? Her *only* flesh and blood, I might add." Sarah's voice had risen. She hadn't meant to express her anger, obviously much deeper than she'd realized. But it was always there, inside her, and today had been a crappy day from start to finish. That Cassandra had pulled another of her stunts was so typical. Sarah was even angrier with herself for not foreseeing it.

Before Natalie could answer, the roar of an ATV drew suspiciously close. Sarah groaned and whipped her head around.

It was the lifeguard again. The older-but-still-younger-than-her man with the too-good looks, the bare chest and the surprisingly calm, competent manner.

He came to a stop and just gazed at her for a moment, his mouth hitched in a half smile, as if he found something about the situation funny.

"What?" she snapped at him.

"Hello, Sam," Natalie greeted him.

"Hi, Natalie. Good to see you again." But Sam had focused all his intensity on *her*. Sarah.

She'd been about to say something scathing to knock him off balance, but as his kind, appreciative eyes swept first up her body, then down, she felt the angry words wither in her throat. She'd forgotten what she was going to say in order to keep the upper hand. He didn't seemed fazed by her anger in the least.

And then his eyes met hers directly—as deep blue as the ocean that had first seduced her, then nearly swept her away and swallowed her up whole.

She felt an uncharacteristic flutter in her

chest. Her head was even dizzy. Yes, it must be the fumes from the cheap towel.

"Whoa," Sam said in his rich, deep voice, then leaped forward to steady her elbow.

She hadn't realized she was wavering on her feet. But the less this man touched her, the better. "To what do we owe the pleasure of your presence?" she asked, shaking his hand off her. "Do all your *rescue* targets receive such hands-on service?"

Now he was full-out smiling. She hated that he reacted to her this way, but it was as if he refused to be ruffled by her bad mood.

Worse, it was as if he saw straight through her offensive shield—over-the-top rudeness and all—and wasn't intimidated in the least. He studied her as if none of what she said was real.

Nobody treated her this way. Except maybe Richard Lee, but she didn't like Richard, and he didn't like her. With Richard it was all business. With her high-tech, artificial-intelligence patents, she stood to make him a fortune, and at the end of the day, that was all he cared about.

Sam-the-lifeguard (yes, she would think of him like that—it was good defense for her), was back to peering into her eyes. Frankly, he looked worried for her health. Well, she was, too, but that wasn't his business.

"I'm fine," she insisted again, sounding unlike herself and too similar to a breathless six-teen-year-old girl, which was just irritating. She wrapped her cheap towel even more tightly around her body. If she could just put her armor back on—suit, expensive shoes, briefcase (even if it *was* full of meditation books)—then she would feel like herself again.

"Sorry to have to bother you," he said to her, "but we've got unfinished business." He shifted his gaze to Natalie. "I have to fill out an administrative report," he said apologetically. "This won't take a minute. Don't sue me, okay?"

Sarah couldn't very well be insulted that he was speaking to Natalie, not her, because she *had* told him that Natalie was her lawyer. "Leave my name out of your administrative report," Sarah told Sam.

"Yes, please do," Natalie agreed. "Sarah is a celebrity, and it wouldn't do to bring that kind of attention down on her or Wallis Point."

"I know who she is," Sam said. "I didn't recognize her, at first, but now that we're at Cassandra's cottage, I fully understand." Both he and Natalie looked at her.

Whoa. Whoa, whoa, whoa.

"You know who I am?"

"Yes. But I didn't know who you were when I rescued you."

"You didn't rescue me," she clarified. "I rescued myself."

"Right," he agreed easily.

Why can't my employees be so agreeable? she thought. Maybe he wasn't that bad.

No. There had to be a catch.

"What do you want?" she snapped.

He gave her a sexy, lazy smile. He backed up a step so he was leaning his hip indolently against the beach buggy, the motor still idling.

She shook her head. She was practically forty. Over the hill, compared to him.

Sam tilted his head at her. "How old are you?" he asked.

She started. "Why?" Was this guy a mind-reader?

"For the report," he said, still calm.

"Don't put me in any of your reports!"

He shrugged. "It'll be anonymous. No name given. Nobody will ever know that it was you."

"Why don't you just pretend it didn't happen at all? Forget about it."

"Can't," he said softly. "The chief of life-guards knows about the incident. You're lucky—it's only because it's early in the season that the medical team wasn't called and ready for you by the time we brought you in—sorry, by the time you brought yourself in." He gave her a teasing grin, showing a smile with really nice teeth. "Then you *would* be in the system—name and all. Police, fire and EMTs—they brook no nonsense."

She crossed her arms. "You're implying I create nonsense."

"We've dealt with VIPs here before, Ms. Buckley. They never complained."

She could feel her face growing red.

"You'll be written up as female, aged whatever," he continued. "That's how our public reports always read. No other identifying information."

"I don't care what you put down," she snapped. "Make something up."

"Nope." He shook his head. "Not falling into that trap. You tell me."

"No."

He pursed his lips. "How about twenty-one? You good with that?"

"Don't be an ass."

He grinned, showing a dimple this time. "You talk just like my middle schoolers. The ones with bad manners, anyway."

"Excuse me?"

"He teaches middle school earth science," Natalie chimed in. "In the local school system."

"Ah. Very funny," Sarah replied to Sam-the-lifeguard who was also a science teacher.

Obviously, he'd wanted her to know that. Wanted her to know he was serious of mind as well as body.

She licked her lips, trying desperately not to look at that body. Toned, sun-kissed skin. Welcoming chest. Really, really hot abs…

Stop. Just tell him you're thirty-five. Not too much of a lie. Or go lower, thirty-two. It was a nice, round age for a woman. Not as preposterous as saying thirty, which was about the age that he looked.

He gave her a kind smile. "My daughter will be happy to know I've met you already. She idolizes you ever since Cassandra showed her the article in *Business Roundup*."

Sarah coughed in surprise. She could feel her eyes bugging out, a blatant show. When she was younger, she'd practiced her "business" face in the mirror. An old mentor had suggested it as a necessity. He'd also suggested that she looked too vulnerable, which she'd been trying to correct, or at least to cover up, ever since.

This was a major fail.

"You think I'm too young to have a daughter, don't you?" Sam winked. "Well, I had her when I was twelve."

She couldn't hold back a bark of laughter.

And yet, he wore no wedding ring. Not even a white tan line to indicate that he'd taken it off.

Not all men wore wedding rings.

"I'm not married," he said, reading her mind again.

Natalie stood by silently. Sarah could swear she was hiding a smile.

It hit her all of a sudden. They were *handling* her. The way she usually sought to *handle* others.

The name of the game is power, her old mentor had taught her. *Others will try to top you— don't let them. It's a sign of weakness and the worst you can do is to show weakness.*

"Thirty-nine." Sarah directed the information to Sam-the-lifeguard. "Put that number in your report." It was the truth. She had almost two weeks until her fortieth birthday.

Deliberately looking *through* him rather than *at* him, she then turned to Natalie. *Enough of this*, she thought. "Where is Cassandra?" She crumpled the envelope the lawyer had handed her and dropped it on the deck. She didn't want to read another one of her aunt's placating notes. She wanted the truth, and she was through with the flaky games. "Tell me what's going on. Stop enabling her."

SAM COULDN'T HELP IT. He was fascinated, both intellectually and physically, by this emotionally fearless, over-the-top woman. Sarah Buckley wasn't like anyone else he knew. She seemed to have this armor about her, clutching at her beach towel as if it was a shield, and her words to him were like verbal jousts. He'd been having fun talking to her, actually.

And his daughter was enamored of her, too. That made it difficult for him. He had to keep his hands off. And yet, he couldn't walk away, either.

Good thing he had Cassandra as a buffer.

He turned to Natalie, feeling pretty confident as to where Cassandra was. She was with Lucy at the town library. Sarah was just going to have to chill out and wait for the two to return home. Yes, Cassandra could have left the house keys with him, but he wasn't fixed to a lifeguard stand this year. He was more of a floating supervisor and therefore more difficult to find than he'd been in the past.

Natalie blinked nervously, shifting her weight from side to side. Sam could see how Sarah would do that to her. Natalie had been in some of his high school classes. She'd been a shy, bookish girl back then. She wasn't like that anymore—she was a lawyer who argued cases in court and won all the time—but Sarah was an overpowering person, to put it mildly.

"Actually," Natalie said to Sarah, "Cassandra

left you the letter because she wanted to explain in her own words where she was. You really should read it." Natalie knelt and picked it up.

A line formed in Sarah's forehead. "She's not *here*, is she?" Sarah asked flatly.

"Well, I'm sorry, no," Natalie replied.

Sarah's face turned red and blotchy. "I'll kill her," she said through clenched lips.

"It's okay." Sam reached out and touched her arm. "She's with my kid. At the town library. She's been bringing her there for the past four days, since Monday."

Sarah stared at him. "You entrusted your *child* to her?"

He sent Natalie a *help me out, here*, look.

But Natalie appeared even more alarmed than Sarah had. She put her hand over her mouth. Blood drained from her face.

"What is it?" he asked Natalie. "Why are you upset?"

"Because my receptionist was given to understand that Cassandra had an emergency and was on her way to the airport to fly out of the country—which she never does—so I assumed it was a particularly bad emergency." Natalie hastily smoothed the balled-up envelope that Sarah had crumpled and dropped.

But Sam felt so sick, so panicked, that he grabbed it from Natalie's hand and ripped open the envelope himself. As quickly as he could, he pulled out and smoothed the two pieces of thick blue stationery.

Thursday morning, Cassandra had written on the heading in bold but shaky handwriting. The next line read, *Dear Sarah*, and that wasn't for him so he stopped reading and lifted his head.

"So, she's only been gone for a few hours?" he asked Natalie.

"It appears that way. She came to my office just before noon. She said she wanted to speak to me, but since I wasn't there, she left the letter and key with my receptionist and said she was on her way to the airport. There was a car waiting outside for her. She left a number at her destination for me to call tonight. That's all that I know."

"Where did she leave *Lucy*? My daughter?"

Natalie looked at him helplessly. "I don't know. What does her note say?"

But as Natalie spoke, Sarah grabbed the letter from him. He struggled to align himself so he could read beside her, but all they ended up doing was bumping heads.

Sarah glanced at each page for about two seconds. "There's not a word here about a *Lucy*." Sarah glared at him. "Just about her damn cats. And *you*. Evidently, I'm supposed to go and see *you*."

"I need to find my daughter!" Adrenaline coursing through his veins, he turned and jumped off the short deck and onto the sand, sprinting toward his house, hoping Lucy was there.

"Wait, Sam! I think I know where your daughter is!" Sarah called, waving the pages as she spoke. "There *is* a mention of a Lucy!"

He turned, still running backward. "Where?" he shouted back.

"The library. Cassandra says she left Lucy at the library!"

His heart thumped wildly, but he gave Sarah a short wave of thanks as he changed course toward the street where he'd parked his truck.

He could be at the library in five minutes. Ten if he hit the two traffic lights on the way. If Lucy wasn't there anymore...

No. He couldn't think about that.

Inside his truck, he grabbed his keys from under the front seat then backed out of his parking space as fast as he could.

Please, let Lucy be okay.

He shifted into Drive and stepped on the accelerator. He was halfway down the boulevard when he realized he was driving in bare feet and wearing only his orange lifeguard shorts and the whistle around his neck. *Crap.*

AFTER SAM LEFT, everything seemed emptier. Sarah stood with Cassandra's letter clutched in one fist, the house key in the other, both arms hanging limply at her sides.

She'd skimmed the whole letter, once. There were excuses, explanations—and as far as Sarah was concerned—rationalizations for why she'd left Sarah *again*.

Her Italian man in Naples. Sarah knew all about that. She'd heard it before, months after Cassandra had chosen to skip her parents' funeral. And again when Cassandra had finally dropped into her life once more—as if her excuses were supposed to make up for another desertion.

How foolish had she been to think anything had changed with her aunt?

"I'm sorry," Natalie murmured. "If I'd been at the office, and I'd known what confusion Cassandra was leaving behind, then I would have attempted to sort it through. When I came out here to see you this afternoon, I assumed she'd fully thought out what she was doing."

"Oh, she's thought it out, all right," Sarah said bitterly. "Trust me."

"But it's irresponsible to leave a child unattended!"

"She once left me unattended for ten months,

Ms. Kimball." Shaking her head, Sarah went back to the driveway where her rental car was and gathered up her luggage. She rolled her suitcases back to the deck and joined Natalie, who was still standing there with that look of concern on her face.

"There's nothing more you can do," Sarah said simply. "She's gone, and that's that."

Natalie's forehead creased. "I'm going to call her tonight."

"Fine. But don't get me involved. I don't want to hear about it." Sarah took the house key and stuck it in the lock. The door opened easily.

"No, honestly," Natalie said behind her. "I want to. My father, before he retired, was Cassandra's longtime attorney. In his files, he has all sorts of her correspondence that I need to read because that is not the way I want to work with her in future."

"Good luck with that." Sarah bumped her luggage and briefcase over the threshold and into Cassandra's inner sanctum. It smelled like paint and turpentine. "Social services tried to reach her when I was twelve. Repeatedly. When the woman decides to disappear, she really disappears." Sarah glanced around at the room. It really hadn't changed that much in twenty-eight years.

Natalie had followed her inside and was turning over papers on Cassandra's kitchen table. "I'm sorry, but I'm not going to let this go that easily."

Sarah just shrugged. She'd spent most of her life fighting in just the same manner. Fighting for answers. Fighting for power. Fighting to keep what was hers.

She should have left well enough alone when it came to Cassandra. She could have gone anywhere for this forced summer sabbatical of Richard Lee's. Hawaii, for one. Tahiti or the South of France.

Sarah didn't even honestly know why she'd chosen to come see Cassandra after all these years.

The meditation stuff…anyplace had people who could teach her that skill.

The rest of her reason for being here was… the subconscious cry of the little girl still inside her who was upset that she'd been abandoned by her aunt and wanted some honest answers why.

Completely ridiculous. Honest answers didn't always come. Time and again, Sarah had learned that the only thing worth fighting for was her own personal power. If she had enough of it, she would always be in charge. And no one could hurt her again.

Cassandra had proven her wrong in that belief, too. Sarah saw now that she could be queen of the universe, and Cassandra would do whatever the hell she wanted to do, regardless of what was going on with the people around her. Even the little people—including her only vulnerable niece.

Natalie stopped rifling through the papers on the kitchen table. "Look at this." She held up a letter. "It's to you, from Sam's daughter."

Sarah snatched it from her. And immediately put her hand to her mouth.

In childish handwriting, a girl named Lucy Logan had written,

Dear Sarah,
I'm so glad you're coming to visit us! I admire you and hope to meet with you soon.
Your friend, Lucy Logan

The girl had decorated the edges with tiny, skillful drawings of seashells and aquatic life.

Sarah just sighed and closed her eyes. "How old is Lucy Logan?" she asked Natalie.

"Eleven, I think."

"And where is her mom?"

"She lives a few towns over. The rest is up to Sam Logan to tell you. Or not." Natalie's lips twisted.

Sarah sat and put her head in her hands. "I really hope that little girl is okay." She looked up at Natalie. "Can you give me Sam Logan's contact information, please? I need to follow up with him."

The lawyer hesitated.

"I need to know that Lucy is okay," Sarah insisted.

"Come here." Natalie beckoned her to the side window. When Sarah had joined her, Natalie pointed to the two-story home with the back porch beside them. "See that house?"

Sarah saw two Adirondack chairs and a grill. A wetsuit hung over the railing, along with a beach towel. "Are you saying that's where Sam lives? Right next door to me?"

Natalie nodded.

If Sarah stayed, there would be no avoiding him.

She didn't know what to think. She was too tired and emotionally drained to even know what her true feelings were anymore. She just knew that her old reaction—to fight harder—seemed futile all of a sudden.

After Natalie left, Sarah brought in her bags and briefcase full of books and set about finding a place to sleep.

Her old room was set up for her. Plus, there were the cats her aunt had mentioned. Two of them, one large and black, the other small with a white belly and paws. They climbed out from under the bed when she sat on it.

She gave a little scream and jumped up. "Dammit, I don't like pets! Go away!"

They both skittered back under the bed. Returning to the kitchen, Sarah saw that two containers with dry cat pellets were set up beside the table, along with two silver bowls full of water. There was also another, more detailed note explaining their care.

Cassandra obviously believed Sarah would feed and water her cats for however long she would be missing. She'd left instructions, but she hadn't left a timeline.

Anger curled in her belly. But who was present for her to be mad at? She was all alone, yet again. Sarah climbed under the covers and pulled the crisp, clean sheet over her head. Before long, she was sobbing her heart out. Pathetic. A Silicon Valley tech executive, reduced to crying on her childhood bed because an aunt she didn't have much of a relationship with anyway had left her on her own. Again.

And then she was vaguely aware of a shift on the mattress beside her.

She peeked out over the covers.

Two purring, furry bodies were snuggled up, one on either side of her.

Sarah had never lived with pets. But she

buried her cheek beside the big one's head. He purred her to sleep, and for a second before she drifted off, she could swear she didn't feel so alone and angry anymore.

CHAPTER FOUR

SAM DOUBLE-PARKED his truck on Wallis Point's Main Street. Then he got out and ran across two lanes of traffic toward the town library, up two short stone steps and through the heavy oaken doors, breathing heavily. He was barefoot and shirtless, but he wasn't going to stop now. The air inside the library was cooler, but his skin was hot. He was filled with panic.

He just needed to find his daughter, and then he could breathe easier. Something must be terribly wrong with Lucy. Wouldn't she have phoned him if she were here and safe?

He stopped just inside the lobby, perplexed. He didn't often come inside this building—his middle school had its own library that he visited with his students—so he looked around for guidance.

A sign for the children's section pointed down a set of stairs. No, Lucy wouldn't be in the children's section. *Try the magazine reading room.* Sam headed in that direction, but the only people there were two old men sitting on overstuffed chairs who didn't even glance up from their newspapers.

Now what? Sam turned, heart in his throat, wondering who to ask for help, when a serious-faced librarian behind a desk called him over.

"Hello, sir." With wide eyes, she looked him up and down and gave him a censuring frown.

He exhaled and held up his hands. "Sorry, but this is an emergency. I'm looking for my daughter, Lucy. She's eleven. Medium-length brown hair. Yea high." He used his hand to approximate her height. "Please, I can't get hold of the woman who was taking care of her. Cassandra Shipp, you must know her? She's a children's book illustrator who lives on Wallis Point beach."

"Yes, of course I know Cassandra." The librarian smiled and stepped out from behind the desk. Luckily for him, she seemed to understand his state of mind. No mention of his bare feet, bare chest or orange lifeguard trunks. "I think I can help you, sir. I know where your daughter is."

"It's Sam," he said in relief. "And thank you. I'm going out of my mind, here."

"It's not a problem." She smiled sympathetically and beckoned him to follow her.

They zig-zagged through stacks of books that gave off a slight musty smell and finally ended up in a small open area with a row of computers.

Lucy was sitting alone nearby at a large wooden table. She was squinting in concentration as she tapped on her iPad.

"Lucy!" He ran over and hugged her to his chest. "I was worried something had happened to you!"

Lucy stiffened and frowned up at him.

The librarian hovered nearby, watching them. At Lucy's less than enthusiastic reception, she suddenly seemed worried. "Is everything okay, dear?" she asked Lucy. "Do you need me to get you some help?"

Sam tried not to be insulted. He knew the librarian was just doing her job. He was trained to be sensitive toward dangerous situations with kids, too, so he understood her response. What he didn't understand was Lucy's reaction. It made him feel sick. But if he'd had a closer relationship with Lucy, frankly, then none of this would be happening.

His serious daughter shook her head at the librarian. "This is Sam Logan. He's my father."

Not a huge recommendation on his behalf.

"Yes," the librarian said, "I understand. But are you all right to go with him?"

The breath seemed to leave Sam. He felt chilled, and when he saw the look in Lucy's eyes, the chill deepened. Was she that indifferent to him? Did he not matter to her *at all*?

"I'm fine," Lucy murmured, so self-possessed for a girl her age that he still couldn't believe it. She went about shutting down her iPad.

"Are you sure?" the librarian pressed.

"Yes." But Lucy didn't look at her.

The librarian didn't seem convinced. She pursed her lips. Her gaze dropped again to Sam's swim trunks. "You're a local lifeguard?" she asked. "At Wallis Point beach?"

"I am," he answered dully. "I also teach earth science at Wallis Point Middle School. Sam Logan. I'm a registered mandated reporter."

This meant he was trained to recognize signs of child abuse and to report them to the appropriate authorities. He took out the driver's license he always kept in the pocket of his swim trunks in case he needed to show his identification on the beach and handed it to the librarian. "You can call my school principal and check on me. I'm sure you know who Tara is."

The librarian squinted at his ID. "Yes, I know Tara quite well. Excuse me."

She walked away, and Sam was quite sure she really was going to call his boss and check up on him.

He couldn't remember if Tara knew about Lucy or not. Lucy didn't live in Wallis Point, so she wasn't a student in his school system. He didn't talk about his personal life to his coworkers much. Maybe he shouldn't have been so private about Lucy.

He definitely should have made her matter to him more. And until now, he hadn't realized how important she really was to him. Until this, the first time he thought that he'd almost lost her.

While Lucy finished packing up her notes and papers, he sat with his elbow on the library table, nose pinched between his fingers. He just felt so beaten down.

Lucy stared at him, and her lip quivered. Maybe he was scaring her with his reaction, too. "Didn't you get our letter, Sam?" she asked softly.

He straightened in his chair. "What letter?"

"Cassandra and I wrote letters to you and to Sarah."

"It's more appropriate to pick up the phone and call, Lucy," he said sternly.

"But I don't know your phone number!" she protested.

"Of course you do, it's—" Sam paused. *Colleen* knew his number. *Colleen* contacted him. She controlled his access to Lucy. And, he supposed, her access to him. In recent years, he'd done nothing to rock that boat.

He shook his head, stunned at his own cluelessness. "Sorry," he muttered. "I'll write it down for you." He glanced at her. "Do you have a phone?" The last he'd checked, Lucy didn't have one. But it was dawning on him not to take anything for granted. He knew so little about her.

Lucy shook her head and rolled her eyes. "Mom won't get me one."

Then he would get her one for her birthday in two weeks. It was a safety issue.

Okay, one problem solved. He took in a breath. "Where *is* Cassandra?" This was the real question, and he knew he should be discussing this with the adult and not the eleven-year-old, but Cassandra wasn't here and Lucy was.

"Well," Lucy said, "this morning Cassandra got an emergency note from Claudio's son in Italy. Claudio used to be Cassandra's boyfriend. Sam, he's dying and he needs to see her."

Claudio. This was the "gentleman friend" in Naples Cassandra had told him about. "I thought he was coming in August."

"I don't know about that," Lucy said, confused. "I don't think that's right."

Sam remembered that was supposed to be his secret with Cassandra. "Maybe I'm mistaken. What happened then?"

"I let her use your home phone to call him. Sam, he was in an accident yesterday, and he's in the hospital. He *needs* to see her. I told her she had to go. Then we went to the beach to look for you, but we couldn't find you anywhere."

"What time was this?" he asked.

"Early. Like, nine o'clock."

He'd been out in the boat, leading swimming drills for the young lifeguards. All the chairs would have been empty at that time.

"Well, why didn't you contact lifeguard headquarters and have Duke call me on my cell?"

Lucy stared blankly at him. Of course. She didn't know what lifeguard headquarters was. She didn't really know Duke, either. She'd met him few times in the past, but she'd been younger then, and Sam hadn't connected the two in recent years.

Bottom line, Duke was Sam's best friend and had been his boss for the past twelve summers, and Lucy didn't know him. That was *Sam's* fault.

"Cassandra could've left me a note at my house!" he said in frustration.

"She did!" Lucy raised her voice to match his. "Didn't you see it? It's taped to the sliding glass door! How could you *possibly* miss it?"

Sam groaned and held his head in his hands. Lucy looked like she was going to cry.

He glanced up. He had to get control of this situation, and quickly. "Okay. It's all right, Luce," he said quietly. "Where is Cassandra now?"

"Flying to Italy. She called for a car and then

we went to the lawyer's office because she needed to talk to her. Then they brought me here. Then she took the car to the airport."

"Lucy…you should have stayed at home and waited for me!"

"I wanted to come here! I come here every day! You said that I could!" Lucy was close to sobbing.

Did Cassandra even know what a storm she'd unleashed? *Oh, never mind.* Cassandra wasn't Sam's worry. His daughter was. And right now, she was extremely upset with him.

Sam touched her shoulder as gently as she could. Other than red, swollen eyes, she seemed physically okay. "Would you like to go home and get something to eat?" he asked in his most soothing voice. "You must be hungry."

"No." Lucy shook her head vehemently. "I ate the peanut butter sandwich I made at Cassandra's house this morning." She wiped her eyes. "And drank an orange soda. Cassandra bought me a case."

Mighty good of her, Sam thought bitterly. Attuned to the details, but not the big picture.

But how could he blame someone else for what was *his* fault? He'd "hired" Cassandra. No, it was worse than that—he wasn't even paying the woman. Maybe if he'd paid her, she would have treated the job of caring for his daughter more seriously.

He sucked in his breath. That was it. He'd made his decision. He was quitting his lifeguard job tomorrow so he could concentrate on taking care of Lucy. He would make sure to do a better job from now on.

"Is Sarah Buckley here yet?" Lucy suddenly asked, her eyes brightening.

"Luce," he sighed. "Let's just go home." He didn't want to open the can of worms that was Sarah Buckley.

"Is. Sarah. Here?" His daughter's voice was strident.

Sam stood, his head pounding. The last thing he wanted—or the situation warranted—was another angry scene with Lucy. He smiled as a woman walked by staring at them, a library patron. She glanced at his bare feet and shot him a frown.

He just wanted to get of here. With Lucy. Beyond that, he had no intention of letting his daughter have anything to do with Cassandra's niece. She wasn't who Lucy thought she was. Sarah Buckley was the last person in the world he would ever consider for Lucy's role model.

"Let's go," he ordered, eager to get away from the woman who was still staring. "My truck is parked out front."

"No! You didn't answer my question!"

"Lucy, let's go," he said through clenched teeth.

"I hate you!"

A buzzing started in Sam's ears.

"I wish I wasn't here!" Lucy wailed.

"Lucy," he said quietly.

"I want to see Sarah!"

He let out a breath. How could he tell her that Sarah Buckley wasn't the person she expected? She would blow his daughter off in a heartbeat and crush her on her way out the door.

Sarah Buckley certainly wasn't worthy of emulation. *He* might have been amused and struck by her as a person, but as a role model for a kid, Sarah was terrible. She was rude. Bossy. In his opinion, she wasn't someone that an eleven-year-old should be interacting with at all.

"We'll talk in the truck, okay? Let's go."

Just then the librarian reappeared. "Sam, I talked to Tara and she vouched for you." But then she noticed Lucy's distraught expression, and a fresh look of concern appeared on her face. "Are you *sure* everything is all right here, Sam?"

"Yes," he answered, nodding seriously at her. He couldn't even fake a smile anymore. He felt like a completely different person from the man he'd woken up as this morning.

He turned to Lucy. "Please come with me," he outright pleaded with her this time. "You can show me the note you and Cassandra left for me. I'm really interested in seeing it."

"Only if you let me see Sarah," Lucy said sullenly.

"Yeah. Sure. Okay," he said. The librarian was staring at them both. If she knew Cassandra, she more than likely knew who "Sarah" was. Sam had to watch what he said about Cassandra's niece in public.

"Right now." Lucy folded her arms. "We'll drive to Cassandra's cottage."

"Well, yeah. Okay."

Lucy stared at him. "You're lying to me, aren't you?" She wasn't budging from her spot by the table, and he couldn't very well drag her off. Not with the audience he currently had.

There was nothing left to do but tell Lucy the truth and hope she saw reason.

He focused fully on Lucy. "You said that you left Sarah a note, correct?"

Lucy nodded. "Yes."

"Then she'll definitely read it and know that you want to see her. So if she comes to see you at our house tomorrow, then I give my blessing to have a visit with her. As long as you both want one. But we're not going to bother Sarah Buckley tonight because she's tired from traveling. She's just arrived from California and it was a long flight. Frankly, she's in a bad mood right now." And quite frankly, he was in a foul one himself.

"All right." Lucy stood. She must have appreciated his honest talk, because she ceased arguing and instead slung her loaded backpack onto her thin shoulders. "Let's go."

Relieved, Sam stood, too, and prepared to herd her the hell out of here. He avoided meeting the librarian's eyes because he'd lost his cool completely, and that embarrassed him. He felt as if he'd never met a middle schooler in his life. Dealing with his own child was completely different from handling students in his classroom.

The librarian stood aside as he and Lucy retreated from the battered library table and left the community room together. From her sagging body language, Lucy seemed to be drooping in spirits. He couldn't blame her for being tired and emotional. Cassandra's impulsive stunt had drained the energy from all of them.

Outside on the street, Sam's double-parked truck had earned him a parking ticket tucked beneath the windshield wiper. Halfheartedly, Sam removed the slip of paper and tossed it inside his truck. Then he walked to the passenger side and unlocked the door for Lucy. It was a big step up from the street, so he held her backpack as she hoisted herself inside.

The top of Lucy's backpack was open, and Sam saw that she'd packed her teddy bear. His heart squeezed. His outwardly angry, near-teen daughter was also a vulnerable little girl who still needed the security of a teddy bear enough that she took it with her wherever she went. Maybe if he'd been a better father all along, this wouldn't be so.

Yes, Cassandra's sudden departure had pushed them to this crisis. But *he* needed to make some changes.

THE NEXT DAY, Sam called in sick. It was easier than giving notice just yet; this way, Duke wouldn't come over to try and talk him out of it. Sam couldn't deal with that stress today. He'd made his decision and he didn't want anybody trying to change his mind.

Besides, Sam couldn't leave the house right now. Lucy was home, alternating between snapping at him and giving him sullen silences. Gone was the adult-like kid, and in her place was a girl who acted more like a wounded animal than a child.

He knew she was unhappy, mostly because Sarah Buckley hadn't called on her yet, and Sam had stuck to his original decision about allowing

Sarah to take that lead with his daughter. As a result, Sam could hear Lucy speaking heatedly with someone in her bedroom. She didn't have a phone, so it had to be through a messaging app on her iPad. Likely, Lucy was talking with her mother. He didn't have a problem with that, per se. He would never begrudge a daughter talking with her mother, even if Colleen talked to him as little as she possibly could.

Still, waiting for the fallout from Lucy's upset phone conversation put Sam on edge all morning. He fully expected Colleen to phone her lawyer who would then call Sam's lawyer, who would then call Sam. It promised to be a stressful headache, and Sam hated stress.

But by noon, his fear hadn't come to fruition. Sam trudged upstairs to the spare room he'd designated as Lucy's bedroom—even though she'd never slept over before this week—and knocked on the door.

He received no answer.

"Lucy, I just want to know if you're ready for lunch?" he called. Still no reply.

He opened the door and found her asleep on her bed, fully dressed. She'd obviously been exhausted. She slept with her arms tucked under her head and that tattered teddy bear on the second pillow, beside her.

Sam swallowed. He noticed that Lucy's window was open and the curtains blew inward. Since it was supposed to rain later, he shut the window and draped a light blanket over her. Then he sat on the chair beside her bed, watching her sleep.

He'd spent eleven years without having his daughter spend the night in his house. He'd let Colleen and the family courts call the shots. He hadn't fought them personally, and he'd told himself it was because he hadn't wanted to damage Lucy by fighting back. But by doing nothing—by letting things happen, and letting his lawyer give Colleen mostly what she wanted—it looked as if he'd caused a lot more damage than if he'd fought to see Lucy more often.

These ten weeks were his opportunity, he realized. This summer, he could cobble together a more solid relationship with his daughter—if he worked on it and didn't stand passively by.

That meant he might have to fight. Like yesterday. He might even have to be rude sometimes, like his new neighbor, Sarah Buckley.

He stood, went downstairs to the kitchen and made Lucy a peanut butter and jelly sandwich. Then he climbed back up to her bedroom and left her lunch on the desk beside her iPad. He didn't have any orange soda, and he didn't want to run to the corner store and leave her alone in the house like this, so he brought her a glass of water, instead.

When she woke, he was going to have as much of a heart-to-heart talk with her as he could. Until then, he decided to do something he hadn't had the time or foresight to do before Lucy had shown up at his door a week ago—make space for her. He wanted to show her that this was her home, too.

To start, he tossed stuff away. Work papers, mostly. Junk in his cabinets and drawers that had nothing to do with family life and everything to do with old hobbies he'd dropped along the way. He made room for Lucy's things. And he boxed up all the beer bottles crowding the refrigerator, except for one. That beer he would save for himself. One last, relaxing goodbye to his old life.

He had no idea what he was going to say when Lucy woke. He would take it moment by moment and keep his Zen as much as possible.

Beyond that, whatever ended up happening… well, it depended in a large part upon Lucy. He only hoped she wasn't too disappointed if their rude neighbor never called on her. Or, worse, if Sarah did come over and Lucy saw that she wasn't the heroine Lucy had conceived her to be.

AT DUSK, SARAH smelled steak being grilled from the direction of her neighbor's porch.

She lifted the kitchen curtain and glanced outside. Until now, it hadn't appeared that anyone was home next door. But over on Sam-the-lifeguard's deck, a barbecue was fired up and smoking.

She wanted to see him. Before Sarah made any decisions about where to travel next, she needed to know that the girl her aunt had left behind—Lucy—was really all right. After that, she fully intended to pack up and leave Wallis Point.

Sarah settled the kitchen curtain back into place and quickly checked on her two feline companions, her comrades in being left behind by Cassandra.

The big cat had moped all day. The little one had possessed the gall to hop into the shower with Sarah that morning. Sarah had actually screamed in surprise, until she'd seen that her aunt had jerry-rigged the curtain setup in such a way that the little tuxedo cat could sit on the ledge of the tub and watch her without getting wet.

"I don't even know you," Sarah had said to him.

She hadn't known exactly how to feed the cats, either, despite Cassandra's instructions, so the little one had squawked at her—he was the talker and seemed to be in charge of the show—

and the big one had led the way to the cat-food cabinet. He'd pawed it with one big, furry black paw, and then had gone and sat by his food bowl while the little one yelled at her to hurry it up and fill their dishes.

She'd split a can of unappealing-looking wet glop between them. Salmon turkey, the label said, though the contents in no way resembled either salmon or turkey, to Sarah's mind. Surprisingly, though, the cats' meal didn't smell half bad.

"Goodbye, you two," Sarah said to the funny duo, bending down to pet their little heads. "Don't get into any mischief while I'm gone." She shook her head, shocked that she was warming up to these cats, given that she'd rather they weren't here at all.

She put on a gauzy cotton dress and a pair of flip-flops because the outfit seemed beachy and cool. Then she picked up the shopping bag she'd packed and headed through the soft sand and muggy evening air toward her neighbor's house.

While she trudged over, Sam stepped onto his porch.

His presence was a good sign. If he was at home barbecuing, then his daughter had to be physically okay, at least. Sarah relaxed a bit.

"Hey, Sam!" Sarah lifted one arm and waved at him. He turned in her direction but said nothing in reply. He looked quiet and angry as he studied her up and down.

She paused in the hot sand, hoping that his bad mood didn't mean his daughter wasn't doing okay, after all. Sarah had a soft spot in her heart for any kid who got caught up in Cassandra's pretend web of caring. When a person found out how false that care was, it was a hurtful thing.

Sarah decided it was best to avoid mentioning Sam's daughter at all for the moment. She had an armload of cargo she needed to unload.

"Knock, knock." She stepped up to Sam's deck and held out the two six-packs she'd brought. "I come bearing gifts." One was a Belgian beer she'd picked up when she'd been out shopping earlier and the other a six-pack of orange soda that had been left on Cassandra's kitchen table. "Consider these peace offerings." She plunked them down on Sam's outdoor table and turned to study him.

He still looked wary and therefore not likely to offer her anything to drink.

"Um, do you mind if I have one?" Sarah indicated the beer. "I'm thirsty."

Sam pursed his lips. "You like beer?"

"Sure, I do. Just because I'm from the San Francisco area, am I supposed to be a wino?"

He cracked a smile. Her sassy sarcasm had

nudged him from his bad mood. "Hold on a second," he said. "I'll be right back."

He disappeared into the house and came back holding a bottle opener and a beer with an unfamiliar-to-her label. "Don't drink that commercial stuff. Try this, instead. It's a private label." He popped the top and passed the beer to her.

She read the label. "Lifeguard Lager?"

"Just try it."

"I don't know, Sam." She had a feeling a friend of his had made it, and she decided to play with him a bit. What was the difference—she was leaving soon, anyway.

She winked at the younger-than-her lifeguard with the nice biceps and tanned face. "After my experience with your lifeguard teams, it might leave a bad taste in my mouth."

"What are you complaining about? We saved your butt, didn't we?"

"That point is still in contention," she said lightly and gave him a smirk.

"Then I dare you to taste it, Ms. Buckley." He said it with a twinkle in his eyes and a hint of the humor he'd shown yesterday.

She liked this Sam better. "Dare accepted."

Tipping her head back, Sarah put her lips to the bottle and took a long, deep swallow. Cool, good-tasting beer. A mild lager, yet distinct. And fresh.

Surprised, she lowered the bottle and gazed at Sam. The hunky lifeguard had his arms crossed and his head tilted. He held the grill spatula like some kind of medieval battle apparatus.

"What do you think?" he asked.

"I like it." She gazed at him. "I do." He wore shorts and a blue T-shirt that suited his tanned complexion and his dark blue eyes.

"I'm glad." Then he turned and went into the house, leaving her alone on his deck.

He returned carrying a box, the flaps open, which he plunked down on the table beside her gifts.

"What's this?" she asked.

"Beer. The last batch I made. It's for you. Take it."

She selected a bottle and studied it. So *he* was the one who'd made the beer. "That's kind of you, Sam, but you don't have to give me all your beer."

"I'm making room in the house for Lucy. I can't keep this in the house with a kid," he said helplessly.

"Sure you can," she replied calmly.

He shook his head. "No. I want to be a good father to Lucy."

"My father had the occasional beer after work, and he was a great father. What's wrong with beer in your refrigerator?" She peered at him. "Are you an alcoholic, Sam?"

"No," he said, looking insulted. But then he reddened, shaking his head. "I remember being a young teen, is all. My older brother and I used to sneak beers and experiment with being more grown-up than we really were. A time or two we got into trouble because of it. I want to be a better parent to Lucy than mine were to me, is all."

This touched Sarah to her heart, which irritated her, frankly. Sam shouldn't matter that much to her.

Really, she was here to ask about his daughter only because Lucy's situation hit so close to home.

"Just take the box and say thank-you," Sam said, an edge in his voice again.

She sat down at his table and made herself comfortable, instead, drinking the bottle of Lifeguard Lager. He sighed, put the box on a corner of the porch and straightened, crossing his arms. Yes, she could tell when she'd irritated someone, but she'd never been bothered when people disliked her. She was not an "eager to please" person.

She'd come over for a reason. "I've been thinking, Sam." And she had. Though Sarah was never going to admit that her banishment had been right or fair, Lucy's situation had shown

Sarah a new perspective. As had dealing with Cassandra's perfidy, yet again.

"What have you been thinking about, Sarah?" And then Sam turned away and flipped his steak over on the grill. This made it easier for her to say what she needed to, because she wouldn't have to look into his probing blue eyes.

She took a breath. "Actually, I came over here to check on your daughter, to see how she was doing. *And* to apologize to you." She took another breath. "I was rude yesterday. I'll admit that. You did save me from the ocean, and I'm grateful." She took another sip of the beer.

His back seemed to stiffen. She almost wished he had his lifeguard outfit on and not his casual clothes, because then she would have had the pleasure of seeing his back muscles ripple.

Warily, he turned to her. "Really? You're serious about apologizing to me?"

"I am," she said softly. "How is Lucy?"

"She's fine. In fact, she'd like to see you." His voice had turned hard. "But since she and I are about to eat dinner, I'd prefer you come back to see her in an hour."

It was clear that Sam was giving her the brush-off. Fine. She understood. In fact, she was hungry, too. His steaks sizzling on the barbecue smelled so good. Sam was obviously a much better cook than she was.

"Do you mind if I ask you a favor?" she asked impulsively. "May I bring over a steak for you to grill for me? I went shopping today. Actual car-in-the-parking-lot-walk-into-the-store shopping." She shuddered. She'd been so irritated that she couldn't use her grocery delivery app because it didn't work in Wallis Point. "But I'm not used to cooking, because I have a personal chef at home. I would've eaten at one of those nearby diners, but…" Sarah shuddered again.

"Really, Sarah? I ask you to leave, and you respond by asking me to *cook* for you?" Sam shook his head, appearing as if he was trying hard not to laugh. "You are something. How do you know I'm up to your fine standards?"

She ignored the sarcasm and instead eyed the steaks he was putting onto a plate. They smelled and looked so good that her stomach growled. "Because I know quality when I see it. And you look like you have good hygiene," she added.

He barked out a laugh.

She grinned at him.

"And I was so determined not to like you," he said, shaking his head as he set the plate down and sank into an Adirondack chair bedside her. He laughed again. He laid his head back on the edge of the Adirondack chair and kept on laughing.

"Excellent," she said cheerfully. "Let me go

get the steak I bought." She rose. "I can bring over a salad for you and Lucy to share if you'd like."

"No, I already made one. But tell me." He leveled his gaze at her, suddenly serious. "Why should I even do this? All you seem to do is insult people, and frankly, I'm not up for that when it comes to my family."

"But… I apologized to you," she said.

"Oh, boy!" He gave her a mock cheer.

"Look, I never apologize, Sam! Apologies admit weakness. That's what my first mentor always told me. So this is a first in the history of the world for me—be flattered."

"You're quite self-centered." Sam paused and grinned at her wickedly. "And I never insult people—be flattered."

Were they *flirting*? How strange for her. But she really kind of liked it.

"A first in the history of the world?" she asked him cheerfully.

Sam barked out another laugh. His grin stayed on his face, and she felt this was a genuine grin, one he really felt.

She *could* be a loveable person. She'd always known this, but not many people seemed to see that side of her. The problem she hadn't been able to articulate to Richard Lee was that he just hadn't hired the *right* people, who understood her, to staff up their company. The company was *her*. If he hired people who didn't think like her, who abhorred her or who were frightened of her personal style or just plain didn't like her, then how was that supposed to work for Sarah?

Was she was supposed to learn how to be a different person just so the underlings he'd hired would *like* her? No. It didn't make sense.

But Richard had all the power. Just as Cassandra had held all the power when Sarah was young.

She gazed at Sam. "We really should think of each other as two people on common ground— we were both hit upside the head by my aunt. As was Lucy. I came to see how she was doing. May I see her now, Sam?"

"As I said, we're about to eat. In fact, you're making our food cold. Go." He made a shooing motion with his hand. "Go get your steak."

"Thank you." She smiled brilliantly at him. "I'll be right back." Before he could respond, she stood and literally ran back to Cassandra's refrigerator, where she scooped up the uncooked steak, still packaged, and plopped it onto one of Cassandra's dinner plates.

When she returned to Sam's outdoor table, he was sitting across from the seat she'd just vacated and drinking the Belgian beer she'd brought over. His expression seemed distant again. And thoughtful.

"Caught you," she said to him, sitting beside him. "The beer I chose is good, too, isn't it?"

"It's an ale," he replied. "Completely different from what I make. But, yes, it's pretty good." He eyed her. "Did you bring this to try and sway me into cooking your steaks for you?"

"Oh, I would never do that." She handed him the plate from Cassandra's kitchen containing the steak she'd bought.

"Sure you would." He hefted the plate. "And this is a better cut than mine."

"Well, then you can have it if you want. I'll take one of the steaks that you cooked already."

"Still trying to sway me." He smirked at her. "No, those two are for Lucy and me." Then he just looked sad again.

"Yes, I figured," She took a breath. Something was wrong. Here was where she was taking a chance, because it was obvious he wasn't especially keen on having Lucy meet her. Not that it bothered Sarah that Sam felt that way, but the note the girl had left her had been so sweet.

"Is Lucy okay, Sam?" she asked in a soft voice. "Honestly, I've been worried about her."

"Yeah. Me, too." He closed his eyes and sighed. "Physically, she's fine. I found her in the town library sitting safely with her iPad. But emotionally…" He shook his head.

Sarah felt bad for him. Maybe it would help to see his daughter's note to her. Sarah took it from her back pocket, smoothed out the creases and showed it to him.

His face seemed to crumple. The girlish handwriting was sweet and innocent. "She *idolizes* you," he said. "She talks of nothing other than you. She's up in her room, mad that I wouldn't let her go knock on your door to say hi."

And Sarah was painfully aware that it was hurtful to him that his daughter preferred to meet Sarah, a stranger, over spending time with her own father.

Sarah expelled a breath. She owed Sam. For agreeing to cook her dinner. For saving her from the ocean yesterday. "Well, here's an idea," she said cheerfully. "How about if I bring Lucy up her dinner? I'll talk with her and…" She glanced at him. "You're a good person, Sam. I'll do what I can for you. And for her." She paused. This was more than she'd wanted to admit to anyone, but she would make an exception here. This was important to her. Besides, it wasn't like she was going to see either Sam or Lucy ever again after tomorrow. "And because Lucy and I were both treated similarly by Cassandra when we were about the same age, I want to help her, in particular."

He folded his arms. "Your idea of help makes me nervous. Lucy is eleven and she admires you. I can handle it when you're blunt and forthright, but I'm not sure she can."

"Well…of course I'll be kind to her. That goes without saying."

He snorted.

"What happened to the friendly lifeguard?" she asked.

"He's resigning from his job on Monday in order to take better care of his daughter."

"What?"

"Go inside and get the roll of aluminum foil on the counter for me," he directed. "My steak is getting cold because of you. We'll talk as I wrap it up to keep it warm."

Normally, she didn't like being ordered around, but she made an exception because he *was* cooking her dinner. So far, her stay in Wallis Point had been all about exceptions.

Sarah went into his kitchen and grabbed the roll of foil off the counter.

But when she came back, she saw that Sam had a visitor. Another lifeguard with the distinctive orange shorts and a bare chest. He'd driven up beside the porch and now sat astride the small ATV that Sam had commandeered the day before.

From the gray streaks in this lifeguard's close-cropped hair and the crease marks around his eyes, Sarah judged him to be older than Sam. Maybe another manager.

She walked right up to her former spot at the table across from Sam and sat down, too. The manager glanced over at her, nodding, but kept right on talking to Sam.

"I heard you called in sick today, is that right?" he asked Sam.

"Yep, I did," Sam said tightly.

"Are you okay now?"

"I'm fine, Duke," Sam answered.

"You've haven't missed a day from as far back as I can remember." Duke waited, but Sam didn't reply.

"I was gonna stop by at lunch and check on you," Duke continued, "but then I figured I'd wait until now." Another pause as Duke studied Sam's face. "You look okay. Are you sure everything's good?"

Sam darted a look at Sarah. She'd made herself comfortable by drinking from the Lifeguard Lager he'd served her. He was cooking her dinner, after all.

Sam swiped his hand through his hair. He wasn't polite, and he didn't introduce her, but she didn't much care about that. Sam would get to her when he was ready, and besides, Sarah got the chance to eavesdrop this way. Something else was going on with Lucy. Sam hadn't told her all of it.

"My daughter is here for the summer," Sam was saying to Duke. "Did I tell you that?"

"That's great, Sam. No, you didn't tell me Lucy was here."

"Yeah, well, I thought I had childcare lined up. It fell through in a big way, though."

"I'm sorry to hear that."

Sam gave a long sigh. "I was gonna see you on Monday to tell you, but... I'll need to take the summer off."

"Seriously?" Duke asked.

"Sorry to spring it on you like this."

"Have you thought about working part-time?" Duke suggested. "You could work in the morning and spend afternoons with Lucy." He shifted in his seat. The engine on the ATV surged, so the rest of his sentence was drowned out and Sarah missed it.

"Look..." Sam turned and stared at Sarah. She waggled her brows at him and lifted her beer bottle to her mouth. Sam sighed, but he turned back to the squat lifeguard in his orange shorts. "I'll have to get back to you. We'll talk more on Monday morning."

"Right. We'll figure something out. We can't lose you entirely, Sam. You're too important around here." The older lifeguard gave his head one more shake and then motored off.

Sam put his hands on his hips and faced her. "Do you have a habit of listening to people's conversations?"

She smiled up at him. "Why, yes, I do. How else would I learn anything?"

"You see, this is exactly why I'm hesitant to have you meet my daughter. You have bad manners."

"I'm practical. Please, Sam, I'd like to try talking with her now." In a lowered voice, she added, "I won't hurt her. And I understand Cassandra *very well*, so maybe I can help with that."

Sam lifted his hands. "Fine. I suppose if I send you away, then Lucy will be more upset with me than she already is."

He brought the tinfoil-covered plate into the kitchen. She followed him, grabbing the edge of the screen door and pushing it wider so he could pass through.

He gave her a tired look. Sam struck her as a man who was tired about everything.

She felt the same way. It took a lot of energy to be angry, and at this point, she just wanted to do what it took to get back to her job and stop wasting energy raging over things she couldn't control.

She stood in his kitchen, waiting for him to take her to Lucy, while he took down a big plastic tray and set cutlery, a napkin and the plate piled with meat and vegetables on it—a well-balanced meal. *Good dad*, she thought.

"Can you bring me in one of those cans of that orange soda you brought over?" he asked her.

"Sure. I figured Cassandra bought them as a treat for your daughter. I don't drink soda regularly, and she never did, either."

Sam just grunted.

She went to the deck and grabbed a can from the grocery bag, along with the Lifeguard Lager that she'd started drinking earlier. She plopped the soda on Lucy's dinner tray.

He nodded, giving her a look as if to say, "Here goes nothing," and then headed down a short corridor to a stairway. She climbed the stairs behind him, then followed him down the hall to the closed door of a room facing the street. Sam's house was twice as big as Cassandra's, which didn't even have a second floor. Sam's place was also a lot more modern and updated.

He balanced the tray on one arm and knocked on Lucy's door.

"Leave me alone!" came a muffled voice from inside the bedroom.

"I brought dinner," Sam announced in his life-guard voice.

"I can smell it from here. Is it steak? I don't eat animal meat. It's horrible that you eat innocent, defenseless animals."

Sam sighed and shrugged at Sarah. "Something else nobody told me about," he muttered.

Sarah swiped the orange soda can off Lucy's tray. "It'll be okay, Sam. Let her get herself her own dinner later, when she's hungry enough. I'll go in and see her now. You and I will eat together afterward. How's that? We can talk about your daughter and appreciate our nice meal."

"Not a bad idea." Sam cocked a brow at her. "I like your way of thinking."

"Thank you." Sarah knocked on Lucy's door. "Is this Lucy Logan I'm speaking to?" Sarah called. "Because if it is, I got your note. This is Sarah Buckley."

A thump sounded inside, like a girl jumping down from a bed, and then the door whipped open.

A preteen who looked remarkably like Sam—with light brown hair that had the same cowlick in front—stood blinking at Sarah. She wore a *Girls Code, Too* T-shirt and pink shorts.

"Sarah Buckley! You came to my house!" Lucy exclaimed.

Sarah heard Sam let out a breath behind her.

Maybe it made him happy that Lucy had called his house "my house."

"Yes," Sarah replied calmly, "I got your note." She patted her pocket, acknowledging that she'd kept it safe. "I brought you some orange soda from Cassandra's stash." She peeked inside the girl's bedroom. "May I come in?"

"Yes! Oh, my gosh, yes!"

Sarah stepped inside the small bedroom, and without ceremony, Lucy shut the door in her father's face.

Well. Sarah bit her tongue. She couldn't call Lucy out on that, because Sarah quite often shut her own office door in people's faces, too.

She hoped Sam would eavesdrop on their conversation. Sarah would, in his shoes.

CHAPTER FIVE

SARAH SAT ON the edge of Lucy's bed. The girl was neat; Sarah had to give her credit for that. The sheets and coverlet were made up, and her clothes were folded and stacked on a dresser. However, the room held remnants of things Sarah was sure belonged to Sam. A treadmill in the corner. Some free weights stacked up beside it. Sam obviously used this room as a home gym when Lucy wasn't here.

"That your dad's stuff?" she said to Lucy.

Lucy snorted. "It's *his* room. This summer is the first time I've ever slept over at his house."

"How come?"

Lucy shrugged. "Because I only see him two Saturdays a month."

"Do you like those two Saturdays?"

Lucy folded her arms and said nothing.

"Well, as you know, I only just met your dad yesterday. But he was telling me he really wants you here, so that's a good thing."

Lucy gave her the side-eye.

Sarah glanced at Lucy's iPad at the end of the

bed. It was open to a messenger app. "Who are you talking to?"

"I'm waiting to talk to my mom," Lucy explained. "I want her to come and get me out of here." She had a forlorn expression on her face. "I really miss her."

Sarah felt sorry for the girl. She knew about being left behind and missing people. "Could you tell me what's going on with Cassandra?" she tried to keep her voice steady and matter-of-fact. "What did she say to you before she left?"

"Oh!" Lucy's face brightened. "I was supposed to tell you something. I kind of forgot in all the excitement." She poked her scraggly hair behind her ears. "Cassandra said to tell you that she was sorry she had to leave. But she hoped you would understand once she sees you in person and can talk to you about it."

"Uh-huh." Sarah said dryly. *Right.* "Let me guess, Cassandra went to see Claudio, right?" Sarah couldn't help adding. "In Naples."

"Yes!" Lucy nodded vigorously "I want Cassandra to finally get her happy ending, but I don't know if she will, because it turns out Claudio is *dying.* That's why she had to leave so quickly."

Mm-hmm. "His son called—excuse me, wrote to her—I presume?"

"He called her lawyer's office, and the office sent a note by messenger."

"What do you think of Cassandra refusing to get with modern technology?" Sarah couldn't help asking, indicating the girl's iPad.

"It's kind of weird. But Cassandra didn't grow up with computers, like I did."

Sarah snorted. That wasn't it at all. Sarah knew ninety-year-olds who used email, but that didn't matter to this conversation, so Sarah gestured at the iPad again. "So, now you've decided that you don't want to stick it out with your dad this summer. Is that what's going on with you?"

"I don't really want to talk about Sam," Lucy said.

Sam. Ouch. "Okay. Where's your mom, if you don't mind my asking?" Sarah smiled at Lucy. "In case you didn't notice, I'm a very direct person. I like to get the facts all out in the open with the people I'm dealing with."

Lucy nodded, brightening again. "You're a woman of substance."

"Damn—I mean *darn* straight." Sarah crossed her arms and nodded at Lucy. "And you are, too. I see that you're a coder." She referenced Lucy's T-shirt.

"*That* is what I wanted to talk to you about!" Lucy said excitedly. "I'm working on a programming project this summer for the Future Tech Scholars competition."

Sarah blinked at the girl. She kept her expression neutral, but inside, she couldn't have been more surprised. "How did you hear about Future Tech Scholars?" she asked cautiously.

"From Cassandra."

How? Cassandra had never even been on a computer, as far as Sarah knew.

Once, a long time ago, Sarah had won the annual Future Tech Scholars competition for teen programmers. Back then, the technology had been much more primitive—no apps or touchscreens—but the contest win had changed her life. And Cassandra had had nothing to do with it.

But that wasn't why Sarah was excited. She was excited because, though Sarah didn't have much to do with the contest anymore, *Richard Lee* did. It was a pet project of his, in fact.

"So…tell me about your project," Sarah said coolly. She would treat the conversation as she did when one of her employees brought her a good idea.

Lucy sat beside her, moving to rest against the pillow, and cracked the pull tab on her orange soda as she did so. "My throat is very dry," Lucy apologized.

"No worries. Take your time. No need to be nervous when you pitch to me."

A buzzer on Lucy's iPad went off. Sarah assumed that was a notification that her mother was calling back. Lucy bent and turned the buzzer off without answering the call.

Interesting, Sarah thought. For Lucy, pitching an idea to Sarah outranked the call she'd been waiting for, her opportunity to ask her mom to come and get her. Sarah thought that was a good sign, for Sam's sake.

The girl scooted back, surreptitiously shoving her teddy bear under a pillow.

"Here is my pitch," Lucy said, plunking down her can of soda on the bedside table. She sat up straighter. "What happens when you get to the beach, and too late, you find out that it's high tide and there's no room for your blanket? Or that it's a land breeze, not a sea breeze, so it's even hotter on the coast than it is back at home? Or worse, that the water temperature is a frigid forty degrees? Or that the waves are so high you can't use your boogie board? Or that boogie boards are against regulations? Or there are rip current warnings? Wouldn't you have liked to have known all that before you put the effort into packing up your kids and your stuff and sitting in traffic for an hour?"

"Interesting. It sounds like a basic weather

and travel destination app. Tell me how your idea is different."

"Actually, my app isn't that basic," Lucy explained. "Yes, the information will all be contained in one place and all in real time. Weather, traffic, oceanic conditions. We'll tie in fishing and boating information, too. Even the lifeguard, police and fire updates. It will eventually cover all the beaches in the region, plus road conditions and traffic. If parking lots are full and where there are open meters. Right now, that information is available in the public domain, but it's spread across a dozen or more internet sources that most people don't even know about. Mine is a one-step, inclusive application. But Sarah, to answer your question, here is the best part. I'm hoping to embed the artificial intelligence technology developed by your firm. That is what will make my app unique."

Sarah just stared at the eleven-year-old. *Wow*, she thought to herself. *Wow, wow, wow.*

And she was only eleven? Yes, there were students that young who entered the competition, but not many. Lucy was certainly ahead of her peer group.

Treat her like she's any developer giving a pitch. That's how you can best help her. "What's the competition for your app?" Sarah asked. "Tell me about the competitors in this market space."

"Nothing else like this exists," Lucy said. "There are no apps at all for Wallis Point beaches."

"You'll need to think beyond the Wallis Point market, Lucy."

"Yes!" She nodded excitedly. "You're right about that."

"And the price you'll charge?" Sarah pushed. "Projected sales?"

Lucy waved a hand. "That's for you to decide, Sarah. I'm just the developer." She coughed. "But Cassandra and I did check on trademarks at the library yesterday."

"Cassandra? Who doesn't even have a land-line, never mind an internet connection?"

"She said that's her personal choice," Lucy protested. "Just because she's chosen a quiet, unconnected life, doesn't mean she doesn't read. She knows what trademarks are."

Okay, then. Maybe it was better if they kept the Cassandra topic off-limits. "What did you do with the information you learned?"

"Well, since my title idea is unique, I bought the domain name." Lucy smiled proudly. "Cassandra let me borrow her credit card. She said I can pay her back after I make my first million."

Sarah snorted. But, really, she was impressed with the girl. Firstly, because Lucy really did have a decent idea. Sarah didn't say that easily. And she hadn't cut Lucy any slack over her youth and inexperience.

And secondly, that Lucy had managed to rope Cassandra into being so supportive of her project. At least until Cassandra had ditched Lucy when Claudio came calling.

Sarah sat back on the bed, crossed her legs at the ankles and stared at her new sandals, thinking, absorbing everything she'd just heard.

"Well?" Lucy asked, crossing her arms and mimicking Sarah's pose. "What do you think? Will you help me with my app?"

"You mentioned Future Tech Scholars," Sarah said, thinking more of herself than of Lucy. "Do you intend to enter the competition formally?"

"Yes, I do."

"And I suppose you're telling me all this because the general strategy was for me to assist you with that?"

"Would you mentor me, Sarah? Oh, please!"

Sarah was pretty sure that, despite her absence, Cassandra had had something to do with this meeting. Regardless, the wheels were spinning in Sarah's mind. This could really benefit her if it was something Richard approved of. "The way I remember the competition is that you first submit an application to compete. This includes all your parental permissions, plus a video explaining a high-level overview of your project—in this case, your beach app."

Lucy nodded. "Right. It's still that way."

"And then, once the application is selected to proceed"—a shoo-in for Lucy, in Sarah's opinion— "you're officially accepted into the competition. At the end of summer, you present your completed app to the committee. They choose a winner, who receives a full scholarship to attend Future Tech Scholars Academy." The most prestigious school for young techies in the country. "Is this what you want?"

"Oh, yes, Sarah!" Lucy's eyes were shining. "Will you help me?"

"Let me ask you a few questions first. Have you filled out your application form?"

Lucy sighed. "Not yet. I wanted to talk to you about it first."

Sarah nodded. She would need to check out the deadlines and the current entry requirements to see if Lucy was able to enter. This competition wasn't something Sarah kept up with every year. Richard did, though. In fact, she was pretty sure he was part of this year's committee, if not the committee head. "Do you have your parental permissions in place?"

"Yes." Lucy nodded. "My mother knows."

"Where *is* your mother?"

Lucy glanced at her iPad. As if worried her

father might be listening, she cupped her hand and whispered into Sarah's ear. "She's in Vancouver today." Lucy got up and pulled a piece of paper from her backpack. "This is the schedule for her cruise ship job. Sometimes she's off duty, and then it's okay for me to video call her."

"Can't you message her any time?"

"Yes, but it has to be an emergency, and this doesn't qualify as an emergency. She'll get mad if I bug her too much."

"Ah." Sarah nodded. "So you've been waiting to talk to her in person today?"

"We talked for a few minutes, but…" Lucy sighed. "She has a lot of practices this week. She's filling in for a big stage show, last minute. She has a lot to catch up on."

"Well, I think it's good that you're in touch with her." Almost every day of her life, Sarah had wished that she could be in touch with her mother, too. But that wasn't to be for her. "Lucy, if you want to apply to be accepted for the Future Tech Scholars competition, then you need parental permission. Isn't there a form that needs to be signed by your parents and sent in, either online or by hard copy?"

"Yes, I know all about that," Lucy said calmly.

"So you've completed the application form and just need to get the parental signatures?"

"Well, yes, I don't have them yet. Cassandra and I were working on it, but I didn't get a chance to finish in time so my mother could see it. It's her signature I need. Sam can't do it."

Sarah sincerely hoped that Sam wasn't listening through the door at this, because it would break his heart. She also assumed this meant Sam wasn't the custodial parent, and that jibed with what he'd already told her.

"So…let me get this straight. If you do get hold of your mother, and you ask her to sign the application electronically, and then you convince her to remove you from Sam's house for the summer like you want, then logistically, how would I mentor you? Even if I could do it remotely…wouldn't that be kind of awkward, with me living next to Sam?"

Lucy jumped on the bed and screamed. "Are you telling me that you'll do it? You'll mentor me with my app?!"

"Calm down! No, did I say that yet? Geez! Think about staying with Sam."

"I will!"

The door opened and Sam stuck his head inside. "Is everything all right in here?"

"Yes, Sam." Sarah turned back to Lucy. She would need to put in a call to Richard Lee, of course, but she had an idea. And if it all worked out as she foresaw, then meeting Lucy Logan *could* end up being a very lucky break for Sarah.

"I need to make a phone call," Sarah said to both father and daughter. To Lucy she added, "You and I will meet in the morning after I confer with my business partner about what we just discussed."

Lucy's grin went from ear to ear. "Nine o'clock, sharp."

"So you'll stay here, then. No packing up and leaving. And you'll get the electronic signature from your mother tonight, right?"

"Oh, yes!"

"Wait, what's this about leaving?" Sam took another step into the room.

Sarah smiled at him. "You've got a good kid here. And nothing to worry about." She would never tell Sam this, but his daughter had just proposed a perfect solution to Sarah's dilemma.

She left Lucy's room, shutting the bedroom door behind her and motioning for Sam to follow her downstairs. He sighed but did as she asked.

In the kitchen he gripped the edge of his island countertop. "What's going on with her?"

"Didn't you eavesdrop on us?"

Sam looked insulted. "Hell, no."

"Well, that's just stupid."

"You can't come in here and say rude things," Sam said, teeth gritted. "You need to chill out and get your head straight."

"So I've heard," Sarah said sarcastically. "Fine," she decided. "*You* can teach me to 'chill out and get my head straight.' I have a whole bunch of meditation books in my house that aren't doing me a damn bit of good right now."

Sam stared at her. "Cassandra asked me to help you learn how to meditate while you were here. You still want me to do that? Are you serious?"

"I am." Learning to meditate with him would be her Plan B to regain control of her company, just in case her project with Lucy didn't pan out. "Teach me to meditate, Sam, and I'll help you with Lucy's childcare dilemma. You saw us together—Lucy wants me to be her mentor."

He went from looking irritated to thoughtful. Then, with an anguished twist to his expression, he asked, "How is she? What's going on with her?"

"Lucy is building an app for a summer project. She plans to enter a competition—Future Tech Scholars. Evidently, Cassandra was intending to hook her up with me. Your daughter wants me to help her enter the competition—but I need to make a phone call first to see if I'm able to do it. And if I do decide to help her, then I'll need you to participate, mainly because her beach project app involves lifeguarding and other beach information. At least for now you'd still be able to keep your job if you want to, because I'd be with Lucy while you were working. Do you see what gift I'm handing you on a silver platter, Sam Logan?"

Sam just stared at her.

HIS HEAD WAS SWIMMING. He needed to pay a lot more attention to the childcare setup this time. He doubted he—or Lucy—would survive another Cassandra situation. Sam had to do better. Maybe even push back a bit on Sarah, despite her enthusiasm.

"We need to talk about this." Sam eyed her as she moved around his kitchen like a shark on the hunt, staring at her phone. "We need to get a few things straight first."

"Sorry, Sam." Sarah stopped and looked up at him. "But what did you say?"

"The thing is, Sarah, I really do need you to chill out when you're around Lucy."

Sarah held up her phone. "I need to make my call now. I'll be out on the porch. Don't disturb me, Sam." Abruptly, she left him alone in the kitchen.

He sighed. Typical Sarah. If Sam had thought his life was complicated a week ago, it was doubly complicated now. The trouble was, he wasn't sure he trusted her with Lucy. The woman was selfish, presuming, rude—a lousy role model for an eleven-year-old.

In his opinion.

But his eleven-year-old wasn't speaking with him, and she *was* speaking with the extremely irritating Sarah Buckley.

An *app*? Lucy wanted to make an *app*?

He didn't know a whole lot—nothing, actually—about high tech or the software business. However, he could find no fault with something so educational and positive for Lucy.

He watched Sarah through his sliding screen door. She paced across his deck, her phone glued to her ear.

When she spoke, her whole face lit up. She'd pinned her hair up, and loose tendrils fell over her collar bone, framing her heart-shaped face.

To look at her was to see an attractive, beautiful woman in the prime of her life. But to hear her was to be jolted by her brash tone.

Sam couldn't hear *what* she was saying. He could only imagine.

This whole thing was outrageous. Even if he *personally* enjoyed watching her—and liked having her around to spar with—it was still an all-around bad situation for him with his daughter. He knew he should give up lifeguarding to be with Lucy, yet having Sarah as her tech mentor would make Lucy happier. And he would like not to have to give up his job after all.

He shook his head, watching her some more.

He would not be attracted to Sarah Buckley.

He could not be attracted to Sarah Buckley.

But Sam had to admit that he was.

"I KNOW IT'S a good idea," Sarah was saying to Richard Lee. "And you know me, I wouldn't have brought this proposal to you if it wasn't a winner."

"I just don't think you're the right person to mentor a young girl," Richard insisted in his snotty voice.

But Sarah refused to be deterred. "The girl *brought* me her project because she *wants* me to mentor her. She's a local girl from the town I grew up in." Sarah coughed. She needed to lie a little. So what? "Her family knows my family. She knows me. She respects me, Richard."

There was a silence on the other end. "Interesting," he finally conceded. "The thought of you working successfully with a young girl and her family is…"

"Proof that I am sufficiently rehabilitated and able to return to my capacity in my rightful role at the company," Sarah finished for him. She half expected Richard to snort in reply, but he didn't. He was silent, and that was a good sign.

That meant he was inclined to agree with her proposal.

"So," Sarah pressed, "I just checked the timeline for the application deadline." She'd done so on her phone while Sam had been nattering on back in his kitchen. "As you know, I'm a past winner myself, Richard. I'm the perfect person to mentor the girl. That means we would need to have her video presentation ready for the committee before the July fifth deadline. I will send it directly to you, to submit to the committee yourself. And then after she is accepted for the competition, I will be returning to my office in California where I will be able to mentor her remotely for the remainder of the summer." This stipulation was extremely important to Sarah—it meant she could return home in two short weeks rather than the ten long ones that Richard had banished her for. "I'm not taking Lucy down this road," Sarah stressed, "unless I'm able to return early. I need your firm agreement on this point."

There was another silence on the line.

"Her father is a lifeguard," Sarah said. "He's Mr. Chill. He teaches meditation on the side, and I'm enrolled in his private sunrise meditation class." *Are you happy now?* she wanted to snap.

"I'm not averse to that idea," Richard said calmly. "Not at all."

Of course he wasn't. That's why she'd embellished her pitch to him like she had. "So, is it a go? Are you on board?"

Another silence. Damn, she'd pushed him too hard. *You need to get your head on straight* had been his parting shot to her that day in his office. Echoed only moments ago by Sam.

She held her breath. *Do not push it*, she told herself. *Stay calm...*

"If you can work successfully with an eleven-year-old and her family, if you can keep calm and show compassion to a young adult, while still helping her to succeed, then yes, Sarah, yes, I will welcome you back in two weeks."

She let out her breath. She couldn't help it—she gave a little skip of enthusiasm.

"I have one requirement," Richard added. "Before you turn in the signed application to me, along with the video presentation by July fifth, I want the parents to be given my direct office phone number in case they have any questions."

She didn't want to argue with him. She didn't want to push her advantage. "Yes, Richard," she said obediently. "I will do that."

"Furthermore," he specified, "I'm delegating future communication between you and me to Gregory." Gregory was his assistant. "I'll be on a retreat, and I don't wish to be disturbed. My electronics will be with Gregory. He will be handling my communication. Which is what I also suggested to you for your sabbatical, if you'll recall."

If Sarah had to deal with that worm Gregory, she would. Gregory knew how important Future Tech Scholars was to Richard. He would be fair about following through with that.

"Fine. Let Gregory know that he'll hear from me before the fifth. I'll send him the video and the completed application for you to view at your leisure. Other than that, I will not be in contact, with you, or anyone else."

"Very good," Richard murmured, appeased. "I'll certainly look for the video and the application package. Gregory knows when to make an exception to reach me at the retreat."

WHILE SARAH WAS on the phone, Sam went upstairs to check on Lucy. Her door was closed, and he heard her proud, impassioned voice. Speaking to Colleen, he guessed. He touched the door with his palm, wishing he could let Lucy know he was happy for her, happy she'd found something she loved to do. He ached that she didn't confide in him or even talk to him much, at all.

He went back downstairs. Mainly to take his mind off things, Sam set the plates and silverware on the inside table and then added candles, cold beer, warmed-up steak and the green salad he'd already made. He was just sitting down when Sarah hung up her phone and joined him.

He tried not to notice how smooth her skin looked in the candlelight, how attractive the light in her eyes was. Or how nice she smelled, sitting so close to him at the small table that her knees bumped his once she'd seated herself.

With her cheeks rosy red, she lifted her bottle of beer to him. "To the upcoming weeks of working together," she said. "To meditation classes at dawn and to Lucy's progress on her beach app."

He took a slow sip of beer without clinking his bottle against Sarah's. "Tell me about this beach app."

"I'll let Lucy do that. Her lifeguard father inspired her, even if it's difficult for her to articulate that to you right now."

He chewed over that information as he cut a piece of steak. Then he remembered he'd forgotten the corn, so he went to the counter and brought back the serving bowl filled with the cobs he'd grilled while Sarah and his daughter were up in the bedroom.

"That smells very good," Sarah remarked.

"Thank you," he said noncommittally and began to serve himself.

Sarah put her beer bottle down. "You need

me, Sam," she said softly. "And I need you. Don't fight this."

He glanced up, and in the flickering candle-light, he met her eyes.

Azure blue. Like liquid pools. With her dark hair and long, dark lashes, the woman was simply stunning. And he felt like he could say anything to her, truthfully, and she wouldn't shut him down or run away. "Honestly, if you can help Lucy not be so angry with me, then that would be forever appreciated on my part. I think I could overlook your brashness, in that case."

"My brashness," she murmured.

"Don't get me wrong—*I* like your brashness. I'm just wondering if it'll work with an eleven-year-old."

Sarah stopped chewing and stared at him. "She's a driven child on her own without me, Sam. And she's highly communicative. She's got a Skype link to her mom, in case you didn't know."

"I know." He tried not to be envious of this. It didn't escape his attention that Lucy wasn't communicative with *him* at all. "It's good for Lucy to have access to her mom when she needs her."

"Yes, and it's also good for Lucy to have access to her dad whenever she needs him, too."

"She *has* my undivided attention," he insisted.

"*Now* she does. But what about all those

years when you only saw her two afternoons a month?"

"I can't change the past, Sarah. And you're just mad at me because I called you brash."

"Hi. Sam?" Lucy's small voice interrupted them. Sam's heart seemed to leap in his chest as he looked up to find his daughter standing there, appearing contrite.

"Would you like to join us, Luce?" Sam offered, quickly standing to find her a plate, determined to stay calm.

Lucy glanced at Sarah. It occurred to him that his daughter actually cared and worried about what *Sarah* thought of her.

"Please do join us," Sarah encouraged.

Thank you, Sam thought as he set Lucy a place at the table. "We have salad and corn," he said, indicating the bowls. "Do you eat dairy and eggs?"

Lucy shook her head. "No, but I like tuna."

"Okay. There are cans of tuna on the bottom shelf in the top cabinet by the stove. The can opener is on the counter."

Lucy paused, but she went into the kitchen, and opened and closed several cabinets. He forced himself to stay still, letting her explore her new surroundings.

He got Sarah's point—he had years of neglect to make up for with Lucy. But he was determined that things would be different now. He'd meant everything he'd said to Sarah.

Sarah stayed uncharacteristically silent. She appeared to be studying Lucy. And him.

He cleared his throat. "Sarah told me about your project, Luce. I think it's great. And if you and Sarah want to work here, that's fine with me." He glanced at Sarah. "Lucy can give you the Wi-Fi password."

Sarah opened her mouth as if she was going to argue with him again. He understood that her first instinct would always be to argue with him. So be it. "If you want to work at the library, that's fine, too. But you should probably know that I had a run-in with one of the librarians." He took a bite of his salad.

Sarah smiled and raised an eyebrow. "*You* had a run-in with a librarian, Sam? I find that not only amusing, but difficult to imagine."

"Save your amusement and your imagination for tomorrow morning," Sam replied, "when you and I have to get up at dawn together."

Lucy joined them at the table with her plate of tuna, while giving Sam a funny look.

"You're welcome to join us tomorrow morning, too," he told Lucy. "We're having a meditation session."

"I'm not a big morning person," Lucy replied, reaching for the salad bowl.

"Okay. That's good to know." If there was one thing he'd learned today, it was to take things slow with Lucy. He had eleven years of rebuilding to work on, and it wasn't going to happen in a single week or even in a single summer. But Sam had patience.

Sarah however, was patience-challenged. He shot her a look as she fiddled with her phone.

Sarah scowled at him. But then she looked at Lucy and tucked her phone into her pocket. "Good idea," she said to Sam. "We'll talk about Lucy's app." She smiled at his daughter. And when she thought he wasn't looking, she slipped her phone under the table and glanced at it again.

He chuckled softly. "You're just like the kids I work with. You wouldn't believe how creative they get when it comes to hiding their phones."

"You know," she said pointedly. "If electronics are off-limits at dinner time, then why are lifeguard managers allowed to stop by to visit on their all-terrain vehicles?"

"Point taken." He grinned at her. "You both have my undivided attention, Sarah."

Sarah looked jarred by that. Lucy stared back and forth between them, fascinated.

"I don't know if I've told you," Sam said to his daughter, "but I grew up in a family that went through divorce." He was aware that Sarah's eyes widened, while Lucy continued to stare at him, rapt. "I was thirteen at the time, and it was pretty much the worst thing that had ever happened to me. You know your uncle Michael. I've invited him to come up next month. He'll tell you the same thing, if you ask him."

"I think I will," Lucy said.

Sam nodded. This wasn't an easy line of discussion for him. He breathed slowly, willing himself to calm. He had a point to make and he didn't want to lose sight of it, despite all the old emotions flooding back.

"One of the good things I remember from before all the bad stuff happened was that we regularly ate meals together," Sam said. "The four of us." It genuinely was one of the best memories he had. "We talked about our days and what was going on with us. When we stopped doing that was around the time when things seemed to come crashing down."

They were just staring at him, unimpressed. He rubbed his head. "All I'm saying, Lucy, is that you and I have a chance to try something different this summer. Having dinner together could be part of that." He met his daughter's eyes. "I'd like to hear about what you guys are working on every day. I'm interested in your project."

Lucy took a bite of salad. "Why did Nana Bea and my grandfather get divorced?"

Sam stilled. The pain was still there. It never totally went away, no matter how far removed from thirteen he became.

But he ignored that and focused on Lucy. He wasn't going to avoid talking about things with her any longer. The time was long overdue to fix this. He needed to include her more in the details of his life—the big stuff and the small. And it had taken Cassandra's leaving and Sarah's arrival for him to see that.

"Well," he said slowly. "Nobody really knows what goes on in a relationship except the two people in it. But from what I could see—or what I've figured out since—it started because they each wanted something different from their futures. They got job offers in two very different places." He sucked in a breath. "And Michael and I had to choose who to live with."

Sarah's eyes widened again. He would just bet she understood how hard that had been for him.

He'd bet Lucy could, too. She'd grown up with two parents who wanted nothing to do with each other. He wasn't sure how much she knew, but essentially, she was the product of a one-night stand. He wasn't proud of that fact, but it was the truth.

He and Colleen had both been so young. And they really had tried to get along for the sake of the coming baby. Sort of.

But they'd failed miserably, to the point that each had a lawyer to handle their relationship for them. Now that Sam was older and more mature, he saw how idiotic that was. He should have tried harder. No, scratch that. He should have tried smarter.

Starting today, he was trying smarter with Lucy. And since Sarah was part of the deal, she was part of the discussion, too.

"I hated it," Sam said to Lucy. "It affected me permanently, I guess."

Sarah made a soft snort. She seemed like she wanted to say something, but was restraining herself.

Lucy noticed, too. She was so attuned to emotional nuances. She didn't miss much between them all. "Were your parents divorced, too, Sarah?"

Sarah pressed her lips together. She looked angry.

"Oh, I'm sorry," Lucy said quickly, covering her mouth in self-censure. "That's right. Your parents died in an accident when you were twelve. I apologize. I knew that."

Sarah reached for her phone and pressed the button so the screen lit up. Then she stood.

"Where are you going?" Sam asked.

"To make another phone call."

"Please don't back out on us," he said quietly.

Lucy stared at him with big eyes.

Sarah gazed from Lucy to Sam. She balanced her fingers on the table and leaned toward him. "You two are the family. I'm not part of this."

He wasn't surprised by her reaction. To go on the attack was a very Sarah-like thing to do. He was starting to understand her. She seemed to keep control by dominating others, and that made her feel better. She'd lost her family young, and that must have been horribly traumatizing. Sam further supposed, as long as he was psychoanalyzing them all, that *his* family background made *him* want to avoid attachments, especially emotional ones.

But that just wasn't possible anymore. Not with Lucy, at least. And if Sarah was going to work with his daughter this summer, then he needed to fight more on Lucy's behalf. His daughter's well-being was at stake.

"Yeah, Sarah," he said calmly. "Family is too strong a word for it, but you *are* part of this discussion. You'll be with my daughter during the day, and you'll need to get used to seeing me, too."

"Do *I* have any say in this?" Lucy asked.

"Yes," he said turning back to her. "Please. What're you thinking?"

Lucy squinted, as if choosing her words.

"First, I think you should keep your lifeguard job. Don't quit it just for me."

He nodded slowly. "I'll consider it. What else?"

"Um…" Lucy glanced at Sarah. "Can I bring Becker and Simmonds into my bedroom? I've always wanted pets, but Mom won't let me have them."

"Oh, hell, yes, please take them with you!" Sarah exclaimed.

"Don't you like cats?" Lucy asked Sarah, confused.

Sarah hesitated "Well, no. I am *not* an animal person."

"They're not *animals*. They're *pets*."

Sam was biting his lip to keep from laughing. "Um, maybe Sarah is allergic to their fur, Lucy."

"*Are* you allergic?" Lucy asked Sarah.

"No."

"Then what's wrong with them?"

"I'm emotionally allergic to them, on principle."

"What does that mean?"

Sarah appealed to Sam. "Did you know that my aunt trained the little yacky one to get in the shower with her? It's creepy. I'm a private person. Tell me, would you put up with that?"

Sam smiled at the image. "Yeah, I can see your point."

"Becker loves to play in water!" Lucy exclaimed. "It's his bonding time with you to do that! That's what Cassandra says. You two are so weird."

"Well, I'm just saying." Sarah shrugged. "If you want to take the two cats, Lucy, I won't stand in your way."

"How about this," Sam suggested. "What if Lucy went over every morning and afternoon to feed them?" He glanced at Sarah. "Would that work for you?"

"Yes. Actually, it would."

"Great," Lucy said. "So, Sam, you'll go to work. I'll take care of Becker and Simmonds. And Sarah will come here, to our house with the Wi-Fi and the air-conditioning, to help me with my app." She smiled at Sam. "And you and I will turn off our electronics every night for dinner. Which I get to cook sometimes."

"You cook?" Sam asked, surprised.

"Yes. It's my job at home." Lucy wrinkled her nose.

He hadn't known that. "You cook *every* night?"

"No. Just when I'm left alone."

Sam was getting an uncomfortable feeling. "Is that often?"

"Sam, Mom doesn't want me to talk to you about her."

"Right," he agreed. A little progress at a time.

He cleared his throat. "I'm okay with our arrangement. I just have one favor. Can you call me Dad, please? I don't care what your mom calls me, but to you, I'd appreciate being Dad."

"Okay."

He blew out a breath. "Sarah? Do you have anything to add?"

Her lips were pursed and she seemed to be restraining herself, but she just shook her head sharply.

Something was up. Something he would press her on tomorrow. "Great. I'll see you at dawn for beach meditation."

Sarah's eyes widened and her cheeks turned red, but he continued to smile at her.

Her jaw snapped shut and she stood. "Fine. I'll be ready." She glanced to Lucy. "Will you be joining us, too?"

"Nope." Lucy shook her head. "I prefer to sleep in."

"Not anymore, you don't," Sarah said tightly. "The cats start bitching and moaning for their wet food at dawn."

Bitching and moaning? Sam mouthed to Sarah. This was what he'd meant by her brashness.

Lucy narrowed her eyes at Sarah. "They do?"

"Oh, hell, yeah. They were howling like crazy this morning."

"Well, I'll feed Becker and Simmonds tomorrow morning when you're both at meditation practice," Lucy said. "Then I'll go back to bed." She licked her fork, content.

"Are you happy?" Sarah snapped at Sam. "Do you *like* what's happening here?"

"Yes, actually," he said, smiling. "I do."

SARAH SAID NO to dessert, then went back to Cassandra's cottage and locked herself in for the night with the little squawking, tuxedo-wearing creature and his big, black furry enforcer.

Both cats stared her down as if to say, "What? No steak for us?" Sarah was sure they had smelled the meal cooking next door and were outraged that she'd neglected to bring them home a doggie bag.

She selected a can of cat food from Cassandra's dwindling stash and opened it by the snap pull. The contents of this particular can stunk to high heaven.

With thumb and forefinger pinching her nose, she scooped out the beige, lumpy mush and prepared to foist it on them, but their two ceramic dinner bowls were dirty. She couldn't serve them dinner in those. Instead, she found two clean human bowls in the dishwasher and divided the wet mess between them.

Becker squawked at her in protest over this deviation from routine, while his compadre betrayed him by digging in without protest.

Becker gave her one final squawk to indicate his displeasure before settling in beside Simmonds.

Sarah washed her hands and headed to her bedroom, firmly shutting the door behind her.

What had she gotten herself into, both with Sam and these little furry creatures who were so intent on shaking up her life and making her be part of things that made her feel so uncomfortable?

On second thought, she got up and cracked open her door. The two little guys were still in the kitchen, eating. She felt a stab of disappointment they weren't rushing into the bedroom. Maybe sleeping beside them last night hadn't been so bad…

She covered her face. It wasn't only the cats who were getting to her. Cozying up and playing house with Sam Logan—the hot lifeguard who scared the hell out of her, if she was honest—and his smart, sweet daughter? How could that possibly be a good idea? She was an independent woman.

But to regain control of her company, she

needed Lucy. Sarah had no doubt that Lucy would pass muster and be approved to compete. With Sarah mentoring her, she fully believed the girl could take it all the way to the finals.

The grand prize was a full scholarship to the most advanced private tech school in California. Sarah had once won this prize, and it had changed her life. From there, she'd gone on to Stanford, also on full scholarship, and then on again to Harvard Business School until she'd dropped out to start her own company.

But she was getting ahead of herself. Their big goal—to get Lucy on videotape giving an excellent pitch—was tough enough. The girl was unpolished—even if her idea was good. Sarah would have to do some serious coaching.

Lucy needed practice with her presentation. She needed to learn good pitch delivery skills and to refine her camera presence.

This would include an appropriate wardrobe and styling. The competition was fierce—every little thing mattered.

Excited, Sarah set about writing up a list for tomorrow…

It was funny, but she hadn't figured Sam for a concerned, involved dad. That made her life more difficult, but she would handle it. She had to.

What was *not* doable for Sarah was thinking

too much about her morning meditation session with a hot lifeguard.

She hoped that Sam wore more than his orange swim trunks and a whistle on his chest.

CHAPTER SIX

JUST BEFORE SUNRISE, Sarah woke and prepared to gird herself for battle.

First, she showered. She washed her hair, shaved her legs and used Cassandra's rose-scented soap. Even in her still-jetlagged condition, she was determined to be on her toes and keep Sam at arm's length.

She pulled out her suitcases and sorted through the clothes she'd packed—an outfit for every occasion because she liked to be prepared—but in the harsh light, everything looked too fancy. Too expensive. Too out of place.

She sat back and crossed her arms. The two cats curled up on the bed she'd made with Cassandra's cotton, Victorian-themed bed sheets. Simmonds yawned, showing a gaping mouth filled with sharp, pointy teeth.

At least they weren't screeching and yowling at her. It was still dark outside. Early, even for them. Under their watchful gaze, she selected a comfortable, oversized T-shirt that she'd brought mainly for sleeping and put on an exercise bra beneath it. She felt bound up like a boy, which was good. She completed the outfit with a pair of calf-length yoga pants. She was expected to go barefoot, she supposed.

She set her pen and a notepad in a book bag near the door, because she intended to take notes. Shaking out her arms, she also supposed she should put something in her stomach, but it was just too early to eat. She added a water bottle to her bag instead.

Sam was right on time. He wore shorts *and* a T-shirt. Sarah watched him through her side window as he left his house, sliding his squeaky screen door open and then shutting it with a thunk. His hair was rumpled and the T-shirt skimmed his chest loosely. The board shorts showed off his slim hips.

What was she thinking? He was so young. She was...middle-aged.

She stepped away from the window, rubbing her eyes, and immediately almost tripped. Simmonds had wrapped himself around her ankles. Little Becker sat on her book bag. Probably shedding all over it. Cat fur already clung like needles to everything she owned.

Sam knocked on her door. Swallowing, she let him in. Of course he was gorgeous in the morning. He was always gorgeous.

Wiping his sleepy eyes, he smiled at her. "You look nice."

Nice? Was that nice, as in old-lady polite, or nice as in *nice*?

He swiped his hand through his hair. "Is this too early for you?"

"No," she insisted. She *was* a morning person. Got all her best work done before other people got into the office. Besides, the East Coast was awake three hours earlier, and she often had conference calls to participate in.

He bent down and unwrapped the big cat from around her ankles. "Well, let's get started. I run the morning training for the lifeguards later on, and if this weather holds, we'll be out doing mile swims."

His eyes looked impossibly blue, and Sarah couldn't *not* stare into them, especially after his bare arm grazed hers.

"I can't even conceive of that," she managed to croak out.

He tilted his head at her, probably remembering her caught in the rip current. "If you ever want to take a break from meditating, some morning I could work with you on your swimming form," he offered.

Work up close with him in a swimsuit? "No, thanks."

"Okay. We'll stick to meditation."

She kicked at her bag. "I read a lot of textbooks about it during my flight, but honestly, I'm not impressed."

"Forget the textbooks."

"That's how I learn, Sam."

"Meditating isn't really something you learn, Sarah. It's something you practice."

"Isn't that the same thing?"

He smiled at her. There was something about that smile that made her go all gooey in the knees.

"Shall we?" he asked, and leaning forward, held Cassandra's cottage door for her as she stepped outside.

Damp, salty air invaded her nostrils. It wasn't unwelcome. She felt hot and bothered just being near him.

But Sam hadn't looked her up and down, so there was that. Unfortunately, there was just so much…awareness on her part. Chemistry.

But Sarah's mind went blank and she found herself unable to trade barbs with him. She was pretty much helpless on his turf. She couldn't just march in and take over as she had done regarding Future Tech Scholars last night.

Her heart thumping strangely in her chest, she followed him down the beach. Outside it was cool, not quite light, and the sound of the waves rushing in from the sea was comfortably familiar. It was high tide.

"There's less soft sand between the sea and Cassandra's cottage than there was when I was younger," she heard herself murmuring to him.

"The sea always changes," he said idly in return.

"Wait! Stop!" Lucy shouted as she ran across Sam's porch and onto the sand toward them. She was dressed in a baggy T-shirt and shorts and she was barefoot.

Out of breath, Lucy stopped before them. "You didn't wake me up," she complained to Sam.

"You seemed peaceful, so I decided to let you rest."

"Yeah, but I promised to feed Cassandra's cats," Lucy said.

"That's good. You're responsible," Sarah remarked. She was grateful for the girl's interruption, because it had snapped her out of her Sam trance.

Sarah reached into her pocket and held out the house key Cassandra's attorney had given her. "I'm trusting you with this," she said to Lucy in all seriousness. Sarah had discovered where Cassandra hid her spare key, so she could get in and out of the cottage using that copy. "You'll be feeding the two cats morning and night. Do you know where their food is?"

"Of course." Lucy crossed her arms. "Cassandra showed me how to feed them. And also, Becker and Simmonds eat the wet food in the morning and dry food in the afternoon."

"Okay. Great. Glad that's settled." Sam gazed up at the clouds and held out his hand. "Come on," he said to Sarah. "I only have so much time before work starts."

They left Lucy behind, and Sarah marched beside him, matching his gait. The beach was silent. They were the only two people as far as the eye could see.

"Shouldn't we meditate right here, in front of the house?" she asked.

"Why? Are you nervous?" He turned to wink at her.

Put that way, as a challenge, she couldn't argue her choice. "It might rain," she said defiantly.

"Not yet. And it's better for us to keep walking to where it's quieter."

"But what about Lucy? Shouldn't you stay close?"

"She's fine for a half hour. Besides, she has my phone number." He patted his knapsack. "Any other objections?"

She clamped her lips shut. Why couldn't she

get the image of the two of them sitting close together out of her head?

She stopped again.

"What is it?" he asked her.

"I need to go back. I forgot my notebook."

He stared at her. "What do you need a notebook for?"

"To take notes," she said patiently. "I'm a kinesthetic learner."

He shook his head. "You don't need notes for this."

"You don't understand. I need notes for everything new to me."

He sighed. "Come on, Sarah."

They trudged on. "How far are we going?" she asked.

"Why?" He glanced at her. "Are you tired of the walk already?"

"No! I'm not that out of shape." She swallowed, intimidated by his muscles, and turned away. But in her nervousness, her need to avoid thinking about sitting alone with him in some far deserted place, she blurted the first thing that crossed her mind. "How long have you been divorced from Lucy's mom?"

She winced even as she heard herself saying it.

He was silent as he trudged along. His mood

seemed to change, as if he was deciding how to deal with the question.

"No divorce," he finally answered. "We never married in the first place."

"Oh!" She hadn't expected that. She slid a glance at him. It seemed to shift her entire opinion of him, though that didn't make sense. What really surprised her was that she'd been forming preconceived notions about Sam since she'd first seen him on the beach, and at each turn she'd been proven mostly wrong.

"Was Lucy's mom a live-in girlfriend?" Sarah guessed.

His jaw tightened. "No."

"A fiancée?"

He snorted. "Wrong again."

She knew she had no right to the information, but she couldn't help wanting to know. "What is it then?" She stopped and crossed her arms. "Why don't you just tell me what the situation is?"

He stopped too, and faced her. "Does it make a difference to you?"

This was obviously a sore spot with him.

"No!" she sputtered back. "Of course not." But this did bring up a question she'd thought of, and it was relevant to her project with his daughter. "I saw part of Lucy's application form last night. Her legal name is Lucy Logan? How can that be?"

"Because it's what her mother decided to name her. I had no input." He crossed his arms. "Can we stop with the personal questions now?"

"I'll ask Lucy. She'll tell me the scoop."

He threw up his arms. "Why do I bother trying with you?" he exclaimed.

Wait, what? "What do you mean, *trying*?" she asked. "Am I that unlikable to you? I thought I did well last night. I thought your daughter was happy to work with me. I thought you were okay with our arrangement. I'm just trying to figure out all the angles of what that means."

"You're blunt, Sarah. You just…say what you think."

"Well, I didn't realize you were so sensitive."

"I'm not. I'm private. There's a difference."

She started walking again, and he matched her pace. But he was breathing heavily, and he was a fit guy, so his panting wasn't just from the exercise. Which brought up something else she'd been thinking about. "Sam, if you're seeing anybody right now, as in a girlfriend, I would appreciate you telling me."

"Why is that important?" he asked again.

"Because I am working with your daughter, so I'd like to know what I'm dealing with."

"Really?" He peered at her. "Are *you* interested?"

"No!" She didn't like his sarcasm. "I'm old enough to be your mother."

He laughed at that. "You're thirty-nine to my thirty-two."

"Well, I'm forty on the fourth. I'll be in a different decade from you." She expected that to make him run away from her.

"Honestly?" He stopped walking. "July Fourth is your birthday?"

She winced, regretting that she'd told him. "Yes," she said reluctantly. "Independence Day."

"Interesting." He smiled, tilting his head. "Lucy's birthday is four days after yours."

She would have to remember that—Lucy was important to her. But Sam walked on, and she followed beside him, saying nothing.

They were quiet for a long time as they continued to trudge down the beach. Sarah listened to the wind settle around the sand dunes and tried to keep her mind clear. It was impossible, of course.

"What was bothering you last night at dinner?" Sam asked. "After Lucy joined us, I mean."

"Nothing. I was glad she came down."

"So, you're okay with the three of us having meals like that occasionally?"

"Why wouldn't I be?" she snapped.

He glanced sideways at her. "You're awfully touchy today."

"As are you."

"No, it's different with me." He was silent again. "Don't take this the wrong way, but Cassandra told me a little about your background. Maybe I should have mentioned this before, but I know she left you in foster care."

"What?" She stopped short. She couldn't believe the audacity of it. "Cassandra has a big mouth. Why would she tell that to strangers? And Lucy..." Her voice trailed off. Tears were threatening, burning the edges of her eyes. This entire conversation was not at all what she'd intended.

How much does he know?

Most of what Lucy had said about Sarah's past to Sam last night wasn't in that business article. She'd had to have heard it from Cassandra's lips. And still, Cassandra had done nothing to step in and rescue Sarah when she'd been a girl. In fact, Cassandra had deserted her a second time this summer.

Sarah sniffled suddenly, drawing her hand to her mouth. That small, unfortunate noise she'd made seemed to break Sam's spell.

He put his hand on her shoulder, to her mortification. "I'm sorry. I shouldn't have brought it up."

"Then why did you?"

"I guess I was wondering why you really came to Wallis Point," he said quietly. "You could have gone anywhere to learn to meditate. I'm wondering if deep down, you came here to confront Cassandra about it."

She slowly expelled a breath. Savagely, she wiped her eyes. "I really do need to learn how to meditate."

"Why, specifically?"

Maybe because his eyes were so kind, she answered him truthfully. "My company's major investor asked me to. I'm too…difficult with the younger workers he's hired. He wants me to get my head on straight, as you so eloquently stated last night, as well."

Sam's hand didn't waver on her shoulder. "I shouldn't have said that," he said.

She didn't feel like he was judging her in the least. In fact, she got the distinct feeling that he was comforting her.

"Cassandra shouldn't have done that to you, either," he said.

"She did it to you, too, Sam. Just two days ago."

"Not like what she did to you," he said softly.

"Not even close. I wasn't the kid that she left in foster care."

Sarah crossed her arms and felt her cheeks burning. "You knew last night and you never said a word until now."

"Yes. I'm sorry. I never would've said anything at all, but…maybe I'm sensitive about Lucy being the product of a one-night stand, and when you brought it up, I overreacted." He laughed drily. "Me, who usually never does that."

He shook his head again. "I'll tell you straight, Sarah—you know your worth. You're strong and capable. No matter what happened to you, you didn't let those childhood experiences beat you down. That's what important."

"That's because I had a great childhood. My parents were…they were really great people." Sarah's voice cracked. "I was an only child. I was doted on by both of them. We used to have the best family dinners together…" Her eyes teared up.

But he steadily met her gaze. "So that's why our dinner last night bothered you," he said softly.

"I don't know." She shook her head. "After my parents died, I…had a different foster family every few months. I hated everything about that. I hated the way I was treated. I hated feeling small and weak…" She shivered. Enough said. "Nobody physically abused me, so get that thought out of your head, Sam. I'm just an achievement-motivated woman who knows what she wants. If that can't work with you, I'm sorry. But I am who I am. I believe what I believe."

He pursed his lips, nodding. "I respect that. Of course I want to work with you."

She shifted, waiting. There was more to come, she sensed.

"You know, I'm a private person, too, Sarah. Especially with my personal life. And for the record, no, I'm not dating anybody. I haven't in a long time, if ever. I tend not to get too close to people. And it's not that I'm ashamed of Lucy or anything like that—on the contrary."

He took a long breath through his nose, as if bucking himself up. "Honestly, I'm just getting to know Lucy for the first time, really. Before this summer, it was safer not to let myself care too much about her, in the situation we're in, because I had no…" His voice trailed off, for too long.

"No control?" she offered.

He looked off to sea. "There was no way the three of us were ever going to be a family. Colleen was angry about that. I was afraid Lucy was getting caught in the middle, and that the conflict would devastate her. So I backed off. It seemed to be best for Lucy then. But now things have changed, and it's not what's best for her anymore. I mean, Colleen and I are never going to be a couple. But I can't keep holding Lucy at arm's length."

"No," Sarah said, "you can't. It's not good for you, either."

"It's not. Let's find that meditation spot." He walked on.

She hurried to catch up to him. "I know a little bit about being left behind, Sam. Colleen—excuse me—Lucy's mom—just up and left her for the summer. Lucy doesn't say much, but she's mad about that. I sense it."

Sam stopped short. He swiped his hand through his hair. "Okay. Yeah, I know you're right. And that's where I need you to help me," he pleaded. "I'm trying to make things better for her. But I just keep missing the boat. I hate to say it, but you seem more clued in to her than I am. Between the tech stuff and the app project and the business knowledge…"

Sarah appreciated his faith in her. That made her want to help him, and for more than just her own selfish reasons. But the only advice she could give him as far as winning his daughter's affections pertained to the things she wished others would do for her.

"It's not just the interests that matter, Sam,"

she said softly. "Keep an open communication with her. Be there for her, no matter what happens. Don't give up on her."

Amazing how empathetic she had become in just two days.

He gazed at her as if he was really listening to what she said. "You're right," he said gently.

"I am?"

"Yes." He nodded. "And here we are." He turned and gazed up at the sand dunes. Then he pointed. "Right there. That's where we're going."

She shaded her eyes and looked, too. It was an absolutely private part of the beach. No one was here at this time of morning. It was just the two of them.

"Come on," Sam said.

He climbed the slight hill until they faced a rounded-out hollow between two natural sand dunes. Swaying green grasses blew with the breeze. The sun hovered just below the horizon, in that quiet part of the dawn Sarah had always loved. The mood was quiet and relaxed and…

But he was so *physically* close. Not just emotionally or mentally. She felt terrified of this sudden intimacy. The hollow inside the sand dunes might be peaceful and contemplative, like Richard had wanted for her, but she was with Sam, and how she was feeling about that scared her.

"I'm not like you," she blurted. "This isn't easy for me."

"I'm not asking you to be like me," he murmured in her ear.

"Then *why* are we here?"

"Look." He turned around and pointed. They were standing up high, completely enclosed and separate from the rest of the beach, but below them the panorama of blue ocean spread as far as she could see. It was majestic and beautiful, and perched up here, she felt like a queen.

She exhaled, loving the feeling.

"To sit and look out over the ocean together with no stress or worry," he said. "That's all I wanted for this first lesson in Sam's method of meditation."

She smiled at him, relaxing more. Of course. It wasn't like this handsome, young lifeguard/ teacher wanted to make love to her in the sand dunes. That just wasn't her life. She didn't need to worry about that.

"It's time to shut off your brain, Sarah. Stop thinking so much."

He touched her elbow, and they continued the few steps up the hill toward the hollow in the sand dunes. And she went willingly alongside him because…

Wow. "The sun is rising," she said stupidly. She saw it first reflected off him, his face turned to the sea. The sky seemed to brighten all of a sudden. He smiled at her.

She turned, gazing at the sparkling water. The waves at the shore lapped softly in an easy rhythm. Receded and came back. Receded and returned.

Sam held out his hand to her. She took it and he pulled her down with him onto the cool sand.

She scooted aside, keeping about twelve inches between their bodies. He sat cross-legged, and she did, too.

He leaned over and put his elbows on his knees. "Just close your eyes, and start by paying attention to your breathing—"

"You're doing it wrong," she told him. "I read in the book that you're supposed to sit up straight and put your palms up, on your knees."

He opened one eye. "Yeah, you could do that."

"Could? Or should?"

He smiled at her. "There is no right or wrong."

"Sure there is, Sam. There's a technique to everything."

He shook his head. "Nope. Not with this." He just kept on smiling. "Your goal is to relax. There are lots of ways to get to that goal."

She fidgeted. "I really don't think this is for me, Sam."

"Give it a chance. It won't come all on the first day."

"But I learn everything fast!"

He smiled at her again. And then he went back to closing his eyes and turning his face to the sun.

"You can't just make up your own technique, Sam!"

"Sure I can," he murmured. "So can you."

She sat there, turning that thought over in her mind. If he and Richard could do this, why couldn't she? Or maybe she should get a professional guru to teach her meditation? Sam didn't seem to know what he was doing.

He chuckled. "Here we are, in a beautiful place, with a beautiful sunrise happening, and you just can't let yourself relax."

"This is because of you," she snapped.

"No, it's not," he said calmly.

In that case, she would have to admit that it was because of *her*.

She swallowed. As she watched him, calmly meditating, she felt tears stinging again. It just was no use. She didn't *get* it.

I'm defective.

"Try lying down," he murmured to her.

They were seated on a gentle slope. It would be a natural thing to lie back with her feet downhill. Gritting her teeth, she laid her head on the soft sand.

No. It still wasn't working. She was as jittery as ever.

She cracked open one eye. Meanwhile, beside her, Sam had closed his eyes and settled into a relaxed, easy pattern of breathing.

As the sun continued rising, she found herself studying him. The way his light brown hair curled over his ears slightly. The tiny birthmark, shaped like a cross, on his back, near his neck over his right shoulder blade. The way his biceps curved, solid and tanned. The Z-shaped white scar on his knee. He'd probably been an active little boy.

Sam shifted back on his elbow until his mouth was next to her ear. "Think of this," he said in a low voice. "Think about how happy you'll feel the day you return to your job in California. You're relaxed. You've done it. You've earned everything that you want. What does that look like?"

She *saw* it. Her company was public. A large sum of money had been deposited in her bank account. She could look at Richard Lee, smile at him, walk out that door and be happy that they'd pulled off such a big deal…

In fact, she could start another business and do it all over again if she felt like it.

She gasped, startled at how thrilled that thought made her.

"What?" Sam asked.

"Nothing. Something I never realized, that's all." She turned to him, genuinely curious. "What is *your* end-of-summer visualization, Sam?"

He smiled at her. "Easy. It's Lucy happy. And me with a daughter I see more often than two Saturdays a month."

"That's really all you see her?" Sarah asked.

"Yeah. That's what the court hammered out for us years ago. But it's time to change that agreement."

And then he picked up her hand and took it in both of his. She was feeling jumpy, almost out of her skin at his touch.

He held her hand for a few seconds, and her breath left her.

With his golden face turned toward hers he said, "So, basically, this is how I meditate. If you want to join me again tomorrow, then you're more than welcome."

She opened her mouth but couldn't think of what to say, beyond squeaking, "Oh."

"And Sarah, if there's anything I can do for you this summer, anything you need, just ask. If you want to find somebody else besides me for meditation practice, that's fine, but I hope you'll still help Lucy. You're right, you have a lot to offer her."

And then he rose. "I'm off. My lifeguard class will be starting soon. But I meant what I said. I won't desert you, Sarah. Not like Cassandra."

She watched him descend the hill and jog back down the beach. She stayed where she was, watching the vast sea, watching the sun's rays dance across the little peaks and valleys in the waves. The rays made a path to the center of the ocean, dark and inviting in the distance, and in her mind's eye she followed it.

For a moment, she felt connected to something bigger than herself, something that made her feel weightless and expanded and not quite in her own body.

But she looked for Sam and saw that he was out of sight, and then she went back to feeling like *Sarah* again.

She used the rest of her meditation time to plot the next moves with Lucy.

CHAPTER SEVEN

"WHO WAS THAT woman at your house last night?" Duke asked Sam.

Sam jolted back to reality. Duke had just caught him daydreaming about his morning with Sarah. It alarmed him that Duke was even asking him about her.

He'd wanted to kiss her when they were alone in those sand dunes, so badly. In another place, the old Sam would have done so. But Sarah was stripping layers from him that he hadn't known existed, and it had felt, strangely, more intimate *not* to kiss her, but to keep it to the meditation, which she didn't know how to do yet, but he did...

"Sam?" Duke waved his hand in front of Sam's face.

"Yeah. I'm here." Sam shook himself, squinting into the sun as it blazed low across the water. He and Duke were leading morning training, and they sat at the end of the lifeguard motorboat, idling behind a group of ten swimmers doing a mile-long workout to the pier.

"Well?" Duke nudged him. "Who is she?"

"Sarah is my neighbor for the summer," Sam admitted reluctantly. He needed something innocent to say, to throw Duke off his trail, otherwise he would be relentless. "Sarah is watching Lucy for me. For childcare purposes. She's the reason I don't need to quit my job, after all," he added.

"Then I think I like her already." Duke took a sip from his water bottle and glanced ahead at the swimmers they followed. "You know, I haven't seen Lucy since she was about three. In my mind's eye she's always that age, I suppose." He turned to Sam. "How old is she now?"

"Eleven," Sam said automatically. When Lucy was three, Sam used to sit her on his lifeguard chair during duty sometimes. Those were the old days, when rules weren't as strictly enforced on the beach. Now Duke wouldn't be able to turn away from breaches like that. "So, yeah, she's in the middle-school years now."

"It gets better. Just wait until the teen years," Duke cracked. He had two teens in the house, a daughter, fourteen, and a son, thirteen. No wonder the guy looked harried.

Sam didn't like to think too far down the road. Lucy already seemed a bit rebellious to him. But maybe she was practicing for her teenaged years. She'd be twelve on July eighth. Four days after Sarah's birthday...

"So, you got a hot babysitter?" Duke mused.

Hot? Sam's neck bristled. He didn't think of Sarah that way. He thought of her as... Sarah. Blunt and direct. Riddled with flaws, like him. Interested in helping Lucy. Surprisingly sensitive, beneath all her prickly layers.

"Sam," Duke said, breaking into his reveries again. "Melanie and I were talking this morning. She wants to host a barbecue next weekend, just you, us and the kids. Becky and Shane are fairly close to Lucy's age. Shane's just two years older. And you could bring your neighbor along, too, if you'd like."

Sam stared. "You mean, bring her like a date?"

"Why not? In all these years we've never gotten together like that. My wife's always bugging me to arrange something, but I'll have you know I hold her back."

"You know I don't date locally."

"This lady isn't local. She's a summer person, right? No one at school will know about her."

"Duke," Sam warned.

"I'm just saying that she looked real cozy with you, sitting on your back deck last night and drinking your Lifeguard Lager."

She had. Sam grabbed his seat for balance because the boat's engine had kicked up. His colleague Dennis was driving. Dennis looped the boat around to check on a swimmer who'd suddenly stopped and was bobbing in the waves, treading water instead of swimming.

It was Charlie, one of Sam's first-year lifeguards. Sam recognized him by his shaved head. Maybe he was having leg cramps. Or more likely, he'd been out partying too late last night. Some of the younger, newer guys still needed to learn that in order to get up at seven o'clock and do a mile-long ocean swim, it was helpful to ease off on the beer drinking the night before.

In any event, tending to Charlie gave Sam a good excuse not to reply to Duke's comments. Or to have to give an answer to Melanie's offer.

With any luck, Sam wouldn't end up alone with Duke for the rest of the day, either.

He reached over the side of the boat and gave Charlie a hand to pull him up and over the side. The young lifeguard's face was pale and if he hadn't been sick, he was going to be soon. Charlie moaned and lay down in the small flood of seawater he'd brought into the boat with him.

"You gonna be okay?" Sam asked the young adult.

Charlie shook his head. And then he staggered over to the edge of the boat and hung his head over the side.

"I'll cover for him this morning," Sam told Duke. Sam was a "floater" again today, designated to move from position to position, covering the staff for breaks as needed. Charlie was posted at the far end of the beach, which would mean that Sam wouldn't be near Sarah and Lucy and the cottage, but maybe he could still see them at lunch.

"Head back to position following the swimmers," Duke instructed Dennis, then went to sit up front beside him.

Sam sat in the back monitoring Charlie. Watching the kid struggle to maintain control gave him time to think about his personal dilemma.

Sam looked out over the ocean. His problem was, he basically *liked* Sarah. Yes, she was the opposite of him personality-wise. She was stubborn, blunt and often rude. Initially, they'd been adversarial when it had come to his rescue agenda, but they had gotten past that. They needed each other for a specific reason—him for Lucy, and Sarah for meditation and companionship since Cassandra had left.

But more than that, there was an undercurrent that ran through all their interactions. Not just attraction or amusement, but solid, mutual respect. They each strove to understand the other.

It was a different way of going about being *interested* in a woman. Something new for Sam.

As he watched Charlie moan and wipe his mouth as he lay on the bottom of the rescue boat, Sam couldn't help thinking that he was getting too old for this young-guy, partying lifestyle. He just wasn't a Charlie anymore. At the moment, Sam would really rather be hanging out with Lucy and Sarah at home, anyway.

Of course he wasn't going to *date* Sarah— her work with Lucy was too important to risk.

Sam wondered how their coding was going, and if Lucy had decided to redesign the home page of her app like she'd been telling him about before bed last night.

The first spare moment he found, he was going to see them.

"HOLD STILL," SARAH said to Lucy. She was applying mascara to the girl's eyelashes. "Done!"

Stepping back, she checked out her handiwork. "You look very professional."

"Let me see!" Lucy picked up the mirror and studied herself. "Ooh, I really do. I look older." She glanced at Sarah. "Will this help them accept my ideas?"

"Yes. Though it's not obvious you're wearing makeup, it conveys a subtle professional polish that works well with the camera and the lighting. *Polish* is what the committee executives are hoping to see. It adds to the strength of your good ideas."

"Okay." Lucy put the mirror down and resumed studying her script. She seemed more interested in *what* she was going to say on the video than in how she was going to look saying it.

That was a good sign, Sarah thought. Lucy wasn't obsessed with the external stuff. Still, Sarah knew how much it could count—even subconsciously—with the judges.

She checked the white bedsheet she'd pinned against the wall as a backdrop. Sarah's phone camera was set up on a makeshift tripod so the frame would be steady. They'd decided to work at Cassandra's cottage instead of Sam's house today because the lighting was better for filming. Sarah had let Sam know they were both here so he wouldn't worry.

"Okay, I need to comb your hair, Lucy. I'm going to spritz some styling gel in it first, okay?"

Lucy giggled. "Look at Simmonds!"

The green-eyed Maine Coon cat had plopped himself before their camera backdrop. He had a white milk beard that stood out against his long black fur.

"Simmonds, you are so funny!" Lucy knelt and hugged him to her.

"Don't get milk on your good sweater," Sarah warned. She shook her head, reminded of what a child Lucy still was. It was risky to bet her comeback on another person, never mind an almost-twelve-year-old girl whose birthday was a few days after hers.

Lucy suddenly blinked, serious. She stood up and carefully brushed the black cat hairs off her red sweater.

"I really want to win this," she said matter-of-factly. And at that moment, she seemed grown-up again. Sarah felt like she was watching a ping-pong ball veer back and forth. Indicative of the age Lucy was at, Sarah supposed.

"If you want to win the Future Tech Scholars competition, we need to focus and get serious, because we don't have a lot of time," Sarah told her.

"Do you think I'll win?"

"Of course."

Lucy was silent for a moment. "You didn't tell my dad about the scholarship prize, did you?"

Sarah's hand stilled on her phone. "What do you mean?"

"About how I'll have to move to California and go to school there if I win the competition and earn the scholarship prize?"

"No, I didn't say anything to him," Sarah said slowly. That hadn't even been on her radar.

"That part of the contest is relevant to the custodial parent, which is your mother."

"Yes, I know that," Lucy said. But still, Sarah felt blown away. It hadn't occurred to her until now that Sam would be devastated if Lucy moved across the country.

Shaking her head, she said, "You got your mother's permission and signatures, correct?"

"Right here." Lucy patted the folder on the counter. Colleen had emailed them to Lucy last night. Sarah already knew this because Lucy had shown her first thing this morning before they'd even gotten started, but now, in Sarah's shock, she'd been compelled to check once more.

"If there is *anything* your mother needs clarification about," Sarah repeated to Lucy, "then I have a phone number she can call directly. You told her that, right?"

"Yes, I told her," Lucy said calmly. "Trust me."

Still, the unspoken words hovered between them. *Lucy hadn't told Sam.*

What was Sarah supposed to do about that? It wasn't her place to talk to Sam about Lucy's mother's permissions. He'd said himself that he didn't have those rights.

"Your father will be disappointed if you don't tell him," was all she could think to say.

"I'll handle it." Lucy added quickly, "Don't

worry. My mom said she'll move to California with me if I win the scholarship."

"Are you sure?"

"Yes. She'll be happy to have a reason not to be near Sam."

Sarah's heart sank. "You don't think they get along?"

"They don't talk at all. My mom pretty much hates him."

Oh, great.

But then a heavy step sounded outside on the deck. Sarah sucked in her breath then flicked a glance at the clock. *Twelve-fifteen.* Sam was here for lunch.

Biting her lip, Sarah strode forward and opened the door. He grinned at her, hand in the air, midknock. "Why, hello, Sarah."

She really hadn't wanted to *hide* anything that she was doing with his daughter. "Hi, Sam."

He winked at her and walked inside. He looked good to her, but he always looked good to her. And it was more than the external. There was a spark within him that drew her to him like a moth to a flame. Or a fish to the sea.

His sun-darkened skin was puckered a bit from the cold wind, and he wore a lifeguard windbreaker to match his shorts. He was barefoot, as always, but she liked his feet. And his calves. And his…rear view…as he turned and dropped his whistle and radio into his baseball cap, which he deposited on a side table next to the door. He was busy wiping his wet, sandy feet on a rug that Cassandra had installed for just that purpose, so he hadn't seen Lucy yet.

Sarah glanced over, but the girl had disappeared along with Simmonds. The red sweater that Lucy had been wearing earlier was draped carefully over a chair back.

Sarah swallowed, turning back to Sam. A part of her had been looking at him differently since their talk this morning. There was much more to him than she'd realized. She'd already decided to keep doing meditation with him, because she'd come so close to *finding* something at the end of their session. She'd felt that brief, not-in-her-own-head moment that had seemed like it should be right for what meditation was all about, given her limited understanding.

She had no doubt that that breakthrough had something to do with Sam as a teacher. There was a manner Sam had with her, the pushback that didn't include pushing her away—he'd come right out and said he wouldn't desert her like Cassandra had—which made her that much more apt to stay open to him.

Not to mention the fact that she needed his daughter's help to get her own job back.

"Sarah?" His wide smile lit up his face. His

blue eyes studied her, drinking her in. "How has your morning been with Lucy?"

"We're working hard on her project," she informed him, wanting to tell him everything, but not sure she should mention the part about California. "How is your work going this morning?"

"Quiet, but that's to be expected today because of the weather."

"Oh. It's raining out." She glanced toward the window. The sun had turned to gray skies and drizzly moisture, but she and Lucy had been so busy filming their preliminary shots that they hadn't even noticed.

"Yeah," Sam said. "There was a mass exodus around an hour ago. Still, I helped one lost kid get reunited with his family."

"A lost kid? How does that happen when the beach is practically empty?"

"Ah. Well." Sam shrugged. "I guess when you have six kids and everything gets confusing in the mad rush for home, and the second-to-littlest one decides to hide in a sand dune because he doesn't want to leave the beach fun even if it *is* raining…then that's how."

"Unbelievable." Sarah was appalled at the thought of a kid being left behind. "It sounds stressful dealing with that."

"No biggie. The kid—Joey—promised never to do it again."

"So, how did you find his family in time?" she asked.

"Ah. I noticed him crying, and then I radioed it out to all stations. Then I walked with Joey. We have a system for that. Luckily, his harried parents realized he was missing before they'd driven out of the parking lot. We met them on the main walkway. They were frantic when we found them."

"It must feel good to save the day." Honestly, that part of his job seemed appealing to her. "Any sea rescues?" She was personally dying to hear that somebody else besides her had gotten stuck in a rip current. It would make her feel less incompetent.

"Just one—during morning workout. One of my charges was a bit, ah, under the weather, so Duke and I hauled him onboard the beach patrol boat."

"Is it bad if it makes me feel better to hear that?"

He laughed. "Nope. It makes you human."

She sincerely hoped he remembered that.

"Besides," he added, "we were just doing our jobs, ma'am." He glanced around the kitchen. "Where's Lucy, anyway?" Then he took a folder from his backpack and withdrew two sheets of paper. "After I helped Joey find his family, I stopped by headquarters and picked up this information for Lucy's app. I thought it might be helpful."

Sarah glanced at the pages—maps of the beach parking lots. "I'm impressed. Lucy can scan these in and add them to her app. That will be a good feature." She glanced up at Sam. "But, just so you know, this is *her* project, and I'm here to guide her, not to do it for her."

"Spoken like a great teacher," Sam said. He turned and looked at the screen she'd set up.

"We've been recording," Sarah explained.

His forehead scrunched. "What for?"

"The first phase of the project is a video pitch. If Lucy makes it past that hurdle, then she's in the running for the next phase."

"There are phases?"

Her heart skipped a beat. Sam obviously didn't even know the basics. She needed to make a choice about how to handle this...

"There's a prize, I assume," he kept right on speaking. "A scholarship or a title, which would bode well for the college application process—"

"Dad!" Lucy's voice rang out from the doorway to the bedroom.

Sam's smile spread from ear to ear. *That's all he wants*, Sarah thought, remembering his visualization at the sand dune. *That's all he wants out of life—just to be Lucy's dad.* And Sarah swallowed, understanding, because she would give anything to see her own dad again. The emotion rose in her throat, flooded into her tear ducts. But no, that wasn't good for her to think about. Not ever, ever, ever. Crying was the least productive reaction possible. It changed nothing. It brought no one back. All it did was make a person weak. And show that weakness to the world.

"Sarah, what's going on?" Sam's voice had an edge that snapped her out of her funk. "My eleven-year-old daughter is wearing *makeup*?"

Sarah blinked, dabbing her eyes with a tissue. Lucy had already removed the neutral lipstick that Sarah had applied, but the mascara and beige contouring eye shadow remained, as did the thin layer of foundation blended into her young skin.

"The makeup is subtle and done only to help Lucy look her best on camera." Sarah pressed the used tissue discreetly into her pocket. "The panel is looking for a certain level of polish in their young tech entrepreneurs."

"These are children," Sam protested.

"Yes. And they are also tech entrepreneurs."

"I thought tech entrepreneurs wore hooded sweatshirts and jeans. And flip-flops."

"Actually, that is changing," Sarah said. "I know the selection committee, Sam. Lucy has an in. She's got this, but we still need to do our best, anyway."

"So you're saying you're going to cheat for her? Pull strings?" He looked confused.

"No!" she said, insulted. "I'm saying that I'm an expert consultant and that you need to trust me." She never would have taken Lucy on in the first place if she didn't think the girl could actually win!

But the word *trust* seemed to hang in the air. Sarah swallowed, feeling herself blanching. She was fast realizing that maybe Sam's concern was valid. Not that she was trying to cheat for Lucy, but that she hadn't been open with Sam about what it could mean for him if Lucy's beach project won. Yes, it was Lucy's lie of omission, but shouldn't Sarah have made sure Sam was completely in the loop before agreeing to be her mentor?

She looked at Lucy, who was licking her lips and glancing from face to face. Lucy had kept back the truth from Sarah on this, as well. The difference was that Sarah was the adult.

Swallowing, Sarah went and deliberately sat in one of the two chairs at Cassandra's tiny kitchen table. The rest of Cassandra's seating was ridiculous, and Sarah wasn't going to deign to sit in an old beanbag chair or a hippie hammock that reminded her of her wayward aunt.

Feeling angry all over again, Sarah poured herself a glass of water from the pitcher Lucy had set on the table and took a break.

"May I see the video you're working on?" Sam asked Lucy, standing in the midst of the room with his arms folded.

"It's not finished yet," Lucy replied, flopping onto one of the beanbags. "We've recorded a few pieces and when we're finished, we'll edit it all together. Then we'll give you a big reveal."

"Where is this editing equipment?" Sam asked Lucy.

"It's on Sarah's laptop."

Sarah drank her lemon water without glancing at either of them. She wanted to keep calm and not get involved in the drama that Lucy had created. Let the two of them hash it out.

"May I see the permission slip for this project?" Sam asked Lucy.

"Hold on," Lucy said, reaching over to grab her pile stuff from the couch. "I have the application right here on my iPad."

Sarah continued to calmly drink. *Do not interfere...*

"Look," Lucy said to her father. She held up the iPad screen. Sarah assumed she was showing him the last page of the application, the one with Lucy's mother's signature.

Sam took the iPad and peered at the screen

for a long time. Sarah held her breath, waiting to see if he would swipe the screen or page down to read the whole document, but he didn't. He was reading the fine print on that one page. Or just staring at the signature.

"Your mother signed it, I see," he remarked.

"Yes, she did sign it, last night," Lucy said. "Do you want to talk to her about it? She's off this morning. We can Skype her. She said she's carrying her phone, and that I can video call her anytime I want."

Thank you, Lucy, Sarah thought.

Sam shook his head. "No, Luce. I trust you."

To Sarah, his face seemed haunted. He didn't have the power to question Colleen's signature. At least, not yet.

"Thanks for helping her with the project," Sam said to Sarah. "It wasn't my intention to offend you."

"I'm not offended. I know you want to be a good dad." Sarah gazed at the slice of lemon gently floating in her water glass. "Lucy," she couldn't help saying, "you're a lucky girl to have a dad who loves you. Don't ever forget that."

Lucy gazed solemnly back at her. She picked up Simmonds and pressed him to her chest. "I'll make you both lunch," Lucy said finally.

"That's nice of you," Sarah replied. "I have

ingredients in the fridge. Do you make salads, Lucy?"

"Of course. My mom lives on salads. I do, too."

Sam looked confused. "But Luce, you only eat peanut butter for lunch."

"No, that's not true." Lucy calmly opened Cassandra's refrigerator and took out the shopping bag Sarah had stashed in there. "I only eat peanut butter at your house, Dad. It's our tradition."

Sam seemed to be chewing that over. He pulled out the other chair at the kitchen table and sat. "It's like I'm seeing my daughter in a whole new light," he said to Sarah under his breath.

They watched Lucy unpack the shopping bag contents on the table. Lettuce. Tomatoes. Cucumbers. Feta cheese. Bottled ranch dressing.

Lucy turned to them. "You two will need to scoot together because I need the table space to chop vegetables. This kitchen is tiny. When I grow up, I'm going to have a great big one." Lucy opened a drawer and rummaged for a cutting board and a knife. "And I'm also getting one of those refrigerators where you can touch the glass front and light up everything inside. You don't even need to open the door to see what you have."

"I have one of those," Sarah remarked.

"See? This is why I need to be a tech mogul," Lucy explained to her father.

A smile played on Sam's lips. "My daughter is a capitalist."

Honestly, Sarah could see he was just happy being there with them. It did something to her, too. It put a happy, safe feeling into her heart. One she couldn't remember experiencing since she was Lucy's age and her parents were still alive.

Like a good chef, Lucy washed her hands before preparing their meal. She expertly set up her chopping board and knife then proceeded to wash the vegetables.

"Does it seem strange to you that we have a kid cooking for us?" Sam asked her.

"No. I rather like it." Sarah smiled at him.

Sam shrugged. "I'm taking you both out to dinner in appreciation, just so you know."

Another warm glow shot through Sarah's heart.

"Someplace nice," Sam added. "I've got a place in mind, though we might have to wait a day or two because I'll need to make reservations. Do you like seafood, Sarah?"

"Love it," she replied.

"Hey, Lucy, do you eat seafood?"

"No crustaceans, but fish caught humanely using lines and nets are acceptable."

"She knows what crustaceans are," Sam said proudly, nodding toward his daughter. "I taught her that."

"Does that mean lobsters?" Sarah asked. "I thought they were a local delicacy here."

"They are," Sam mouthed. "And I love them." He glanced at Lucy to be sure she hadn't heard.

"The way they're cooked is inhumane," Lucy said calmly, chopping the head of iceberg lettuce like a pro. "How would you like to be dropped into a pot of boiling water, Dad?"

"I wouldn't," Sam said. He squinted at Lucy. Then at Sarah. "Where did she get the makeup, anyway?" he asked. "You don't wear any."

Sarah most certainly did. She raised an eye at Sam. "At work I do, all the time."

Sam gazed deep into her eyes. "I like you how you are now."

"With no mascara? No lip gloss?"

He gave her a slow smile. Under the table, he briefly touched her hand.

Lucy's dad was *sweet* on her. The shocking realization made Sarah put her hand over her quickening heart.

But this was a secret not for Lucy to know, so Sarah needed to act low-key about it.

Just as the details of what Colleen had signed were not for Sam to know, at least not yet. She needed to be low-key about that, too.

CHAPTER EIGHT

SAM NEVER DID reply to Duke's wife's invitation. Instead, two nights later—after he'd taken Lucy and Sarah down to Newburyport for dinner on a dockside table at his favorite seafood place—Sam phoned Duke at his home number.

It was just after eight o'clock. Lucy was up in her room, probably Skyping with Colleen, and that didn't cause any tension for Sam in the least, because the crisis of Lucy being angry with him seemed to be over. She loved her app project. Loved working with Sarah. She even seemed to be more comfortable with him, and more so every day.

In fact, all seemed right with the world as far as he was concerned. Sarah was in Cassandra's cottage, not fifty yards from where he was standing on the beach. The light in her bedroom was on, and he could gaze at it here in the warm June night air, listening to the waves slowly lapping onto the shore, and thinking about his time with her tonight.

Sarah had been at her entertaining best, upbeat and making funny Sarah-like comments. The three of them had driven down the coast and back together in his truck. Lucy was in the backseat, and after she'd run into the house to make her Skype deadline with her mother—evidently, the cruise ship sailed promptly at five—he and Sarah had finally been alone.

While telling him a story about the first time she'd ever been fishing as a kid, Sarah had touched him on the arm. Clasped him, warm and solid, which was remarkable, because he knew she was uptight about the age difference thing. His goal had been to make her forget about it. They'd been leaning against his truck in the darkness, laughing about nothing important, as if they had all the time in the world.

That's what was surprising to him about being with Sarah. The adventure of getting to know her was completely different from the way he usually felt when he went away to places like... Scotland, for example.

He hadn't *escaped* from anything. He was actually living his real life in Wallis Point with his real name. And his real job. And his real kid.

And yet, he didn't mind getting to know Sarah this way. It felt even better than staying anonymous. Different, but he was fast getting addicted to hanging out with the very intense Sarah Buckley.

This possibly explained the insanity of the call he was making now.

"Sam," Duke said when he picked up the phone. "I didn't expect you. What's up?"

"I know. Hope it's not too late, but, ah…" Sam glanced at the light in Sarah's bedroom. Somehow this nudged him to go on. "This is, ah, related to what you asked me two mornings ago on the boat."

"Oh, yeah," Duke said. There was noise in the background that sounded like the baseball game on TV. "Do you want me to tell Melanie to set something up with you three, then?"

You three—Duke was referring to Sarah, Lucy and him. "No. I mean, yeah." Sam laughed. This felt so weird to him. But good weird. Right weird. "No, actually, it's Lucy's birthday next week." Sarah's, too, but he wouldn't mention that. "So I was, ah, thinking of having a birthday party. Something small. Do you guys want to come over and help me celebrate?"

"Which day?"

"I want to do it early, on the fourth." He would have to pull it together—get a cake and such— in a little over a week. He could do that, he figured. There would be fireworks on the beach, so that was a draw. There would be crowds and traffic, of course, but he had available parking for people on his lawn…

"Sam, you always have a house party on the Fourth of July. We were planning on going this year, anyway."

Yes, Sam usually had a big blowout with crowds of people—lifeguards, teachers, friends—whoever could squeeze their vehicle into his front yard. Cassandra usually let him use her driveway for guest parking, too.

"Actually, I'm thinking about something different this year." Because *he* was different. "No blowouts. This will be a small *birthday* party. Yes, it will be during the holiday fireworks on the beach, but that's the fun of it." Lucy had already said she would share her day with Sarah. "Plus, Lucy isn't big on crowds, and neither is Sarah, so—"

"Sarah. That's your neighbor. You *are* seeing her, aren't you?"

Sam let out a breath. He'd slipped in mentioning her name. He hadn't meant to do that. Technically, he wasn't seeing anybody, but he didn't like getting into the particulars with Duke. "No," he said shortly. "She's close to my daughter. Her name is Sarah Buckley."

Duke paused. "Sarah *Buckley*? That Sarah? Isn't she the high-tech woman that was written up in a magazine article? Cassandra Shipp's niece?"

"You heard about that?"

"Sure. Cassandra showed the article to every-body at the library. You know my daughter is a summer volunteer there, right?"

"No." Sam cringed.

"Sarah Buckley is famous. You knew that too, right?"

"Duke, she's a regular person. My daughter loves her. Can't we just…be normal about this?"

There was a long pause. "Okay. We'll be there on the Fourth. But I warn you, people aren't going to accept that you're not having your reg-ular Fourth of July blowout. They're not going to accept it. They'll show up anyway, trust me."

As Sam turned it over in his head, he saw the wisdom in what Duke had said. As long as he lived here, there would be a blowout. He had to keep in mind what he could and couldn't change.

"Let me talk with Lucy, and I'll get back to you." He had to figure out a solution to make everyone happy.

THE NEXT MORNING, Sam met Lucy at the bot-tom of the stairs. He was on his way to Cassan-dra's cottage to pick up Sarah for their morning meditation session. Lucy was on her way to feed Cassandra's two cats.

On the walk over, in the predawn light, Sam asked Lucy outright. "I'd like to get a cake for your birthday. I was thinking of doing it on the Fourth because that's when the fireworks are."

"No, Dad." Lucy stopped. "That's *Sarah's* birthday. We need to do something for her *special*. My birthday is on the eighth. We'll do something else for me then."

"Okay," he said pragmatically, slogging through the cool beach sand in his bare feet. "Out of curiosity, did Sarah tell you about her birthday?"

"She mentioned it when she saw on the Future Tech Scholars application that my birthday was right after hers." She glanced up at him. "I *really* want to give her a surprise party. Just you and me. Please?" she wheedled. "Can we do it for her?"

"You've really gotten close to her in one week, haven't you?"

"Six days. And yes. I want to be just like her when I grow up."

They had come to Sarah's cottage door. "Well, I'll let you plan it, then," he said as she inserted the key Sarah had given her into the lock. "One more thing. How do you feel about big Fourth of July parties?"

"I've never been to one, but it sounds like fun." She paused. "Sarah won't like it, though."

"No?"

"No." Lucy shook her head decisively. "She'll

love a small, separate party, like the one I'm going to plan for her. We should do it in the morning, but not too early. After you come back from meditating will be best. I'll get everything ready, and then we'll surprise her."

"Okay. You have a week to take care of the details, Luce."

"I know. Seven days," his very precise daughter said. She pushed open the creaky door, and Sam saw that both cats were sitting still beside their food bowls, waiting for Lucy.

As she bustled about getting cat breakfast served, Sam waited for Sarah. She came out from the bedroom with her hair pinned back and wearing a pair of shorts this time.

"Are you ready?" She grabbed her phone from the table where she'd been juicing it up. "I'm going to take a video of you today while you meditate."

He paused. "Why?"

"Because you know that 'what do you want at the end of summer' visualization thing you said to me that first day? That was the closest I've come to feeling something. I thought maybe if I filmed you and studied it and then practiced some more—"

"Let's just take a walk, okay?" He smiled at her and shifted his backpack onto his other shoulder. He knew she was impatient to *feel* something, as she put it. "Let's skip the whole sitting-meditation thing for today. We'll do a walking meditation, instead."

"Sam…no. I need to learn."

He liked the way she said his name, but he didn't like that she appeared to be panicking. He held out his hand. "Come on, Sarah. This will help. It's part of the process. I promise."

She didn't take his hand, but she did brush past him. He would do everything he could to distract her from thinking about what she couldn't do and, instead, try to help her relax. This was most important.

He noticed Lucy watching them as he turned to close the door. Sam gave her a thumbs-up. Lucy nodded.

He felt like he and his daughter were coconspirators. *Finally.*

His heart swelled. Working with Sarah was bringing him closer to Lucy, and for that he was grateful.

As for the blowout, they would figure it out when the day came.

THREE DAYS LATER, Sarah sat in Sam's living room, setting up her laptop on his glass coffee table. She still didn't get this whole meditation thing. It was particularly nerve-racking because she had less than a week—five days—before she would be able to return home. Plus, she'd promised to show Sam Lucy's video before she sent it to Gregory and Richard, and she couldn't very well renege on that promise, much as she would like to.

Sam handed her a glass of sparkling water. Raising a brow, he sat beside her on his couch.

"I'm actually kind of nervous to see it," he confessed.

Yes, she was, too. Sam *had* to sign off on the video. If he didn't, Sarah's entire plan would be ruined, and as such, she was treading carefully. She did her best to remain neutral and nonchalant.

"Luce," he called upstairs. "Are you coming down to watch?"

Lucy stuck her head into view from the stairwell. "No. I watched it twenty hundred times already."

"Well, it's my first time." Sam moved closer to Sarah and patted a spot on the couch on the other side of him. "Care to join me?"

"No way. I'm too nervous that you'll say no after you see it." Lucy scooted out of view.

While Sam frowned, Sarah called up the computer file, her heart beating in her chest. She was nervous in a new way now, because Sam was sitting so close to her that his leg brushed hers. Her whole body felt prickly with yearning, as if her skin was begging her to ask him to touch her. All over. Slowly.

She squirmed on the couch. The shorts she was wearing rode a little higher, putting pressure on a part of her anatomy that was just screaming for Sam's caress...

They'd been working and living beside each other for going on two weeks now. Not enough time to know someone completely, but more than enough hours, minutes, days together to know she really, really liked having him around.

He was funny. He was smart. He was thoughtful.

He even cooked for her. They'd eaten three meals together yesterday, once without Lucy, who'd been happily distracted by skipping ahead with her project and loading her app with maps and tidal charts.

Sarah hugged her bare arms. She felt barely dressed in short shorts and a thin sleeveless blouse—first, because it was hot outside—not muggy, just hot in the sun—and second, because she had this strange, driving need to feel sexy for once.

Sam *made* her feel sexy.

He got up from the couch and then came back with a bottle of his Lifeguard Lager. The pretense of not drinking it around Lucy had gone by the wayside. Lucy didn't care. Her mother drank wine, she'd informed Sam, and it wasn't a big deal to them.

Sarah opened the computer file, and Lucy's face came up, superimposed with a big white arrow. All Sarah had to do was hit the arrow, and the video would begin.

This could go either way, and Sarah was nervous as hell. The pitch was damn good. It might make Sam proud or it might freak him out.

Lucy was freakishly advanced for her age. In Silicon Valley and as a scholarship student at the Future Tech Scholars Academy—well, she would just be one of the crowd. But here in Wallis Point, Sam might be very surprised by what he was about to see.

Sarah hoped he wouldn't be upset. "Are you ready?" she asked him.

He reached over to her laptop and pressed the start button himself.

Lucy came into view, standing up straight, smiling pleasantly and professionally in all her confident glory.

Her hair was pulled back and she wore a light layer of what Sarah called "stage" makeup, to make it clear to Lucy that wasn't an everyday thing, even if she was accepted into the Future Tech Scholars competition.

Lucy's hands were relaxed and her posture erect and natural, just the way Sarah had taught her. Sarah had spent hours in personal coaching, learning to give effective presentations, both in person and on camera. Lucy was a fast learner. Kids naturally were, in Sarah's opinion. They'd worked first from a script, which Lucy had pretty much memorized. In the video she spoke from memory with only a few ad-libs, but the pitch appeared internalized, as if she was having a conversation with the viewer.

Sarah watched Sam as he watched Lucy.

He leaned slightly forward, lips parted. He wasn't smiling. That wasn't a good sign.

Swallowing she turned back to the video. They were at the halfway mark. Soon, Lucy would be turning to her wall maps.

Sarah lifted her glass of water to her lips. She should have asked for something stronger. She was feeling too jumpy.

She moved to stand, but Sam put his hand on her knee. She dared to look at him.

"I can't believe it," he said when the video had finally finished. "Who *is* that girl?"

Her heart hammered. "Because she did such a great job, you mean."

"No. I mean, yeah. I mean…she's just like my mother." He shook his head in wonder. "She's twelve—well, almost twelve. But today, she's eleven going on forty."

Sarah was "going on forty." In just a few days, in fact. She could feel her face turning crimson.

"I mean," Sam said, seeing her embarrassment, "I don't exactly have a great relationship with my mother, to put it bluntly."

"She's a doctor, right?"

"Yeah. Don't get me wrong, I think doctors in general are great…"

"But not that doctor in particular," she finished for him.

He stood, as if shaking off a bad feeling. "You know what, forget I said anything. It doesn't matter. I'm being crazy. Lucy is Lucy. I'm proud of her." He seemed to force a smile.

Then he went to the kitchen and drew another beer out of the refrigerator.

"I'll have one, too," she called.

"Great." He took out a bottle opener and flipped the caps off, then brought them back to the table. "Hold on," he told her. He went back out and got her a chilled glass from the freezer.

She'd trained him well. "Thank you," she said kindly as she poured her beer.

He sat beside her again. He seemed to be far away, deep in thought.

"You're not comfortable with the video, are you?" she asked quietly.

He shook his head absently. "It's the whole competition. And it bothers me that I'm not comfortable, because I know I should be." He turned to her. "Review the process again with me. The video gets submitted to the selection committee. How long does she wait until she hears from them?"

Sarah would send the video and then text Gregory right away, first thing in the morning, in order to set the process in motion. "I estimate that we should hear from the committee shortly after the deadline of July fifth."

"That soon?"

To her, it wouldn't be soon enough. "Yes."

He nodded, taking a drink from the longneck bottle. "And then what happens?"

"And then..." She took a sip of her own beer. This one was crisp, with a bite of summer lemon. "And then..." She wiped a bead of lemony beer from her lip. "And then Lucy gets an email."

"Why not me? Why not the parent?"

Because Colleen was the parent of record, and Colleen hadn't given an email address when she'd filled out her part of the application, so Lucy had copied down her own. "I'm sure Lucy will tell you the moment it comes in, Sam. You'll hear her screams of happiness from one end of the beach to the other."

"Yeah. Yeah, of course." He looked at her. "If

Lucy's not accepted, it will be hell around here. You know that, right?"

Sarah was silent. She had no doubt Lucy would be accepted. Sarah wouldn't have stayed and gone through any of this work otherwise.

"And if Lucy is accepted..." Sam scrunched his brows. "I take it that's when the app development begins in earnest?"

"Yes. She's done a bit of the upfront legwork, but I counseled her to wait on doing too much more. Sometimes the committee give directives or advice on what she should do differently from her plan."

Sam nodded. "That makes sense."

"But, yes, there is a lot of effort involved in developing an app." He didn't know the half of it. And she wasn't going to discuss that now. She fully planned to conduct the rest of the mentorship remotely, from her office in California.

"And the prize for us is scholarship money?" he said.

In a nutshell, the answer was yes, so Sarah answered, "Yes."

"Well, I won't lie," Sam said. "That is very welcome to me. The more scholarship money she can win, the more thrilled I'll be."

"Right," Sarah murmured noncommittally.

"So." Sam slapped his hands to his knees. "We're set, then."

She nodded.

"I'll go tell Lucy to go ahead with the application."

Sarah nodded again, sitting still as Sam headed upstairs.

When he was gone she leaned her head back against the couch. *I just want to go home*, she reminded herself.

And Lucy's admission to Future Tech Scholars would make it happen that much sooner.

CHAPTER NINE

ON JULY FOURTH—her fortieth birthday, Sarah was trying hard not to remind herself—she begged off her meditation session with Sam and didn't rise until late morning.

She tried to relax by taking a walk on the beach in the pleasant sea breeze. But when she stepped outside, she saw Lucy and Sam sneaking across the sand toward the front of Cassandra's cottage. They were carrying something between them in a brown grocery bag. Lucy was wearing a sparkly Happy Birthday cap.

Oh, no. Was Sarah going to regret giving Lucy that key? The two of them obviously had something planned for her birthday.

Sighing, Sarah sat on the back deck and waited with dread. In the past, she would have stormed in and stopped them, but shockingly, she found she cared too much about their feelings to hurt them that way.

What was happening to her?

It could be worse, she supposed. Sam and

Lucy could have thrown her a surprise party with lots of people. This was probably just a small cake they'd brought over for her. She should just chill out and bear it for their sake.

Sarah leaned back and closed her eyes. All of a sudden, she felt a pair of small hands close over her eyes. "Surprise!" she heard Lucy say.

"I'll kill you later," Sarah couldn't help muttering. In good humor, of course.

The hands came off her eyes. Sarah blinked at the bright sun. Lucy loomed before her, wearing a birthday-girl cap on her head. "Happy Birthday, Sarah!" she cried.

"Happy Birthday to you," Sarah said in return, attempting to sound a bit more upbeat and pleasant.

"I love that we share a birthday week. Please come inside and see what I did to celebrate." Lucy held out a matching birthday-girl cap for Sarah. "This is for you to wear. You can wear it on my birthday, too."

"Fine." Sarah sighed. "Lay it on me."

Lucy grinned and looped the elastic chin strap around Sarah's ears. The pointy cardboard cone felt strange on Sarah's head.

It could have been *much* worse. Lucy could have also asked Sarah how old she was. Thankfully, she hadn't. Sarah couldn't help glancing over at Sam, hands in his pockets, as he lounged against the door to Cassandra's house.

Her heart skipped a beat. He was just so damn handsome.

"I made you a birthday cake," Lucy said. "Will you come inside and blow out the candles with us?"

"Only if you share the cake with me," Sarah stipulated.

"Okay. But I'm still making myself another one on the morning of *my* birthday."

"Right. Of course." Sarah hoisted herself to her feet, because…she couldn't disappoint her mentee. Lucy clasped her hand in hers and they walked barefoot, hand in hand, to join Sam.

He leaned in close to Sarah. "Nice hat," he murmured in her ear.

So, so appealing. She gritted her teeth. "Don't pretend you had nothing to do with this," she breathed.

He gifted her a grin with one of his signature dimples. "I've got you a special present for later," he said in a low voice.

She sucked in a little breath. What did he mean by *that*?

He grinned again, and as he passed by her, he brushed his hand against her hip, ostensibly to nudge her aside.

His touch was protective. It was…intimate.

No one she worked with would ever think or dare to touch her, never mind to touch her like that. Her blood seemed to hum with awareness of Sam. Dimly, she blinked as Lucy led her into the house.

The two cats sat, both looking irritated, with little blue Happy Birthday caps perched between their little cat ears. A beautiful round double-tiered cake with pink-and-white frosting and a circle of five blazing candles met her on the table.

Sarah put her hand to heart, blinking away the moisture in her eyes. Nobody had made a cake for her since her parents had died. "I'm touched. I'm really—" Her voice cracked, but she cleared her throat. "I haven't had a birthday party since I was…" She glanced at Lucy. "Your age."

It was true. Not even at work did anyone do this, mostly because she was hostile to birthdays. Also, Sarah was one of those lucky (or unlucky) people who shared their birthday with a holiday, when coworkers weren't in the office.

Outside, a homemade bottle rocket screeched through the air. The people of Wallis Point loved their fireworks. All legal in New Hampshire, of course.

"Shall we sing?" Sam asked Lucy.

"Wait." Sarah pointed at the cake. "What do the five candles mean?" Yes, she risked feeling bad at the answer, but she was genuinely curious. "Do they mean that if you'd put the proper number of candles on it, then the house would've burned down?"

"No." Lucy looked horrified. "There is one candle for you, me, Dad, Becker and Simmonds. Five of us, all together."

"Oh," was all Sarah could seem to say, in a small voice.

Damn, she was going to cry *again*. What was wrong with her?

"Do you have a wish all lined up and ready?" Sam asked Sarah. "Because I'm thinking we should get the singing going so you can blow those things out and we really can avoid a house fire."

She laughed, a teary, happy laugh. The thing was, she wasn't sure what to wish for. What she wanted so badly seemed perfectly obvious. It was the same wish she'd had since she'd been banished to Wallis Point. *Please, may Richard Lee let me go home to my job soon.*

But the sooner that happened, the sooner she would have to say goodbye to Sam Logan.

What should she do? "Um, please give me a minute. I need to consider my options."

"Certainly." Sam sat at the table. "But let me just remind you that the wax is melting into the frosting."

"And I'm hungry," Lucy added.

"Well, in that case, let's get this show on the road. Sing away, please." Sarah waved her hands at them.

Sam stood. On a count of three, he and Lucy began the Happy Birthday song. Sam sang in a deep rich voice that seemed to resonate in Sarah's bones, and Lucy in a soft, girlish accompaniment. When they got to the end, Sam clapped and directed Lucy to get out plates and forks—just in case, Sarah supposed, the girl had designs on singing, "How old are you now?"

It still felt raw to actually be in a new, older decade of life, but it stung a lot less than it had two weeks ago when she'd first arrived here.

"Make a wish," Sam said softly.

Sarah leaned over the candles. Her mind felt uncharacteristically empty and her heart much too full in her chest. She bent her head and softly blew out the candles without even making a silent wish for anything to be different than it was at this moment.

Lucy and Sam cheered. Sarah sat and cut everybody—except for the cats—a piece of cake.

"Now it's time for the presents," Lucy announced.

"Presents? This *is* a surprise." Sarah licked vanilla cream frosting off her finger. It really was the best birthday she'd had in years, even if it was her fortieth.

"It's my own personal recipe," Lucy said.

"Not a bakery cake?" Sarah asked.

"No."

"A box-mix cake, right?"

"Nope."

"Come on. You two did not make this from scratch for me." Sarah gazed at Sam for the pleasure of watching his expression.

He lifted his hands and smiled at her. "Don't look at me. Lucy is the talented baker." He shook his head in wonder. "She had me fooled all these years that she only likes peanut butter."

"I'm a person with many deep talents and desires," Lucy said.

"You certainly are." Sarah tasted the cake. The cake itself was spongy and chocolate. The vanilla buttercream frosting was a perfect complement. "Oh, this is so good." She licked her lips. "What are you making for *your* birthday, Lucy?"

"Well, I'm considering a classic lemon layer cake. But I reserve the right to change my mind at any time."

Sam did a double take. "A lemon layer cake? Where do you get these recipes?"

"Off the internet. Where else?"

"Where else?" Sam repeated.

"Give Sarah credit, too," Lucy said. "She drives me to the grocery store every day."

It was true. Sarah liked to eat good food and that meant she needed fresh ingredients, which she trusted Lucy to select while she waited in the car until the credit card was needed. It was the perfect arrangement.

They ate in silent togetherness for a moment. Despite the sugary dessert and her new advanced age, Sarah felt better about herself than she had in quite some time. Sam had her out walking to their meditation spot almost every morning at the crack of dawn. And while she still wasn't doing it properly—still couldn't see what she was *supposed* to do, besides sit with Sam and enjoy the ocean air—she was giving it a go and showing patience.

"I'll be right back." Lucy ran out and then reappeared after a quick run next door. The screen door slammed behind her. With a shy smile, she held out a package to Sarah. Instead of store-bought wrapping paper, the gift was wrapped with what looked like a piece of printer paper decorated in a colorful inkjet design of pink and red hearts and birthday cakes.

Sarah hadn't expected this. "Why, thank you, Lucy." Sarah had the beginnings of another lump in her throat. She put down her fork and opened the card first.

Lucy had illustrated it with magic marker and colored pencils. She'd even written a personal note inside.

Dear Sarah,
I hope you have a Happy Birthday! I'm so glad you came into my life and are helping me become a woman of substance, just like you.
Your friend, Lucy.

Sarah swallowed and fanned her face. She was getting much too emotional over this. *Must be those midlife hormones.* Blinking fast, she stood and gave Lucy a hug.

A hug? Seriously?

"Honestly, I never do that," she murmured apologetically, stepping back. "I am not a hugger. I usually don't even like to touch people."

"You don't have to explain yourself to us," Sam said, struggling to keep a straight face, probably for Lucy's benefit. "I totally believe you."

"I don't hug people that much, either," Lucy commiserated with Sarah. She clasped her hands together and appealed to her. "Now open my present, *please*."

This means I have to remember to get something for Lucy's birthday, too, Sarah thought.

Which was a strange thought in and of itself. When was the last time she'd gotten *anybody* a present? Unless it had to do with work and she was sucking up to them, of course.

She glanced at Sam's daughter. Lucy wasn't sucking up to *her*, was she?

Not with that sweet, guileless face. Sarah shot her a guilty smile and tore open the wrapping paper all at once, like she couldn't remember doing since she was a young girl at Christmas.

Her present was a beach rock, painted beautifully and personalized just for her, to commemorate their summer project. *To Sarah, Love Lucy.* The words *Wallis Point* were embellished over the face of the design.

Sarah sat motionless, emotion welling in her chest.

"Do you like it?" Lucy asked in a small voice.

Like it? The word *like* was inadequate. Lucy's keepsake would make a beautiful paperweight back home in Sarah's office, and every time she looked at it, she would remember her weeks with Lucy Logan and her father Sam.

Wordlessly, because her throat couldn't seem to work, Sarah nodded at Lucy. Then she shook her head and wiped her eyes. "I'll treasure it forever," she somehow managed to say.

"Oh, I'm glad you like it. I hoped you would."

Lucy turned to Sam. "Dad, where is your present for Sarah?"

"There's no rush. We can do it later. After the fireworks tonight." Sam gave her a secret smile.

Sarah swallowed. There was meaning in his words. She saw it in his intense blue eyes, gazing directly into hers.

"Okay." Lucy bought his explanation. "Um, Dad," she said, staring out the side window. "People are here now for the Fourth of July party. I'm going to put some food out for them, okay?"

"Sure," Sam agreed. "But if you could help me first by directing our guests where to park, then that would be most helpful right now. Do you remember where I showed you?"

"Yes." Lucy made a little skip. "What time are the fireworks starting again?"

"It's her first year with me during the Fourth of July holiday," Sam explained to Sarah. "And I'm sorry I didn't mention it earlier, but there's a party today, followed by firework-viewing tonight." To Lucy he answered, "Ten o'clock."

"Oh. I'm supposed to call Mom at eleven. I want to show her the video that Sarah sent, and it will be eight o'clock her time. She told me to Skype her then."

"Sounds good. You can certainly do both the fireworks and call your mom tonight."

Sarah waited to talk with Sam until Lucy left. "You're having a Fourth of July party?" she repeated.

"Yes." Sam gave her his "buck up" smile. "You're invited, of course."

"To a *lifeguard party*?" she said incredulously.

"Yeah. And I hope you come." He paused. "My original idea for tonight was to host a small party for you, Lucy and my friend Duke and his family. But it turns out that traditions die hard." He held up his hands in a sign of surrender. "I'm the guy with a beach house during the fireworks on the Fourth. I floated cancelling it this year, but there was a general uproar, and I was overruled."

"I'm not a hugely social person, Sam."

"Really?" he asked drily. She had to laugh.

"So will you come over anyway?" Sam showed her his killer dimples. "I'll make it as easy for you as possible. You won't be left alone with any Neanderthals, and I'll be the perfect escort. Close by, but not smothering. Does that suit you?"

How could she say no to him? He and his daughter had just done the nicest thing for her that she could remember anyone doing in quite a long time. And she had a soft spot in her heart for him, which was growing stronger by the day...

Shaking with emotion, she stood. The problem was, she didn't *want* to say no to him. She *wanted* her present from him, later on. After the fireworks…

But she must have seemed hesitant—and she was, because she was so nervous—because Sam said quietly, "I'm not going to force you to do something you don't want to do."

"Maybe I'll find a book to read and then join you for the fireworks," she said.

He stood silently for a moment. Quieter still, he said, "You know, that sounds really good." He abruptly turned and headed for the door.

"Wait!" she called to him. "Please don't go away mad. I just…" She paused. Her heart was thumping. "You'll introduce me to people at the party as your neighbor, right?"

Slowly he shook his head at her.

"Then…what?" She swallowed. She had to get this out on the table. And what did his double meaning about his present for her equate to, really?

"You're my date," he said calmly.

"I thought you didn't date."

"That used to be my policy. What's changed is that Lucy adores you, and I think you're pretty great, too."

"Maybe we should meditate over that," she cracked.

"Why is the idea of going to a party with me so bad?" he asked, his head tilted.

Did he really want to know why? Maybe she should just say it. She was always so brash and blunt. So what was her problem in getting the words out?

"I'm older than you, Sam," she said, flustered.

"No." He shook his head. "That's not it. Something bigger than that is bothering you. Tell me."

Yes. Sarah needed Sam's daughter in order to get her old life back. And to do so, neither Sarah nor Lucy could be completely straight with Sam.

The lure of forming a small, albeit temporary "family" with them was just too tempting for Sarah. In the end, she would be a fool for making this mentoring transaction messy and hurting them all by getting too closely involved with Sam.

Despite the way he and Lucy had touched her heart—the lovely birthday party, the longing she had for the romantic connection with Sam, the way her body so obviously wanted him and her heart tugged at her to be with him—it just wasn't a good idea.

She crossed her arms. When in doubt, it was best to keep her eye on the prize. "It's just not something I'm into," she said in her old brash voice. "That's all."

Sam frowned. But he nodded. How could Mr. Laidback argue with her?

And then Lucy entered the cottage. She'd changed into jean shorts and a red-and-white striped sleeveless blouse—her most patriotic colors—and if Sarah wasn't mistaken, she'd also put on some of the mascara they'd used for the videotape.

Lucy must have sneaked it out in her pocket. "Sarah," she said timidly. "Are you coming to the party?"

"No, Lucy."

Lucy looked stricken. "If you don't go to the party, then I'm not going, either."

Sam seemed to freeze. Then he took a deep breath and headed out the door.

Sarah and Lucy stared at each other. "What's he doing?" Sarah asked. She needed Lucy as her ally. Right now, Lucy was the glue that kept this whole fragile alliance together.

Sarah followed Lucy to the window and watched Sam. He stood on his deck with Duke. Though he was wearing his laid-back face to greet his friends, she could see the tension in his shoulders. She knew full well that she'd just shoved a wedge between them.

"Wait, Sam!" Sarah rushed out the door and across the sand, Lucy following close behind her. Sarah still wore her birthday cap; she felt it tilt in the wind, and she wasn't really fit to be seen in public. But she had to let Sam know she was with him. If it made him happy, she would get through this party. She needed him on her side in order to get back to her job. And how often had she used her schmoozing skills to make it through professional obligations? If she treated his party that way, she could handle it, no matter how personally uncomfortable it might be.

She bumped into Sam and tugged his arm. The fact that she was afraid—of him, of his lifeguard friends, of feeling self-conscious because she was *old* and a brainy indoor girl, and they were young, athletic, outdoorsy people—none of that mattered. She just had to get over that junk *right now.*

Breathe, she told herself. *Stay calm. Just like Sam tells you in his meditation sessions.*

Drawing in a deep breath and letting it all out in *whoosh*, she gave Sam and his friends a brilliant smile. "Sam! Hello! Introduce me to your friends, please."

They all stared at her. Maybe she'd made an idiot of herself. But she smiled gamely at the first person she saw, who just so happened to be that older lifeguard—Duke, that was his name—older than her, even, and when that fact penetrated her brain, she was able to breathe a genuine sigh of relief.

SAM COULDN'T HAVE been more shocked. But he turned to Duke, who was looking at both of them as if he couldn't believe what he was seeing. Sam didn't much care if Duke thought he was acting out of character, but Sarah—he cared about protecting her. He cared a whole lot. And not just for Lucy's sake. He cared about *her*.

Putting his hand on Duke's arm, Sam smiled easily at him. "Remember I was telling you about Sarah Buckley?" Sam turned to Sarah. "Sarah, meet Duke Daniels. He's vice principal of Wallis Point High School and, during summers, the chief lifeguard of Wallis Point beach." Duke was also Sam's mentor and best friend, but he wasn't going to launch into that now. Besides, it was pretty obvious.

"Pleased to meet you, Duke," Sarah said. Despite her fiery, mostly unpredictable nature, Sam was counting on Sarah to be polite. As a businesswoman, she knew how to do this if she was so inclined. He wasn't going to fool himself that she could ever really fall for a guy like him, but obviously, there was some reason she'd changed her mind about coming as his date. He wasn't going to think about what that could be now.

"Duke, this is Sarah Buckley. She's my neighbor and a guest from California this summer."

Sarah's smile didn't falter. She took Duke's hand and shook it firmly. That she was wearing the birthday hat his daughter had chosen for her only made Sam feel that much more for her.

She really was magnificent. *I know how much you're trying*, he thought. *And I appreciate it.*

"Sam has spoken highly of you, Duke." Sarah straightened the pointy birthday cone cap on her head as if it absolutely belonged there and she was proud of it. "Sorry I wasn't here to greet you, but we were having a small birthday celebration back in my cottage."

"Happy Birthday," Duke said.

"Thank you." Sarah cupped her hands together and nodded slightly. "Lucy's is in a few days. Make certain you tell her Happy Birthday. She'll be thrilled to hear it."

"Ah. That explains the cap she's wearing, too." Duke smiled.

"Yes. You should see my aunt's two cats. Lucy found birthday caps for them, as well."

Duke chuckled. Obviously, he was charmed by Sarah. Sam stared at her in amazement. There was no trace of the rude executive he'd first met. In any event, he felt grateful and relieved.

"Let me introduce you to my family," Duke was saying as he led Sarah off into Sam's house. Sarah smiled back and gave Sam a little wave. He should probably follow.

But Lucy skidded by, carrying the trays of cut

vegetables, munchies and cheeses she'd prepared for the party, which had been taking up most of his refrigerator and kitchen table, stacked in neat, plastic-wrapped piles.

"How is it that you knew how to do all this?" Sam asked, catching his daughter's attention on one of her trips past him.

"Mom entertains a lot." Lucy rushed off to help Melanie, Duke's wife, crank up the umbrella on the back deck. Somebody—he wasn't sure which young lifeguard—had brought a baby with him, and the baby needed shade.

Sam stood off to the side, watching everything swirl around him in his own home. Just another Fourth of July party, but not really. Everything had changed.

Lucy was in his life. It struck him again how little he'd known her, how much of her life so far had been a complete void as far as he was concerned. He'd been oblivious to that before this summer.

And Sarah—he just didn't know what to think. She was a whirlwind of energy and action, as usual. Compared to her, he was the calm wave, going over everything, and she was the hurricane, the fierce storm that came in and shook everything up. Including him.

The way she'd first reacted to the party, Sam had been tempted to cancel the whole event, send all the guests home, just because he hadn't wanted to make her or Lucy have to *tell* him to stop. Hadn't wanted to make them feel guilty, like they had to choose sides.

That was super important to Sam.

He stared at Lucy. He doubted guilt was something she felt very often in her daily life. It just wasn't in her nature.

But when he'd been a kid, guilt had wracked him perpetually. He'd been so sensitive about it. It still affected him—that was part of why he'd closed himself off, to dodge that feeling. The great, gaping pain of his life had been the fallout from his parents' divorce, and until recently, he hadn't really thought about that much, either, preferring to stay detached and avoid caring too much about people.

Lucy had changed that. He was caring now.

And it felt amazing.

He didn't want to think about the danger, of how he would feel at the end of the summer when Sarah finally left them. He had to believe she would continue to keep in touch with Lucy. Why not him, too?

Sarah went from person to person, chatting, filling drinks, talking about who knew what. He could only hear snippets of her conversation. Maybe they trained people in business to do this, and maybe she was simply playing a role, but even if she was, that didn't matter. What mattered to him was that she was doing it because of him and Lucy. She couldn't have any other motivation. He and Lucy couldn't help her with business. His meditation lessons didn't seem to be helping her just yet, so it wasn't like she needed him for that. But she appreciated their company.

And somehow, he and Sarah *worked* together. He was letting himself *connect* with her, and that felt good.

LATER THAT EVENING, shortly before it was time for the fireworks to start on the beach, he looked for Sarah. He'd been distracted by the growing number of guests and the fact that the party was getting boisterous.

One of the younger lifeguards—Big-D was what they called him, maybe because he was a huge kid—staggered across the room like he'd had too much to drink. Sam glanced over. He noticed that Big-D, being inebriated, was talking Sarah's ear off. Sam didn't think he'd ever heard Big-D say much of anything unless he absolutely had to. He was "conservative in his words," as Duke put it.

Sam edged over and caught Sarah by the elbow. She jumped a little, but when she saw him she smiled. And she didn't shift away from his touch. In fact, she nestled closer into the crook of his arm.

He took that as a very good sign indeed.

"I need to speak with my date," he said to Big-D, shocking both himself and the young lifeguard, who blinked at him.

"Why don't you find something to eat?" Sam counseled the young man. "You're over twenty-one, right?"

"Yes, sir." Big-D tried to straighten like he was standing at attention or something. "Yes, sir, I am."

"Good." Sam had thought so, but it was good to check again anyway. He made a mental note to be sure his car keys were taken away, if he had any. Sam took the beer from the young lifeguard's hand and gave him a little poke in Duke's general direction. Duke was always the unofficial guy in charge of such things. Certain people were uninvited from future parties if they behaved badly.

Over the crowd, Duke nodded to Sam. Duke was a vice principal at heart. He dealt with disciplinary cases on a daily basis, and relished being the "dad" in charge.

"You didn't need to rescue me," Sarah whispered in Sam's ear. "I was doing fine on my own."

"I know. You're the most competent person I know," he murmured back.

"Boy, you know how to sweet-talk a girl." Sarah smiled at him.

"Is it working?"

"Of course. How is Lucy doing, by the way?"

"She's fine. She's cuddling a baby outside, fascinated by it. I wonder if I should be worried."

"No, that's natural in girls her age."

He tried to imagine Sarah interested in babies.

Reading his expression, Sarah laughed. "Yes, I was once that way, too," she teased. "I was actually the best young babysitter in my Connecticut neighborhood." She seemed amazed by that fact.

"Are you really having a fun time?" He peered at her. "Honestly?"

"No," she said smiling. "But I'm faking it pretty well, aren't I?"

"Do you want to take a walk with me?" he asked. "The fireworks will be starting soon."

"Then who will be in charge of the house?"

"Duke," he admitted. "He's the real reason these parties exist. His house is inland, and my house is the perfect spot for when Wallis Point has beach fireworks. His family loves it. Plus, if anyone gets out of hand, then Duke takes over. He's a natural father."

"Where is *your* father?" Sarah asked. "You've never mentioned him."

No. He hadn't.

Sarah stared at Sam, waiting for him to explain.

But he swallowed the sour feeling in his stomach. Why ruin her birthday with an unpleasant conversation?

Sarah's gaze bored into him, though, and he slid his glance aside, seeking a distraction.

From the corner of his eye, Sam saw Lucy headed up the stairs. He backed away, studying her expression. "She looks unhappy," he said to Sarah.

Sarah turned to watch her. "She does." Sarah didn't sound happy about that. "I noticed her staring at Duke's son earlier, but he's, what? Two years older than her? And he seemed to be looking at another girl." Sarah sighed. "I'll go talk to her. That's probably all it is."

"Thank you," he said. "Boy troubles are out of my league."

"Mine, too."

"Maybe not."

She gave him a questioning look.

"Take our walk in a few minutes?" he asked her.

"Lucy is more important right now."

True. He couldn't argue with that. "We'll meet up later," he said. "I still haven't given you your present."

But Sarah never did come back, not even for the fireworks.

After everyone had left for the night and Sam caught up with his daughter, Lucy told him that Sarah had gone home after she'd talked briefly with her in her bedroom "about nothing important."

Somewhere along the line, Sarah had gotten cold feet where he was concerned.

And he was kicking himself for botching everything. He really should have cancelled the damn party instead of putting it off to chance.

He wouldn't make that mistake again.

CHAPTER TEN

SARAH BUCKLEY'S HEART was a barren place, she knew. Before she arrived at Wallis Point, she'd thought she'd hardened all the old soft spots.

But, as it turned out, she wasn't as tough as she thought. Last night at the party she'd realized she was caring too much for Sam Logan. It had scared her, and she'd decided it was best to leave before she said or did anything she would come to regret.

Sarah sat at her aunt's kitchen table, staring at the birthday gift that Lucy had made for her yesterday. It was quite good—the artwork showed skill and love. The fact that Lucy had personalized it made it something that Sarah would never forget.

She wiped her hand across her eyes. The unfortunate thing about her growing closeness with Sam and Lucy was that the loving gift from the young, talented girl was also proof positive for Richard that Sarah *did* have some human, redeeming qualities. No, more than that. It showed she could work closely with a person from the younger generation, and that she could mentor her and help her achieve something even better than she would have on her own.

Sarah touched the rock with reverence. She treasured this gift, and she always would.

But she was also pragmatic. Yes, the video Sarah had sent spoke to Lucy's innate talent and the merit of her beach app project. But the *gift* showed that Lucy appreciated her. That she hadn't run away screaming as a result of interacting with Sarah Buckley. On the contrary, Lucy Logan *liked* working with her.

Before she could think about it much longer, Sarah used her phone to take a photo of Lucy's gift and then opened her messaging app. Tell Richard I am mentoring the younger generation just fine, she wrote to Gregory after attaching the photo.

No, scratch that. Sarah erased the text—it was too obvious. Instead, she typed, A birthday gift from the lovely young woman I've been mentoring. Please be sure Richard watches her video today.

It wasn't quite so blatant, but the underlying message was clear. *See?* it said. *I've changed. I can do this—I can work closely with people and even inspire them to achieve great things. And I can do so without them hating me for it.*

Sarah pressed Send.

Then she went out to Cassandra's deck with a cup of coffee. It was another beautiful, clear July day. The thing about the summer holiday falling in the middle of the week was that working people tended to vacation on either side of the day off. Today, the beach was jam-packed with vacationers and their sand chairs, colorful beach towels, coolers and shade-throwing umbrellas.

Somewhere in the midst of this teeming humanity, Sam maneuvered a Wallis Point mini emergency vehicle the size of a golf cart, while Lucy was off at the amusement arcade with her cousins, who'd arrived earlier from Boston to visit her for the day.

There was just no *work* for Sarah to do. Nothing to focus on but avoiding Sam as much as possible while she waited for the go-ahead from Richard Lee to move herself back to California.

Hopefully, he would email her this morning so she could make her escape tonight. He'd had the video for two days now, time enough to make his decision. And today was July fifth.

Sarah felt jittery about waiting. Back home in California, today would have been a work day. A big part of her still longed for her comfortable and familiar office space.

Sarah went inside and opened her laptop. Using Sam's Wi-Fi signal, she downloaded a whole bunch of meditation videos to study. Sam had tried to be helpful, but ever since that twinge of out-of-body bliss on the first day, she hadn't come close to feeling what meditation should surely feel like. She had an idea that she needed to double down on her research before she went home. She visualized herself as being able to sit with Richard Lee in his office and show him the effects of her meditation practice, or at least being able to fake it so he thought she was doing it right.

But a funny thing happened. Sarah watched five different videos and still couldn't concentrate. She kept checking her messages and received…nothing in reply.

Worse, the painted rock on her coffee table made her think of Lucy. And the more Sarah thought of her, the guiltier she felt. Sending the photo like that had made her feel like she was using the girl's friendship for her own ends. In the beginning, it had been easy for Sarah to use the mentorship to get what she wanted from Richard. Now, guilt was involved. She'd developed a real friendship with Lucy and Sam, and to treat them with her customary tunnel vision toward her own ambitious ends just didn't feel right.

Becker padded into her living room in his particular, cat-prowling way. When he saw Sarah sitting on his couch, he jumped into her lap, turned around a few times, snuggled in and began to purr.

Even the cat seemed to be bonding with her. A lump formed in Sarah's throat. These were Cassandra's cats—they certainly weren't *hers*. She didn't feed them or change their litterboxes. But she hadn't tossed them out or otherwise been mean to them. She was silent company. She'd brought them Lucy to care for them.

And Becker was thanking her for it.

She closed her eyes. Sam had given her a wonderful gift—his daughter—plus a party that made her fortieth birthday not only not seem so bad, but fun. And she'd repaid him last night by disappearing on him.

Guilt was a horrible feeling. Because the thing was, she was better than this. Her parents hadn't brought her up to be this way. They'd instilled values of friendship and loyalty. After they'd died and she'd been abandoned and thrust amidst strangers, she'd been hurt and angry, and had turned her back on those qualities that had let her down. She'd turned self-focused and ambitious, and she'd done it for pure survival. But those days were past now, and her parents' way was right. Maybe it had taken this place from her girlhood, and meeting a sweet girl and her dad to make her realize that.

She took her phone and instead of dialing work, she dialed Sam. He might have his phone stashed in his backpack, but if he didn't answer, she could leave him a message.

He picked up on the second ring. "Sarah?" he said. There was urgency in his normally laconic voice.

She swallowed. "I…was just thinking of you."

"Ditto here." His voice softened.

"Is Duke with you?"

"Yeah. He's looking the other way while I take a personal call."

She took a deep breath. "I know your brother's family is with Lucy right now and that you'll probably be busy with them tonight, but if I could just see you for a few minutes when you get off work, maybe we could meditate together. I…missed seeing you this morning."

She flinched at her own words. They sounded so stupid. She just felt so miserable and guilty.

"Yeah," he surprised her by saying. "I'm glad you called, Sarah. But unfortunately, I've got a kid here who needs first aid. He stepped on glass and has a cut on his foot. Can I call you back later? Will you be home this afternoon?"

"Yes. Of course." She laughed softly. "I'm in my cottage meditating with my cats."

She hung up, wondering why she'd said that. This was Cassandra's cottage and these were

Cassandra's cats, and she was definitely, certainly not meditating.

She turned off her phone and her laptop and went onto the deck, carrying Becker with her. It was low tide, and the horde of people enjoying the seashore was far enough away from her that maybe she could pretend they weren't there. The ocean made a nice sound that she could even imagine covered their voices and holiday noisemaking. She could sit here and close her eyes, and just tune into the waves...

RETURNING HOME MID-AFTERNOON for his delayed lunch break, Sam saw Sarah sitting on Cassandra's deck. He headed over, put down his knapsack, and immediately did a double take.

Sarah was *meditating*. She hadn't just been making that up when she'd called him earlier. Her eyes were closed and she was breathing slowly, but she was sitting up in the blue chair and she was facing the ocean.

He sat in the Adirondack chair across from her. It felt good to relax and chill out. He'd been assigned as a floater again today during the busy July Fourth vacation week, this time on medical emergency call, and it seemed that every kid within a mile's radius was having an accident-prone morning. He'd bandaged more small cuts and scrapes than he could ever remember. Soothed more worried adults and sobbing kids than he ever hoped to see—or hear—again.

Meow! Simmonds had leaped up on the table and stood an inch from Sam's ear, howling at him loud enough to wake the dead.

Both Sam and Sarah jumped up.

"Oh!" Sarah said. "When did you get here, Sam?"

"A few moments ago." Sam paused. "You were meditating."

"No, I wasn't." She shook her head. "I was just resting my mind."

He smiled at her. "That's exactly what meditating is, Sarah. Congratulations."

She shook her head. "No, I watched some videos this morning. I wasn't chanting or counting breaths, which now that I think about it, is possibly what Richard does when he meditates."

"Well, that's one technique, yes, but maybe it isn't *your* technique." She looked flummoxed, but it really wasn't meditation he wanted to talk about right now. She'd left his party early without saying goodbye to him. That's what he wanted the answer to. "Why did you call and ask to see me earlier? What's going on?"

She sighed, then looked at her hands. "I feel guilty, actually."

"That's the last thing I want."

"I just ran off on you yesterday, Sam. I didn't say good-night, or stay with you for the fire-works…"

"Yeah. I was thinking over the last conversation we had, and I was wondering if it was because you asked me about my family, and I didn't give you a straight answer."

She blinked at him. Had he misinterpreted her?

"No," she said. "It wasn't that. I'm just…"

"Be honest with me."

"Well, I thought leaving like that would make it easier to detach from you when I have to leave. I mean, leave Wallis Point. Isn't…that what's best for both of us, eventually?"

He thought about that for a moment. Of course he knew she had to leave Wallis Point. But he didn't *want* her to detach from him.

Wow. For years, he'd been living under the assumption that if he let himself care about a person—really care—it would only bring him pain. In his experience, people always left. It had just seemed safer to him to keep a comfortable, laid-back emotional distance.

But now, being with her and Lucy this summer…

He pulled his chair closer to her. "You know,

Sarah, two weeks ago I would have agreed with you wholeheartedly."

"But not now?"

He shook his head. "I've missed a lot of Lucy's life because of this way of thinking. Yes, opening yourself up to someone can bring pain when they leave. But if I don't risk that…" He shook his head again. "I miss the good stuff, too."

"So…you don't mind if I leave."

"It will hurt…yeah. I'd always thought it was my worst-case scenario, watching people leave, but…" He couldn't think about that just yet. "All day I've been turning over what you asked me last night. Probably not a good idea when I'm bandaging kids' cuts, but…" He smiled at her. "You asked about my family, and I really do want you to know." He absently stroked Simmonds's fur as he talked. "The thing, is, Sarah, I'm not close to either of my parents. I guess that when they sat my brother and me down and told us they were getting divorced, it was a huge shock. Or it was to me, anyway. My brother, Michael, is older, so maybe he was more clued in to what was going on than I was." He stared at his hands. "I thought, you know, like kids sometimes do, that if I just behaved better, then they would stay together. But it didn't work."

"You were only a kid," Sarah said.

He smiled. "Yeah. A little hellion."

She smiled back. "I can perfectly see you."

He felt his smile fading. "The harder I tried, the worse I made it for myself."

"That must have been so confusing," she said softly.

He stared up at the cloudy sky. "They were fighting so much by that time, wrapped up in their resentment, that they lost all perspective." He took a breath. "My brother and I had to choose which side we were on. Specifically, we each had to choose which parent we wanted to live with. I never did make the decision. I remember I threw up when they asked me. Michael convinced them to keep us together, and he made the choice. I just went along. We went with our mother, but things were never the same with our father. And she didn't seem to care."

He put Simmonds down on the deck then glanced at Sarah, who was gazing intently at him. "The thing was, I still couldn't choose. I stayed detached from my mom, too. I guess that's what I do naturally."

"It's horrible that your parents did that to you!"

Sam nodded slowly. "Well, I didn't realize how bad it was until I was charged with caring for Lucy. I mean, I've always been charged with caring for Lucy, but having her every day is much, much different from when I see her every other Saturday afternoon. Then, it's like a playdate. It's not real life. This…everything that's happened this summer, as messy as it is… it's real. And I tried not to be too attached, at first. Because if you get attached to a person, it never ends well. Or, at least, that's how I used to think."

He blew out a breath. "I've never told anyone this. None of this…what's going on…it wouldn't be happening without you. You've made the difference to us, Sarah." He smiled at her. "So, even if you didn't get to see Cassandra and find closure there, I hope Lucy and I will have been an okay consolation prize for the summer."

"You're not a consolation prize."

Sarah reached for Sam's face and framed it in her hands. Her heart was full to bursting. And, yes, there was guilt in her still—from the photo she'd sent to Gregory to the secrets she still kept—but she knew now that she did care for him, and that was okay. If he was willing to accept her leaving, then they would figure out the consequences together.

She didn't have to be on her guard against that any longer.

She leaned over and kissed Sam on the lips. His skin was sun warmed beneath her fingertips, and his lips were rough from the sea. She wasn't going to be able to give him up easily, but he was hers today. He'd told her and shown her the truth of who he really was, and he'd invited her in to share his family life.

With a groan, Sam stood and embraced her. It had felt too hot to wear a bra beneath her T-shirt, so her breasts pressed against his bare, muscular chest in a way that instantly set her aflame. She curled her arms around his neck and reached for him as he leaned down to kiss her again.

She could get used to kissing him. She hugged him more closely, feeling the hardness in his bathing trunks.

"Come with me to my bedroom," he said.

To his *bedroom*! "Are you sure?" she asked, breaking from him. She could hardly believe what he'd asked. *I'm forty! He's not!*

He responded by threading his fingers with hers. "As sure as I've ever been."

Her heart was in her throat. This was not quite what she'd expected. "But, it's the middle of the afternoon and you're still on shift!"

"Duke's not going to page me. There's a second floater arriving now to take my place."

"Duke knows you're here?"

"Not specifically. He thinks I'm on break, checking on Lucy and my brother's family before I join them for dinner. But I got a message from Michael—he's taking Lucy down to the go-karts with his two kids, and they just want to grab something fast. He told me he'll catch up when he drops Lucy off later tonight. So it's just you and me now."

He squeezed her hands. "Sarah, the summer is short. I know you have to leave eventually. I want to take advantage of what we have while we still can, because before we know it, it will be Labor Day."

"So...you're accepting that I have to leave?" she asked, double-checking. "You're really sure?"

He nodded sadly. "It doesn't mean we can't be a couple now, though, for as long as you're here."

"Well, I..." She paused, shaken to her core. It was true that she didn't want to be just friends with him, that she wanted more. And it was also true that she planned to leave ASAP, much earlier than Sam thought. She hadn't heard from Richard or Gregory yet, but it was early still...

But Sam wasn't letting her *think* through all the angles properly. He wasn't letting her feel bad, either. He was a man of action. His fingers stroked up under her shirt, kneading at her bare skin.

"Sam..."

"Hmm?" His thumbs slipped to her sides and circled the edges of her bare breasts.

"Oh, please don't stop," she murmured. She

leaned her head back, enjoying the touch that she'd been craving from him for so long.

And then her T-shirt was inched up and her belly exposed to the warm breeze, and his mouth and tongue, wet and sensual, scraped across her nipple through the thin cotton material. She gasped with the decadent pleasure of what he did to her.

His kisses trailed up her neck and stopped beside her ear. "Let's go inside," he whispered. He nipped the edge of her lobe. "You can be in charge. Order me around all you want, or you let can let me please you as I see fit."

He stopped kissing and grinned wickedly at her. "Do you want to relax? To *really* relax? You won't even need to meditate." And then he kissed her deeply on the mouth, his fingers running through her hair, massaging her scalp, making her feel as if she wasn't herself but somebody very special. A goddess of sea and sand.

There wasn't an agreement between them. She didn't remember hearing any words, speaking any promises. Any remaining guilt over leaving him early just drifted away. Time seemed to skip ahead in a lovely pattern, as if she were drugged by the warm summer afternoon and the bliss of lovemaking. Soon they were tiptoeing through his empty house, up the back staircase in case Lucy had somehow magically appeared (she hadn't), and then they were inside his bedroom.

He locked the door behind him. She was thankful for this.

He led her to his bed. She was thankful for this, also. The cool air-conditioning whispered across her sun-kissed, heated skin, and the crisp softness of cool sheets embraced her as she relaxed into his firm mattress. She had a quick glimpse of a sparse, bare, masculine room with a hardwood floor, white walls, shuttered windows. She hadn't realized it, but there was a small balcony off his bedroom, with a lone cushioned chair outside. In the corner was a short hall leading to what she supposed was an en suite bathroom.

He was an adult in a home of his own. He had a job. Standing in his community. She shouldn't care that he was eight years younger than her. What did it matter if it didn't matter to him? He offered her no-strings escapism. He'd said so himself.

And besides, in the end…she would have control. Even if she ceded it now, for her own pleasure, she would be the one who left him. Not the other way around…

He stripped off his shirt and then hers. He smiled, kissing each of her breasts in turn. She wasn't a well-endowed woman, but what she had was feeling very good indeed. Stretching, she gave him better access. She would only be vulnerable if she acted vulnerable.

"You're so beautiful," Sam murmured. His dark blue eyes gazed into hers so directly that she had to look away. Gently, he took her cheek and turned it to him. "Come here, Sarah." He touched his tongue to her lips, opening them. And heaven help her, her body responded. She didn't want it to. She didn't want to be at his mercy. "I wondered for so long what it would be like to kiss you like this."

He'd taken off her shorts. He stroked her thighs so easily, so absently, as a matter of course. And while she breathed heavily and concentrated on not caring about him, his rough fingers stroked her womanhood. He dominated her like the sea had dominated her that day when she'd been sucked up in the rip current.

Only today, in his big bed, she enjoyed being carried away. His thumb had found the center of her, the secret hardness of her sex, and it was rhythmically stroking her, carrying her and tossing her about, as if she was floating on the cool, cold waves far out from shore. She felt exquisite shivers of pleasure and was dimly aware of calling out. But her sounds were swallowed up by his kisses. And then her back was arching, yearning for him to enter her. To take control.

He did. His lifeguard trunks came off and he reached briefly beneath the bed, dragged out a small suitcase, and dug inside the pocket, finally sheathing himself with a condom. *Good, safe*, she thought. Because he wasn't real. Sam would be gone once she woke up from this dream and reasserted herself in her life. But for now…

"Please," she sighed, tugging his cool-as-the-ocean hips toward her.

"In a moment, Sarah." He kissed her gently. And the laid-back devil teased her some more with his thumb on her body. Oh, she couldn't stop the pleasure waves. She cried, mewling noises, happy noises. And only then did he enter her, filling her and touching her deeply, pleasuring a whole new set of other, deeper nerve endings.

With each stroke into her, she floated over another wave, and another, crying out in joy at each one. She didn't want it to end. If this was forty, then forty was fantastic, and if all younger guys were like this, then they were the only men she would ever date from now until the end of her life.

But it didn't end yet. He brought her higher and higher, with patience, with, yes—with love, with gentle teasing and slight laughter, until rockets exploded. And it still did not stop.

Her knees somewhere near her ears—*Who needs meditation*, she thought, *when you have Sam Logan to make love to?*—she rubbed against him, laughing and crying, savoring the after-waves, curling and uncurling her toes. He laughed along with her, gently encouraging, until last he couldn't stand it anymore. He released his own pleasure, crying out and then lying limp. Both of them were covered in a sheen of light summer sweat.

He smiled at her as if she'd put him in bliss.

She—old, businesslike Sarah—had done that to him.

He pulled her closer within his embrace. "Sarah, I'm exhausted." He gazed at her in wonder.

She laughed. She felt a happiness she knew she couldn't have forever, but she could fool herself, at least for today.

THEY SPENT THE rest of the afternoon in bed, and it wasn't awkward to Sam at all, even though Sarah knew who he was. She knew his kid's name. Heck, she even knew that he *had* a kid. And he did not feel stress over this. He felt completely relaxed and at home being connected through feelings to his neighbor, Sarah Buckley.

With his arms behind his head, leaning against the headboard, he asked her, "So, what did you do to make this guy, Richard Lee, mad at you in the first place?"

Sarah gave Sam a closed-lip smile, as if she was guilty but no longer cared. She had the sheet wrapped around her middle—he did have the air-conditioning kicked up a little too high, he fully admitted that—and she laughed aloud. "I guess he's just not as tolerant of my enthusiasm and my talents as he could be."

"Come on, what did you do?" He grinned at her, expecting an outrageous story.

"Well, it doesn't matter so much what I did, but why I did it." She rolled onto her side and faced him. "See, Sam, I want to take the company public and then sell it right away. I want as big a payout as I can get. Richard, on the other hand, wants to wait. I think his aim is to see what other tech projects he can get from my engineering team and then spin those out, too."

"Well, if it's your company, why can't you do what you want with it?"

"Because I sold a chunk of it to him, in return for some badly needed capital. I also gave him the right to decide when to take the company public in a five-year window." She rolled her eyes. "I know, I shouldn't have. But I wanted strategic direction from him, because he's the top venture capitalist in Silicon Valley, and his word carries weight. If I ever need financing or help again, he's someone I want as an ally, not an enemy. He has influence and can open doors. He's a true master." She frowned. "Except I don't like the strategic direction he's giving me. I made a mistake in trusting him."

"Can you fire him anyway?"

She laughed and shifted so that she was on her elbow. "You're ruthless," she teased. "But I like the way you think."

"No, really. What do you want to do with your company besides make money?"

"That's really it." She turned to face the ceiling again. "I want to sell it for lots of money. Power money. Money so big that that I can do this again. Start something, watch it grow, spin it off. Build and build and build and build."

Wow, she was scary ambitious. Not that he minded anymore. "The funny thing is, I could see Lucy saying the same thing you just did."

Sarah thought for a moment. "Yes, I can see her saying that, too."

It was so obvious that he was going to lose both of them at the end of summer. Sarah to her mogul ways. Lucy back to her mother.

"I don't want to lose her," he said, feeling the old panic creeping back into his heart.

"Who, Sam?" She stood and was putting her shorts back on. "Do you mean Lucy?"

"Yeah." He got up and opened a drawer. Found a pair of shorts so he didn't have to wear his lifeguard trunks.

"You don't have to," she said. "Hire a good lawyer. File for more custody."

He'd been thinking something along those lines. Slowly, he took a calming breath. "I want to try without a lawyer, first."

"Noble of you," she remarked.

"Yeah. I'm gonna do things my way this time." He smiled at her, feeling more resolved. "You've inspired me. If there's ever a woman who does things her way, it's you."

"I'm glad to see you coming around to my way of thinking."

"I have an ulterior motive." She looked suspicious until he laughed at her. "Don't worry, Sarah. I'm no corporate shark." He thought of something. "In fact, I need to give you your birthday present now."

"I thought you just did," she teased.

"Ha, ha, ha." He playfully swatted her. He liked how they couldn't keep their hands off each other. But he reluctantly let go of her hand and reached for a box on top of his dresser.

"Lucy wrapped it for me," he explained. And

then he held the gift out, feeling slightly embarrassed. "I hope you like it."

She tore it open the same way she'd torn open the present Lucy had given her. He enjoyed her enthusiasm.

She looked at the small box beneath Lucy's wrapping paper.

"Open it," he urged lightly.

With a hesitant touch, she opened the lid of the jewelry box, withdrew a delicate gold chain and held it up.

But her fear—of jewelry, so serious, she surely thought—turned into a peal of laughter. With delight in her eyes, she said, "Where did you find this?"

A little gold shark pendant swung beside a tiny gold heart.

"It says Sarah Buckley all over it," he teased.

"It does!" she agreed. "I'm going to wear the shark proudly into my next staff meeting." Her face clouded a bit. "If I ever have a next staff meeting."

"Oh, sharks always have a next meeting."

She smiled again. She loved to think of herself as a shark.

"I added the heart," he explained, "because you're a lovable shark. At least, to me."

"Yeah, well, don't tell anybody else, okay?"

He crossed his heart. "Your secret is safe with me."

For a moment her smile faded and she looked away. But a moment later she was back to smiling brightly.

A door slammed downstairs. "If it's Lucy, she's back early," he said, tossing on his T-shirt. "Maybe she didn't like the go-karts."

"Oh, no. Where is my shirt?"

"Here, on the floor," he directed. "On the far side of the bed." He admired the view as she scurried over and bent down to retrieve it. Still, he thought, sighing, he wasn't sure how this was going to go over with Lucy.

"I'll go downstairs first," he said. "I'll take the front staircase. It might be a good strategy for you to take the back."

"I definitely would like to take the back," Sarah agreed. She coughed. "We need to have a conversation about this."

Not one he relished. "Sure. Later. I'll go down and see her now." He glanced at the clock. It was after five. "At least I'm officially off duty," he said.

"I hope it was a pleasurable duty," she shot back as she pulled on her T-shirt. He was pleased to see that she then clipped the shark and heart pendant around her neck. "And thank you for the birthday present, Sam. Both of them."

"You're welcome."

"When is *your* birthday?" she asked quickly. "I want to reciprocate, and I'm getting some very good ideas on how to do that."

He grinned at her. "Sorry, Sarah. You'll have to wait many months."

"When is it?"

He grinned harder. "You're not going to believe this, but January first."

"New Year's Day? Your birthday is on a holiday, too?"

"Yes. Another fireworks holiday. See what happens when you put us both together? We burn the place down."

SARAH WAITED UNTIL Sam's footsteps faded down the stairs, then pulled her phone from her shorts pocket. At least the time had passed quickly. She hadn't thought once of her text to Gregory, which was amazing in itself, after all the agonizing she'd done this morning.

She checked her text messages. Nothing. No missed phone calls or voicemails. Nothing. Her emails. Nothing.

She dropped the phone on Sam's bed and sat there. Some shark she was.

Richard might not like Lucy's idea, after all. And rejection wasn't something Sarah had considered.

She clenched her hands into fists. There was nothing she hated more than feeling powerless.

Lucy would be devastated if she didn't hear positive news soon.

And Sarah would be stuck in Wallis Point that much longer.

Tears prickled her eyelids. Not because staying here would be unpleasant—it would be very pleasant to delude herself and hang out with Sam all summer long—but she would never get her rightful place back this way. It was *her* company. She couldn't let Richard run it any way he wanted.

But all Sarah could do was wait. If she didn't hear anything from Gregory by the end of the week, then she would know for certain that Lucy was out.

It just couldn't happen that way. Shaking her head, she went into Sam's bathroom and splashed cold water on her face. He had his shaving things out on the counter. A bottle of hand soap. A neatly folded towel that hung on a towel bar.

He had a beautiful tiled shower that looked big enough for two people.

She studied herself in the mirror, gave herself a little shake. Tidied her hair with a comb she found in a drawer.

What am I worried about? You're a shark, Sarah.

A shark with a heart, she reminded herself.

Satisfied that she didn't look like she'd just been ravaged by a very skilled and sexy lifeguard, she demurely patted her hair and headed down the back stairs.

Where Lucy promptly met her at the bottom. The girl's face was expressionless.

CHAPTER ELEVEN

SARAH PAUSED AND tilted her head at Lucy. "Am I allowed to pass, or do I have to pay you a toll?"

"Are you and Sam, like, *together*?" Lucy asked.

Sarah slowly exhaled, willing herself to stay cool. "What did *he* say about that?"

Lucy rolled her eyes. "Nothing. But he's *whistling*. And I know you were up there with him because your car is still in Cassandra's driveway and you weren't at home. I just checked. Becker threw up in the kitchen, by the way. But I cleaned it."

"Oh, wow," Sarah murmured. "Is Becker okay?"

"Yes, but I was reading on the internet, and I think we need to change his food to get him something to help him dissolve his hairballs. They're too much for him."

"Okay. Yes." *Take better care of our cat children*, Lucy was telling her. "You're right, Luce. We'll do that together." Sarah went to step around Lucy, but Lucy still didn't budge.

Sarah took a breath. "I'm sorry. I don't want to negatively affect your relationship with your dad. Please don't take this in a bad way."

"I'm not. My dad would be lucky to have you, believe me." Lucy thought for a minute. "And I would like it, too. *If* it worked out. Which it probably won't, because of him."

Sarah stared at the girl. Lucy's cheeks grew pink. "I don't want you to get hurt," she muttered.

"Um…" Sarah didn't know what to say.

"My dad doesn't *commit*. That's what my mom says. She's warned me about him."

"Do you still believe that? He seems very committed to you now."

"We'll see," Lucy said ominously. "The summer isn't over yet."

Sarah still didn't know what to say. She glanced up and saw Sam standing there, watching them. Sarah lifted her hands in a gesture of helplessness.

Sam shook his head. Sarah figured he was going to walk away, but he didn't.

"Luce," he said.

His daughter turned. She had the grace to blush before she scurried off upstairs to her room. Both of them watched her leave.

"Now what?" Sarah asked, leaning against the stairway wall and crossing her arms.

"Give her some space. She'll calm down eventually."

Maybe. But Sarah couldn't help thinking of what Lucy had told her. "Did you hear everything she said?"

"Just the tail end."

"She said you can't commit. I think it might be a good time to talk to Lucy and answer any questions she has about the past between you and Colleen. And the future with you and her mother."

Sam's face turned a bit green.

"I know it's a bombshell," Sarah said. "But Lucy implied that she thinks it won't work out between you and her—let alone you and me—because she thinks you leave people. She said that's what her mother told her."

"Wow." Sam shook his head.

"Just so you know, I'm not worried about myself." Sarah's voice shook, but she controlled it. *She* would be the one who would be leaving *him*, after all. "It's Lucy I'm concerned about. I really do think you should talk to her, Sam."

"I'm not going to leave her or make her choose between her mother and me," Sam said quietly. "And if Lucy said that…" He paused. "I don't want to speak negatively of her mother, so let me just say that it's probably Colleen's fears speaking, not Lucy's."

"Are you *really* going to fight for Lucy?" Sarah asked.

A tick stood out in Sam's jaw. He seemed angry that she'd even asked him.

"I, um, have to go back to my cottage," Sarah said. "Lucy says Becker is sick and I need to tend to him."

Sam nodded. He just looked at her silently.

"May I come back for dinner later?" Sarah asked.

"I'm ordering pizza tonight. But, yes, I think you should come back."

"You think or you want?"

"I *want*, Sarah." He pulled her close to him. "I definitely want."

SAM RAPPED SOFTLY on Lucy's bedroom door then opened it a crack. His daughter sat against the pillows on her bed with a book in her hand. *The Witch of Blackbird Pond.*

He entered the room and sat on the edge of her bed. "How were Uncle Michael and your cousins?" he asked.

She shut her book, not looking at him. "Aunt Michelle didn't come with them today."

That was Sam's sister-in-law, Michael's wife. "Did that upset you?"

Lucy's lip quivered. "Do you think they'll get divorced, too?"

Sam scooted her over on the bed and sat beside her. "I don't know, Luce. But I wouldn't jump to conclusions or worry about it until I talk with Uncle Michael." He glanced at her. "Is that why you came home early from the go-karts? Because you were upset?"

She gazed down at her book. "I wanted to meet you when you came home from work," she said in a small voice.

Sam was getting the inkling that Lucy was worried about the relationships of the important people in her life collapsing around her. Gently, he took the book from her hands. "Hmm. *The Witch of Blackbird Pond.* I thought you'd finished it already."

"I did." Her face turned pink.

The story must be a comfort read for her, he figured. "Does it have a happy ending?"

She nodded. "Kit and Nat end up together. They take care of Hannah and bring her away with them. Everybody is safe."

Okay. Obviously Sam didn't know who the book's characters were, but he gathered that Lucy's worries had to do with keeping relationships and families together.

He ran his fingers along the edges of her worn paperback, staring at the stylized art of the teen girl on the cover. "Lucy, I'd like for you and I to continue to have a closer relationship after the summer is over. I'll do everything in my power to sit with your mom and you, and to figure out a better arrangement for all of us than we've had in the past." He would never ask Lucy to choose between him and Colleen, but there was still a lot he could do to make it easier between the three of them. "I'm very committed to you. In fact, you are my most important person. I haven't always been good at showing that, but I'm working on it."

Lucy nestled her head into his shoulder. She smelled like coconut-scented sunblock and fried dough. It pained him that she hadn't been able to enjoy the day with her cousins in a beach arcade because she was so overset by worries about her home life.

"Luce, if you ever have any concerns, I want you to come directly to me. You can talk to me about anything. I won't blow you off. And I won't ever be mad at anything you say."

"Okay," she said in a small voice.

"Do you have any, ah, questions you want to ask?" he said, thinking of Sarah and what Lucy had stumbled upon. That had to be confusing for his daughter.

"No." She shook her head. But he got the impression that there was something else she wasn't telling him.

And it bothered her.

But he let that alone for now.

AFTER SARAH LEFT SAM, she climbed into her rental car and took a long drive to the outskirts of town with the windows rolled down. Time to help Lucy the best way she could at the moment, by shopping for their cats' needs.

Sarah figured Lucy's worry and anger were symbolic, somehow, of the care Lucy felt was missing from Sarah and Sam. Or maybe a cat illness was just a cat illness.

In any event, Sarah *was* taking Lucy's dad's attention away from her. She hadn't intended to do that, at all.

So intent was Sarah on doing her part to help Lucy, that for once, she didn't mind—too much—that she had to suffer traffic in order to reach the local superstore, which she also disliked on principle. Her preference was to internet shop, but the cat was sick and needed special food for his diet *now*, and Sarah couldn't get same-day shipping in Wallis Point. She also couldn't borrow Lucy for this chore. Someday in the future there would be drone delivery. Within-the-hour order arrival—that would be perfect. Maybe Sarah would even have a part in that technology solution.

Inside the superstore, Sarah wandered for miles, it seemed, until she found the pet food. An entire aisle of it. She stood there, feeling lost, until she spotted a can of food that mentioned hairballs. Doing her due diligence, she quickly scanned the label. *Protein.* Yes, that was good. *Salmon*, yes, Becker liked fish of all kinds. Chicken, too. Sarah plopped a bunch of cans in her basket, hoping Becker would eat it and that it would actually help him.

It's true, she thought. *I'm actually becoming a crazy cat lady, or at least a lady who cares about cats.*

But it was Lucy she really couldn't stop thinking about, and the encounter that she and Sam had had with his daughter at the bottom of the stairs. Sarah didn't want to be a bad influence in any way. Lucy was at a difficult age. Duke's thirteen-year-old son clearly appealed to her, so Lucy was aware of boys and relationships, though Sarah honestly didn't know how Lucy felt about Sarah being in a relationship—however brief—with her father, despite what she'd said.

That had been her mom talking. Sarah wanted to know how *Lucy* felt.

It had felt great helping Lucy dig away at her

dreams for her future. Caring about her own dreams—that was what Sarah wanted to encourage in the girl. To depend on someone other than yourself was folly. It never worked. A woman needed to be independent in order to get by in this world.

Sarah stopped at the wrapping paper and card aisle on her way to the register. Lucy's birthday present had already been delivered and was sitting at home in Sarah's bedroom, but it seemed like a good idea for Sarah to wrap and give it to the girl early. That Richard still hadn't called them was a bad sign. A very bad sign.

Lucy would take that news horribly when she found out. Maybe receiving a great present would help.

Sarah found a wrapping paper featuring birthday cakes and cats wearing silly hats. Then she found a funny card that would appeal to Lucy's dry sense of nerd humor.

Sam was the only one left on Sarah's shopping list—just because she liked him and figured he might need the boost after a potentially difficult talk with Lucy. She got him a bottle of fancy beer, Irish stout this time, and one of those horribly unhealthy pastry-cake things wrapped in cellophane that he seemed to enjoy.

She hauled all her loot over to the self-serve cash register—that way she wouldn't have to deal with people—and then headed back out to her rental car, where she promptly grabbed her hand sanitizer and freshened up before pointing the car home.

An hour later—the after-beach traffic was just ridiculous today and Sarah was grateful for the car's upgraded sound system and commercial-free radio service—she was humming along to ABBA, feeling like a Dancing Queen. She pulled into Cassandra's driveway thinking she was coping just fine with all the challenges in her life.

Just in time to see Cassandra exiting a taxi.

Sarah screamed and slammed on her brakes, inches from hitting her aunt with her vehicle.

CHAPTER TWELVE

SAM WAS IN his kitchen on the phone with the pizza delivery place when he heard tires screeching and then yelling coming from the direction of the cottage next door.

His first thought was that someone had been hurt in a car accident. His heart pounding, he bolted as fast as he could out the sliding back door and sprinted over the sand toward Sarah's place.

Cassandra was back?

Sam stood in the driveway, dumbfounded. Just then, Sarah stepped out of her rental car and slammed the door. Sam realized she was the one who'd been yelling.

"Cassandra!" Lucy cried out beside him. His daughter ran to the older woman, waving her arms and tumbling into his neighbor's arms. Cassandra bent to Lucy, kissing his daughter's cheeks and crying. Lucy and Cassandra embraced in a long, blubbering reunion that seemed to go on and on.

Involuntarily, Sam's fists curled. This lady

had endangered his child. She'd hurt Sarah. And she'd made him look a fool.

From the expression on Sarah's face, she was thinking along the same lines. It was doubtful she would ever forgive her aunt. Sarah's arms were crossed, and the superstore bag she held was drooping.

Clenching his jaw, Sam headed over to see his wayward neighbor.

Cassandra's gaze snapped up to meet his. She didn't seem contrite, not at all. Instead she seemed unbearably sad.

"Dad," Lucy said, dragging his neighbor over by the arm. "Cassandra is home."

Sam stopped and slowly exhaled. With a look, he beckoned Sarah to him. She complied without a word. The two of them appeared before Cassandra, a united force.

"You shouldn't have left us the way you did," he told Cassandra.

"She had to—Claudio was dying!" Lucy interjected. "And don't be mad at her for leaving, because I *told* her to go. Plus, it was my fault you couldn't find me. I waited at the library and not at our house like you wanted me to."

"Lucy, please go inside. I want to have a private conversation with Cassandra." His voice rose in a way that was foreign to him. Lucy's eyes widened, but she obeyed.

Even Sarah remained silent. He didn't look directly at her, but he could sense her staring daggers at her aunt.

"What you did was unacceptable to me," Sam said quietly. "Sarah will speak for herself, I'm sure, but I need you to know that actions have consequences. You endangered Lucy, you scared me half to death, and as a result, it's going to be a long time before I trust you again."

Cassandra's gaze faltered. She had a tissue in her hand and she dabbed at her eyes. "I understand, Sam. I'm truly sorry."

She looked completely beaten down. Racked with guilt and grief, and that was before he had compounded her misery with his scolding. Sam stepped back. "Did Claudio pass?"

When she nodded mutely, he said, "I'm sorry for your loss."

"I'm sorry I left notes instead of finding you directly."

Notes. And suddenly he remembered that Lucy said a note had been taped to his door. He recalled snatching it down later that afternoon, when he'd still been furious with Cassandra, but he'd been too angry to read it just then. In the interim, the note must have been lost in the change and confusion that had been his life these last two weeks.

He needed to find that note.

"Sarah, I am most sorry to you." Cassandra's voice was a whisper. "I know how difficult this must have been."

"No," Sarah said through clenched teeth. "You really don't." She turned to Sam. "May I move in with you for a few days, please?"

Sam hesitated. He wasn't sure this was the best timing considering Lucy's recent difficulties. "If not for Lucy, I would say yes. But I'm just not comfortable right now—"

"Of course," Sarah snapped. "My mistake." To Cassandra she said, "I'll be moving into a hotel."

"No, no, no, I will move into the hotel," Cassandra insisted. "You stay right where you are."

Sarah seemed barely able to control herself. Her face was red and she shifted from sandal to sandal. "You're right. I like sleeping with the cats. They're loyal to me and they care. *You* go to the hotel. Sam will drive you there."

And then Sarah turned and stomped into Cassandra's cottage, the superstore bag slapping against the back of her leg.

There was a long moment of silence. Cassandra leaned heavily on her purple cane. She looked as if she'd been through hell. She moved to one of the deck chairs and sat heavily.

Sam was starting to feel sorry for her. She seemed too exhausted to say much.

He picked up Cassandra's small suitcase from the dirt where the taxi driver had deposited it and carried it over to her.

"Thank you, Sam."

Sam sat in the Adirondack chair beside her on the deck and folded his arms. "Your relationship with Sarah may be irreparably broken."

"Yes." Cassandra nodded sadly. "I understand that."

"Why, then?" He leaned forward and gazed at her. "*How* could it be worth it?"

She looked up at him but said nothing.

"The day that you left, Sarah got caught in a rip current while she was waiting for Natalie to bring her your house keys. I was scared for her."

Cassandra's eyes widened. "That's terrible!"

"She's recovered. But I'm not sure she's recovered from you abandoning her once again."

"It was a difficult decision," Cassandra said. She appealed to him with her eyes. "How are you doing with Lucy?"

"Fine," he said. To his mind, Cassandra had forfeited the right to know anything about how he and Lucy were doing.

"May I speak with her before you drive me to the Grand Beachfront Hotel?" Cassandra asked. "Please?"

He blinked. She seemed so resigned to bearing the pushback. She'd never seemed so humble before.

"All right," he said. Lucy would be angry with him if he didn't let her see the woman she considered her friend. "She's upstairs in the front bedroom. Walk over to see her, and when you're ready to leave, I'll meet you out front in my truck. Your suitcase will be in the back."

"Thank you, Sam." Cassandra lifted her cane, and he helped her get up by holding out his arm.

But he didn't help her walk to his house. And he didn't remain to watch her get there safely, either.

Instead, he opened the cottage door and went inside to see Sarah. She had to be hurting.

He found her in her bedroom. She was on the unmade bed, up near the pillows, sitting cross-legged, with one cat on the pillow beside her and the other cat at the end of the bed, standing guard. Sarah appeared to be crying. She was also using tape to gift wrap what looked to be Lucy's birthday present. The wrapping paper was green and it had cats on it, too.

Smiling to himself, Sam headed over to the side of the bed where there wasn't a cat, and joined Sarah up near the pillow. She sniffled, and he put his arm around her.

"I'm just so angry at her," Sarah said.

"I know." He hugged her tighter and they both

slid down a bit under the covers. The window was open, and it wasn't that hot outside, so it felt nice to be cocooned with Sarah in the sea-breezy room.

"What are you doing?" he asked her.

She turned on her side and put her arm around him. "I'm wrapping your daughter's gift. It's way too big and expensive, but please don't get upset with me, because I have the money, and Lucy needs the present."

"Is it electronics?" he asked.

"Yes. Lucy is a smart girl going into seventh grade. She'll be writing papers and reports next year, so it's time she has a decent laptop."

A laptop. Sarah had bought his daughter a laptop, and an expensive one. Sam had planned on giving her an old one of his, but it was clunky and slow. The new ones were much lighter and faster.

"Lucy will be a lucky girl, getting a phone from me and a laptop from you."

"You're not mad about it, are you?" Sarah asked.

"No," he said. "I think it's incredibly generous, and I know you care about her." And then he moved a strand of hair from her forehead. "I care about you, too."

Tears glittered in her eyes, and she wiped

them away. "Thank you," she whispered. "I need somebody to care about me."

"Well, you've got me. And I'm not going anywhere."

Sarah sniffled and nodded. She seemed more emotional than Sam had ever seen her before.

"All I can think of is what *gall* Cassandra has," Sarah said. "Did you know she left me alone at my parents' funeral? I was there without a single member of my family, extended or not. Crowds of neighbors and friends came... everybody in the community showed up. They all loved my parents! But I was the only *family* there. The funeral director honestly didn't know how to deal with me. One of the church deacons handled the details. Cassandra never even showed up."

"That's horrible," he murmured. He'd been so angry at his parents, but this...*this* was far worse. He clasped Sarah tighter, put her head against his chest. She was hot with emotion, this normally cool shark of a lady. They lay together, in each other's arms, in the little bed in Cassandra's cottage with both cats keeping watch over them.

"At first, everyone wanted to help me," Sarah said in a sarcastic, bitter voice. "One of my friend's parents offered to let me stay with them—until it became too inconvenient. Or maybe I was too difficult. I'm outspoken, you see. My parents didn't raise me to suffer or be meek, and some people don't like that. They thought I should be more grateful, I suppose. Then there were some financial and legal tie-ups with my parents' estates. The money—what little there was—just wasn't available for me right away. So the family told the State to take me from them. One day I came home, and my bags were packed and set on the curb."

He closed his eyes. He could see her, young Sarah, at Lucy's age. Stubborn, prideful, angry and hurt. It was a volatile combination, and it could be difficult to understand or to live with. He kissed Sarah on the cheek.

"The State couldn't find someone who wanted to take me—everybody is so busy. But then finally…"

Her voice cracked. "The first family I was sent to had this horrible father. He never touched me, but he was emotionally abusive. The things he said to me were vile. And no one…no one believed me. I was difficult, you see. A troubled child."

Sam hugged her tighter. Inside, he burned. He could imagine exactly the scenario she'd described. He taught in the public schools. He saw such people. He interacted with their children.

Most were beaten down by it, but some, like Sarah, fought back.

She was a fighter.

"I vowed, Sam. I vowed… I would never be in a position where anybody could do this to me ever again. I wouldn't let it happen. I would be too rich, too powerful, too influential for them to *dare* to hurt me."

"And you did it," he said softly, kissing her. "You made it happen by the sheer force of your will and the passionate heart you possess."

She cried harder. He could do nothing but hold her while she sobbed.

"I'm not there yet," she choked out. "I'm not there. And here is Cassandra waltzing in as if she's done nothing wrong and I should overlook *everything*!"

He ached for her. He wanted to know why Sarah had come back to Wallis Point to begin with—what had she possibly expected from Cassandra?

"You could have gone on a retreat and learned to meditate anywhere," Sam said. "I'm glad you came to Wallis Point, Sarah, don't get me wrong. It's the best thing that could have happened to me and Lucy. But…*why*? I know I asked you this before, but I'm asking again. Why did you come, *really*?" He let the question hang there. He wanted Sarah to pick it up and think it through for herself.

"I don't know," she whispered. "Maybe..." She sat up and wiped her eyes. "It's so juvenile," she admitted, cringing as she faced him.

"I will never think less of you. I admire your bravery."

"Well...maybe it was a dumb fantasy. But I'd just been written up by that women-in-business magazine, and maybe I wanted to gloat a little. Maybe hear her say how sorry she was and how impressed by the way I turned my life around for myself." She laughed ruefully. "It's so ridiculous, Sam. Cassandra is who she is. I can't control her actions or reactions to me."

"I know," he said, thinking how much it galled him sometimes to see his daughter lionize Cassandra.

"I'm not going to forgive her," Sarah insisted. "I don't have to. I don't want to."

He just nodded and listened.

She laid back and stared at the ceiling. "She can stay in that hotel for the rest of the summer, for all I care. I'm staying here. I've been banished from my job until I learn to chill out, which may never, ever happen."

He laughed. "I like you just the way you are, you know." He couldn't help grinning at her. "And I'm sorry, I should feel bad that you're banished, but I don't. How would we have ever met, otherwise? It means I get to have you here with me, and that's what I really want."

"Honestly?" Sarah sounded so young and hesitant when she asked him that way. "Honestly, you like having me here?"

"Love it," he breathed. And then his mouth was on hers. And she was twisting in the bed to meet his body. The huge present on the bed—Lucy's laptop—he lifted and moved out of the way.

Sam couldn't stay too long—he had to take Cassandra to the local hotel—but he would be back. And the cats? He wasn't worried about them. They hopped off the bed and left the room to go take care of themselves, independent creatures that they were.

TWO DAYS LATER, Sarah hummed as she signed Lucy's birthday card and taped that to the top of her gift, along with a fancy yellow bow she'd found.

It was evening, and she'd been invited to Lucy's birthday dinner at Sam's house. She slipped her feet into her sandals and smoothed some lotion on her skin. Her legs were tanned from walking the beach with Sam every morning on their way to meditate, and getting a bit muscular from all the exercise, too.

She stretched and smiled. Overall, she felt great. The emotions she'd poured out to Sam had come from her heart, and she'd needed to express them. The benefit was that the more she expressed, the more she felt bonded to him. Sam had stopped by several times since. They hadn't spent the night together—Lucy had been an obstacle to that intent, although not an unwelcome one—and Sarah completely understood. She and Sam were keeping the physical aspect of their relationship private, careful not to touch or show public displays of affection, but emotionally they were close.

Despite that, Lucy knew what was going on between them. She'd let Sarah know that she knew on the staircase that day after she and Sam had first made love. Sam hadn't said if he'd discussed it with her further, but Sarah would be surprised if he hadn't.

Sarah also suspected, but didn't know for sure, that Colleen brought home boyfriends. Lucy had mentioned that her mother had a male roommate on her Alaska cruise—a drummer in the ship's band. Sarah got the impression Lucy wasn't too happy about that, even though she didn't express an opinion to Sarah one way or the other.

Sarah just felt sympathy for the girl. Even though Richard had never called—and Sarah was certain at this point that the rejection email would be coming any day now—she didn't feel personally discouraged. After her big cry a few days ago, she was now enjoying the interlude with Sam. If she was banished for the next month and a half, then so be it. Sarah would take her penance and then go back and fight all the more.

To Lucy, she'd counseled, "We'll stay positive and wait to hear from the committee." It was remarkable to her that she wasn't being as blunt and angry as she normally was. But Sam's kindness and loyalty were rubbing off on her, making her feel optimistic.

Not that Lucy completely bought it. She was miffed that they hadn't heard yet. But Sarah usually managed to talk her out of her moods. They spent all day together, almost every day.

Straightening, Sarah put down the bottle of moisturizing lotion. The cottage was tidied and cleaned. The lunch dishes that she and Lucy had used were washed, dried and put away, and the tiny kitchen smelled like homey lemon.

One cat sat purring beside his empty food bowl, and the other stood guard on the front windowsill.

"Here, Simmonds," she told the big black cat. "You earned a treat today." She was trying to keep his weight down, so she gave him a small portion of whole milk in a ceramic saucer she used for just that purpose. Simmonds bent his thead and lapped happily away. His milk mustache would appear in no time.

Becker clambered down from the sill and pleaded for his portion, too. She poured him just a speck less milk than his big brother received.

"Be good, boys," she called to them. "I'm going out."

And then she heaved up Lucy's new laptop gift into her arms and picked her way in new flip-flops over the short, sandy expanse to Sam's house.

When she got to his deck, she paused. The sun was sinking low over the sand dunes. It was a nice time of evening. Normally she and Sam would share an after-work beer and watch the waves break. The beach was empty at this hour. The day-trippers and lifeguards had gone home. Only seagulls and a smattering of local walkers remained to enjoy the day's remains.

She wondered why Sam wasn't outside, barbecuing something tasty. She heard voices in the kitchen—Sam's rich baritone that sent shivers down her spine and Lucy's high voice, girlish with enthusiasm. Smiling, Sarah let herself in through the sliding screen door.

And immediately stopped. *Cassandra's* purple cane leaned against the kitchen counter.

Please, no. Hoping it was a mistake, Sarah glanced to the chair closest to it. Cassandra sat smiling, her hair in a bun, wearing a turquoise caftan and sipping a cocktail that tinkled with ice and sported a wedge of lime on the rim.

Rage filled Sarah. Gripping Lucy's birthday present with all her might, she searched for Sam's face.

He stood over the table, opening small white cartons that could be Chinese food, could be Thai. Cassandra's influence, likely. Sam never ate takeout like that. He was strictly a steak or pizza guy.

"Lucy invited Cassandra to her party," he said quietly to Sarah. "It's her choice to do so."

Sarah pinned her gaze on Lucy. The girl didn't seem to have a care in the world. By inviting Cassandra, she certainly had no idea of the hurricane she'd opened in Sarah's soul.

If the laptop hadn't been for Lucy, and therefore precious, the old Sarah would most definitely have smashed it on the floor. It was just such an angry reaction that had caused Richard Lee to banish Sarah in the first place.

Shaking, Sarah set the gift down gently. Then she straightened, exhaling as much anger out of her lungs as she could.

Sam came over, ostensibly to greet her. "Zen,"

he murmured into her ear as he kissed her on the cheek.

"Why did you not warn me earlier?" she gritted out in a low voice.

"Because she just showed up in a taxi," Sam answered in an equally low voice. "I couldn't say no to Lucy."

"*How* did Lucy possibly invite her?" Sarah hissed. "The woman has no phone."

"The Grand Beachfront Hotel has a telephone," Cassandra said. While Sarah glared at her, Cassandra nodded. "Hello. You look beautiful tonight."

Sarah wasn't going to be fooled by *any* attempts to charm or appease her. And she *knew* she looked good. She'd worn a short dress and pinned her hair back so it was off her face. She thought she looked quite feminine for Sam's party.

Sarah inhaled a breath. It wasn't appropriate to go all Hurricane Sarah on her aunt. Lucy would be upset. It was Lucy's birthday, and Sarah would show her aunt decency for that reason. Plus, Sam would approve. That was the choice Sarah was making—to tone it all down for the sake of her continued, improved love life and personal happiness.

Lucy eyed her birthday present. "Wow, is that big box for me?"

"Yes." Sarah leaned forward to hug the girl, if a bit stiffly. "Happy Birthday, Lucy."

Lucy hugged her back and then bent down, fingering the yellow bow on the wrapped gift. "May I open it?"

Sarah guessed the girl knew exactly what it was, given that she was nearly panting with desire, her fingers itchy to tear the cat wrapping paper wide open.

"Luce, let's eat first," Sam ordered. He motioned her over to the kitchen table. "This is an informal dinner. Everyone will serve themselves. Why don't you get down the plates? Oh, and bring a plate to Cassandra, please."

Sam looked at Sarah grimly.

I don't like this any more than you do was his message to her.

"Sarah, how are Becker and Simmonds doing?" Cassandra asked pleasantly.

A dozen retorts sprang to mind, none of them remotely civil. Sarah clamped her mouth shut.

"Becker had some hairball issues," Lucy answered, "but Sarah got him some new food, so he's okay now."

"Oh, that's wonderful, dear." Cassandra sipped at her drink.

"They both sleep with me now." Sarah couldn't help getting the dig in.

"She's like Kit in *The Witch of Blackbird*

Pond," Lucy said to Cassandra. "And my dad is like Nat."

"Ah!" Cassandra smiled and Lucy giggled with her.

Now, what was that all about? Who were Kit and Nat? What was *The Witch of Blackbird Pond?*

She shot a questioning glance at Sam, but he just shrugged and handed her one of the Irish stouts she'd bought him earlier in the week. She'd forgotten about that.

"These are good," he murmured. "I like them even better than the Belgian ones you brought me that first night."

"What first night?" Lucy asked.

Sam winked at Sarah. "It's nothing important," he told his daughter.

Lucy pouted. It was her birthday, after all.

"What kind of cake did you decide upon?" Sarah asked Lucy. She took a sip of her stout—very stouty—and licked the creamy moustache from her lips while Sam looked on with appreciation.

Yes, she was behaving rather well, given the circumstances, she thought.

"Well, I decided on a classic devil's food cake with buttercream frosting," Lucy said.

"How many candles?" Sarah asked.

"Thirteen. Twelve, plus one for good luck."

"Why do you need good luck, dear?" Cassandra asked.

Inwardly, Sarah cringed. Lucy would almost certainly be thinking about the Future Tech Scholars competition. She hadn't completely accepted that she hadn't made the cut. She was still smarting over it, and Cassandra was just picking at the scab.

"Because I need luck right now," Lucy said. "Sometimes, it's just a stroke of luck that a person needs to get what they want."

"No, that's not it at all," Sarah said sharply.

Sam groaned. Lucy looked crestfallen.

And Cassandra gave her a censuring look.

Sarah's temper was rising. How dare Cassandra censure *her*? Luck had nothing to do with anything. Will did. Hard work did. Responsibility did.

Something Cassandra, her flaky aunt, knew nothing about.

Sarah put down her plate, her blood pressure feeling sky-high, and stood. "I'm going to overrule your dad, Lucy. Open the present now. You have my permission."

"Awesome!" Lucy didn't need to be asked twice. She skipped forward and dragged the gift to the center of the floor.

"Luce, that's not—"

R-r-r-i-i-p-p-p. It was like Christmas morning and the paper was gone in the twinkle of an eye.

"Oh, look at what I got!" Lucy screamed. She leaped to her feet and hugged Sarah as if she were Santa Claus and the patron saint of all good things wrapped into one. "This is *so* awesome! I will love you forever, Sarah!"

Sarah nodded, rubbing her neck where Lucy had grabbed her. She'd expected the girl to be happy, but joy over simply getting a new gadget wasn't the message Sarah was trying to give her.

Avoiding Sam's gaze, Sarah fixed her attention on Lucy. "I gave you this laptop for a specific reason. Are you listening, Lucy?"

"Yes." She sat up straight and nodded her head vigorously.

"You're to use it to continue with your app project, do you understand?" Sarah said. "No matter what anybody else says about it, do not stop. Do you hear me? Do you promise?"

"Yes, and I—"

"Luck has nothing to do with it," Sarah said sternly. "You can't count on luck any more than you can count on anybody to look out for you besides yourself. Because you can't count on people. Not really." Here, she couldn't help glaring at Cassandra, who seemed to be shrinking into the chair, making herself as small as

she could. *Good! She should be ashamed!*
Sarah thought.

Her rage fueled, Sarah continued on, "Don't
trust anybody else. Don't count on anybody to
help you or save you. There's only you, Lucy.
You're smart and you have good ideas, and I
want you to take that laptop and use it to make
yourself a good life. Because you deserve a good
life! Everybody does!" Sarah stopped to take a
breath.

There was abject silence around her. Lucy's
mouth was wide open. Her eyes were glittering
with moisture. Cassandra was gazing from her
to Lucy and back again, and shaking her head
sadly as if *she*, Cassandra, had failed.

Well, she had.

Sarah swallowed. She didn't dare look at Sam.
She couldn't, anyway.

"Lucy should be able to count on you." Sam's
voice had an edge to it. "That's what you promised, and you shouldn't let her down. She also
has me," he added quietly. "And you have me,
too, Sarah. You can count on me."

Swallowing, Sarah closed her eyes. She was
going to burst into tears. She had to force it back.
She would *not* let herself cry.

"Thank you for the laptop," Lucy said in a
small voice. Sarah wasn't going to open her

eyes to see, but she was sure Sam had somehow nudged her to say this.

"And it's…okay that I wasn't chosen for Future Tech Scholars," Lucy said. "I mean, I would have had to move to California if I won the competition, and I'm pretty sure my mom wouldn't have moved there to be with me, anyway. I know she said that she would, but then I talked to her yesterday and I think she's changing her mind. At least, that's what she said. I'm sorry I kept that secret from you," she said, obviously addressing her dad now. "I know I should have told you…"

Oh, no, Sarah thought. *No, no, no…*

"Sarah?" Sam's tone was bewildered. "What does she mean about keeping a secret from me?"

Sarah opened her eyes. Sam's face was pale, and now it was he who was struggling to hold back his pain.

"Oops." Lucy covered her mouth and looked guiltily at Sarah. "I'm sorry, Sarah. I know I wasn't supposed to say that."

"Explain to me, both of you," Sam said, jaw tight. "Why you couldn't tell me about moving to California?"

Lucy lowered her head. "It doesn't matter anymore anyway, because my project obviously wasn't chosen. I was *rejected*, Dad."

"Well it does matter to me that you conspired to lie to me," Sam said, and his tone had turned cold.

"Outside," he said to Sarah. "With me. *Now.*"

Turning to Cassandra, Sam added, "Why don't you and Lucy finish clearing up the plates and then set up the candles on the cake. We'll be back in a few minutes."

We'll. He'd said *we'll.* Sarah clasped onto that word and held it tight as Sam marched her outside to the beach for what she could see was going to be a difficult conversation.

He was angry with her. And it broke her heart.

She wondered what she could do to fix it. Or if she could fix it at all.

CHAPTER THIRTEEN

"WHAT WAS LUCY talking about in there?" Sam asked Sarah. "After all the times I asked you to review everything about the contest details, you were deliberately keeping the truth from me?"

He tried to keep the emotion from his voice, to act perfectly calm and reasonable and to hold it all in, but he just couldn't do that anymore. "Didn't you realize that if Lucy had won the scholarship and moved away, all the way across the country, then I wouldn't be able to improve my relationship with her? The relationship I've been working so hard to build on this summer? Did you even consider that?" His voice shook.

Sarah faced him in the low light of the setting sun, her expression contrite. "At first, no, I didn't think of that—you're right." She appealed to him, her palms up. "You know me—I had tunnel vision about charging ahead for the win, and I honestly didn't see at first that I was keeping anything important from you."

"At first, maybe." He took a deep breath, struggling to stay calm. "And I realize that you didn't *have* to tell me anything because Colleen is the one who signed the forms, but Sarah…you and I got closer. So much closer."

His voice cracked. "At any point along the way, especially during the past few days, you could have told me the truth. You could have given me fair warning at any time. Especially after I had that heart-to-heart with Lucy. I could tell she was feeling guilty about something, and it was *this*—that she deliberately kept the whole moving-to-California thing from me because she knew it would hurt me when I found out. I see that now. Sarah, you could have helped me prepare for that. Especially after I spent the time comforting you over Cassandra."

"I'm sorry! You know my aunt makes me crazy, and I—"

"That's it, isn't it?" Sam paced, tearing his hand through his hair before he turned back to her. Suddenly, the picture had snapped into place for him. "She *does* make you crazy, and it needs to stop."

"Right. So easy for you to say," Sarah hissed. "Did you really have to let her in tonight? Talk about fair warning," she spat out.

"And now you're angry again. Lucy is a kid— she invited her. Do you see, Sarah? Do you see why you need to deal with this? Because if you don't, it affects everything you do. All your relationships, always."

She stepped back, her mouth open in shock.

"This isn't easy for me to say." He pointed back toward his house. "But don't you see how you're so fixated on your goal of getting back to your job, of being so rich and important and never powerless again, that you used *Lucy*—a child—and me, who cares about you, to get what you want?"

She started to protest, but he shook his head at her. "Let me finish, Sarah. *Listen* to me. Somehow, I'm sure this project with Lucy is helping you get back to your old job, helping you get what you think you need. Your hurt and your anger with your aunt just clouds your judgment and makes you close your eyes to everybody else's feelings except your own. Do you see that? It affects all your relationships."

"Is that really fair, Sam?" She appeared close to crying again.

"Yeah, I'm sorry to say, but I think it is." He took the letter from his pocket, the one Cassandra had written to him, and showed it to her. "Your aunt and Lucy taped this note to my door and I forgot all about it in the confusion until Lucy reminded me the other day. Sarah, her apology details all her reasons for doing what she did. I wasn't going to show it to you because I knew it would upset you, but I really would like to share it now. Just you and me. It will help you."

"Don't tell me you've fallen for her excuses! She did this to me *twice*, Sam!"

His hand dropped, and suddenly he just felt sad for Sarah. "I'm not excusing what she did. On the contrary. But don't you want to seek to understand somebody else's inner pain, the difficult choices they had to make, and the way they've chosen to cope? We're human, Sarah. You are, too. You are. And I'm telling you that you need to get out of your head and away from your own pain so you can drop this resentment that's affecting everything in your life. Not for her sake—for yours. For *ours*."

She stared at him as if he'd betrayed her, as if he'd been the one to abandon her, rather than her aunt. Sam wasn't even sure Sarah had let herself hear most of what he'd been saying. She seemed to have shut off his words and stopped listening to him entirely.

His heart sank. Obviously, she wasn't ready to do this. "Sarah?"

"No." She shook her head wildly. "In fact, I don't want to see Cassandra around here anymore. She's hurt me too badly. And I think it's fair that you give me my request, given the circumstances."

He stared at her, feeling helpless.

"How is that so hard for you to accept?" Her voice rose. "You don't owe her anything."

"Sarah, Lucy wants her around. What am I supposed to say? You really want me to make this choice between you and Lucy?"

"Tell Lucy that she can see her outside of my presence and without me knowing about it!"

He shook his head. "I can't do that. I can't make a choice like that—" He stopped, gazing at her. Her eyes had widened.

"You won't do this for me, Sam?"

He shook his head at her.

"What am I to you?" she asked in a quiet voice. A voice that didn't seem like Sarah's, at all.

Sam took a breath and gazed out to sea. He hated fighting with her. Hated seeing her upset.

And worse, he hated having to make a choice again, between two people he cared about and wanted to get along. Desperately.

Sarah was a lot more to him than he'd realized. The importance of her presence in his life had snuck up and hit him over the head, and he hadn't realized how much he'd grown to depend upon her until now.

Sarah was…she was, after his daughter, the person Sam most looked forward to seeing when he woke up in the morning. When he had a funny encounter or learned something interesting, she was the one he wanted to tell. Not Duke anymore, but Sarah.

She was the person he couldn't wait to see when he got off duty. And the person he wanted to eat dinner with. And the person he wanted to call up and ask to go to the store with him, just for her company.

Before he'd met Sarah, Sam had been trying so hard to stay detached, to be cool and laid-back. But Sarah had come into his life and changed everything. Heck, after she'd been blindsided by Cassandra's presence in his house, all Sam had wanted to do was take Sarah outside, skip the birthday party, and commiserate and strategize with her over what they were going to do next.

Until her blowup and Lucy's revelation, which had made him realize the extent of what Sarah had been keeping from him. And how that affected Lucy. And how the anger and the resentment Sarah harbored weren't likely to go away until she managed to find some sort of peace with what Cassandra had done.

But overlook it? And let the problems continue to affect him and Lucy?

"I'm sorry, Sarah. I can't do what you're asking."

"So, I guess I'm nothing to you, then?" Sarah actually said to him in her pain and her rage, as if she had a chip on her shoulder and she was daring him to knock it off.

And that revelation shook him from his place of indecision. It was how he usually acted when he wanted to stay cool and Zen and not make any rash decisions—no, when he didn't want to make any real decisions at all.

What sucked most was that he'd fallen in love with her.

But he had to make the hard choice and *decide*. "I can't choose you over Lucy," he said.

"You're leaving me?" Her face crumpled completely. Even in the semidarkness he could see how devastated she was by his refusal to wage a war against her aunt and choose Sarah's side.

He couldn't. Lucy would always be his first choice. If Sarah weren't caught up in her hatred and pain over Cassandra, she would understand that. But he couldn't force her to see it.

He slowly backed away from her. He didn't want to leave her, but he had to.

And then he turned and went into the house to salvage what was left of his daughter's birthday party.

CHAPTER FOURTEEN

MISERY. THAT WAS ALL Sarah had left. If she'd thought she'd been in the worst possible emotional place when she'd come to Wallis Point, it was exponentially worse now.

Sam had just dumped her.

And worse, she *cared*.

She had grown to care about him very deeply. She had centered her life here in Wallis Point around him. She had made herself vulnerable, something she just did not risk, and for good reason. It seemed she always got hurt, somehow, whenever she was vulnerable and therefore weak.

She couldn't be weak. She had to act strong.

After he'd dumped her, and she'd been forced to watch him walk away, feeling deeply betrayed by his allegiance to Cassandra, it had felt like her heart was being ripped from her chest. She'd sunk to her knees in the beach sand and cried like a twelve-year-old girl.

But there were still people walking along the

shore here and there, and she'd attracted their curious attention.

Angry, she gotten up and gone home. She'd headed immediately to her bedroom, and Simmonds and Becker, loyal companions that they were, followed her inside. They each had their role. Becker, the little guy in charge, leaped immediately onto the bed and lay down beside her, purring. Simmonds, with his big shaggy Maine Coon body, had blocked the door like a loyal dog.

"That's right, don't let anybody in," she'd commanded him, sniffling, knowing Sam wasn't likely to come, anyway.

She broke into fresh tears. It *hurt* how much she'd grown to depend upon him. She'd been fooling herself, imagining she wasn't living in reality anymore in this summer wonderland by the sea she'd found herself in. Pretending to be a family with a younger-than-her lifeguard and his bright, appealing daughter.

But it had been real. Gloriously, terribly real. And now it was gone.

Her old life in California was where she belonged. And she needed to get it back.

THE NEXT MORNING, Sarah rose early, but not as early as she'd risen when she'd been with Sam. She wasn't going to meet him this morning for meditation—or, as it had been for the past few days, a makeout/talking/laughing session in the sand dunes. It hurt—it really hurt that he'd turned his back on her the previous night.

She rose and went through her daily ritual with her cat protectors. Fed them, showered—with Becker overseeing her safety from his tub ledge—dressed and forced herself to eat some fortifying breakfast.

Then, wearing a pair of shorts and a soft T-shirt, she headed down the beach so she could sit on her own, in a different place from where she used to sit with Sam. Her throat felt tight and her eyes raw, but the harder and faster she walked, the more she seemed to forget about her sorrows.

She found the perfect hollow in the dunes about a hundred yards past the spot where she usually hung out with Sam. She climbed up the dune and over a short rope barrier, into a hollow shaped like a small bowl.

It was completely hidden from view. Tall grass protected her so that when she lay on her back, all she saw was cerulean blue sky and bright green grass. The puffy clouds were shaped like tortoises. She closed her eyes and let her mind drift. Nothing hurt anymore. She was rootless in space and time. The muffled sound of the waves breaking lulled her into a dreamy state, except she wasn't dreaming or thinking about anything in particular. It was as if her mind, that constantly racing motor, just turned off for a bit, and it became the most refreshing, loving, calming place she'd ever been. A state of mind more than a physical place.

She woke up sometime later when she sensed a movement in the sand near her feet.

She opened one eye to find a small brown-and-white bird with a black band above his eyes gazing calmly at her. Holding her breath, she hitched herself to one elbow. The bird turned and hopped into a flat section where the vegetation was sparser. Cautiously, she crawled after him.

It turned out the little brown bird was showing her a small nest of white speckled eggs.

Baby birds, she thought. In awe, she watched the nest with him for a while. It was so calm and peaceful in their protective hollow. The sun's rays felt just right—warm, but not too hot. She and the bird and the little nest of eggs were protected from wind and weather and the presence of other people.

Finally, the bird seemed to wink at her, and she took that as her cue to leave.

Sarah got up and stumbled back down the steep bank. Then she hiked back down the beach to her cottage. She knew exactly where she was going and what she was doing next. Her heart was giving her dictates, it seemed, and it was the most perfectly natural thing in the world to follow what they said.

She showered again, dressed again, made a quick check for directions on her phone, then climbed into her rental car and headed up the coast. The scenery was beautiful. She passed stately homes and marinas. The grounds of a sprawling private school that intrigued her enough to pull in and explore it for a bit. And then she continued on her journey, just over the bridge that marked the border with Maine, to a beautiful rocky cliff overlooking the ocean, where she stopped at a large meditation and yoga studio.

Inside the studio's small shop, Sarah bought clothes and a mat, and then set herself up for the next beginner class. She stayed in the back and just listened, following what the instructor said to do. She didn't need to strive or stand out or…be the Sarah nobody was allowed to ever take advantage of.

It felt nice to chill out and stay off her guard. There was an organic eatery next door to the studio where she ate lunch alone and let her mind slip into a state of calm. No plans or worries to upset her. Just focusing on taking care of herself.

Probably what Richard had envisioned for her in the first place, but Sarah wasn't going to think of him or her company or her home in California or her disappointment about Sam, or Cassandra, who'd hurt her.

After lunch, she treated herself to a foot massage and a pedicure. She saw a flyer for a retreat with hiking paths even farther up the coast, so she headed north to explore that.

By the time she got back to Wallis Point, it was dark outside. Somebody—Lucy?—had recently been inside the cottage to fill Becker and Simmonds's food bowls, and the two furry beasts were eating contentedly, side by side.

Without even looking at Sam's house—and it took some serious effort to do that—Sarah managed to change out of her clothes and into her nightgown, and climbed into bed. She slept the most restful sleep she'd had since she'd arrived.

The next day, she did it all over again. Her brown bird—Larry, she called him—seemed delighted to see her in his sand dune. The two of them meditated together, and then she walked down the beach and back home, and drove first to the hiking retreat center she'd briefly explored yesterday. Later, before she headed back to Wallis Point, she decided to take an evening yoga class on the beach while the sun set.

She didn't waste one measure of concern on

Richard Lee. The day would come when she would confront him, but today wasn't that day.

For now, the New England summer was beautiful, and she was happy just enjoying it as it was.

Sarah was on her third morning in the sand dune with Larry the bird, lying on her back staring at the sky, when Sam found her.

The squawking of his lifeguard radio jolted her out of her lovely meditation. Squinting, shielding her eyes from the bright rays of the sun, she lifted her head.

Sam peered at her over the top of the dune, looking startled to see her there. He wore his orange lifeguard shorts and had a dark, haunted look in his eyes. He looked shaken up and disturbed by something.

Surprised that he didn't seem his normal, laid-back self, she sat all the way up.

"WHAT ARE YOU DOING, Sarah?" Sam asked, and his voice sounded raspy, even to him.

The last two days had been hell. He'd had no idea where she was, though he'd thought it best not to make an effort to find her. The differences between them couldn't be bridged until Sarah decided she was ready to face what bothered her.

But now, seeing her like this, alone in the sand dunes…

He dropped his gear bag and sat beside her in the hollow. She seemed calmer, somehow. Like a different person.

"I'm meditating," she explained to him.

"Ah." That explained her air of serenity. She must have found a method that worked for her. "I'm glad."

His radio squawked again. He reached into his gear bag and turned it off.

"What are *you* doing here, Sam?" she asked.

He pointed to a sign. Forbidden Area. Prosecution Upon Violation. "I got a call about someone in the forbidden part of the sand dunes with the nesting piping plovers."

"Oh." She put her hand to her mouth. "I honestly didn't see that."

He nodded. Unfortunately, that was typical of Sarah. She had a history of focusing on her desires to the exclusion of all else. She didn't always notice external details.

He rubbed his eyes.

"The birds are fine with me, Sam," she said meekly. "Just watch them for a minute. You'll see." She held out her hand.

And damned if the little piping plover guy who appeared caught up in her charms—*poor bastard*, Sam thought—didn't wander over and touched his tiny beak to Sarah's fingers.

"I already know you're magnetic," he told her.

"To me and to the piping plover, which is an endangered species, by the way. Neither of us can seem to resist your pull."

"I'm sorry." She tilted her head to him. "I really didn't mean to endanger an already endangered species." She took a breath, and then met his gaze. Her eyes were different, he noticed, or rather the expression in them was. "And I have to apologize to you. I should have told you everything about the contest. I shouldn't have held anything back." She paused, glancing down at her hands, silent for a moment. He gave her the space to finish her thoughts.

She lifted her eyes to him, those long lashes just slaying him. "Honestly, I was scared for you to know because I was scared of having to stay here for the ten weeks. If Lucy had had to drop out, I wouldn't have been able to use the mentorship as an excuse to get back to the office. I know how bad that sounds. But, worse than that, I was worried that the longer I stayed away from work, the more Richard would realize I wasn't important to my own company."

Impossible. She could never not be important.

But as long as they were talking about mistakes… "I should have looked at the contest rules myself," he admitted. "It was all there, on the forms, and I didn't read them closely enough."

He drew a small circle in the sand with the tip of his radio. "Maybe part of me didn't want to know. It's easier not to care that way." He shook his head. "I've tried so hard not to care, but you snuck up on me, Sarah."

She shifted to her knees and put her hand on his. "Is it so hard to care about *me*?"

"On the contrary. It's hard *not* to, and I know, because for two days I've been trying not to think about you." He paused. She was gazing into his eyes, and he couldn't not be honest with her. "Have you considered what I said the other night?"

"You're talking about Cassandra, right?"

He slowly exhaled. So she was willing to address Cassandra. That boded well. He nodded, treading carefully.

She took the letter out of her pocket, the one that Cassandra had written her. He'd last seen it day she'd shown up in Wallis Point. By now it was mangled.

She stared at it, her lips pursed. "I haven't read it yet. Not really. I mean, I skimmed it once to pick out the basics of where she'd left Lucy, but other than that…" She shook her head. "I just find Cassandra so infuriating. She's bad for my mental health."

He was glad that she was admitting it. He nodded, waiting.

Her smile faded. "How is Lucy?" she asked softly.

Obviously, she was thinking about how she'd behaved at Lucy's party.

"Well, she's been spying on you and reporting your activities back to me, if you really want to know. But even she didn't realize you were hanging out with birds, here in the dunes."

Sarah laughed. He loved the way the lines around her eyes crinkled.

"She's afraid that you're mad at her for being friends with Cassandra and for spilling the beans to me," he confessed.

"I'm really not. Please tell her it's okay, that I think she can be friends with whoever she wants. She doesn't need to hide that from me."

"I'm glad to hear you say that." He paused, treading carefully still. "I'm figuring out that Lucy was as invested in Cassandra's trip as Cassandra was. She says she told Cassandra to buy the plane ticket and go to Italy. I'm also figuring out that Lucy has this thing where she wants the women in her life, especially, to have their happy ending."

Sarah blinked. She seemed dumbfounded to hear this.

Sam took her hand. "It makes sense, if you

think about it. Lucy has lived with her mother's disappointments all these years. She's even worried about my brother and his wife, even though we showed her last night that her fears are unfounded."

"Wow." Sarah shook her head. "I didn't realize…"

He remained silent, letting her work through this. He knew it was hard for her. But she was a bigger person than even she knew.

He pulled Cassandra's note from his bag and placed it on the sand beside hers. His was the sealed note Lucy had taped to his door weeks ago and that he'd finally read himself the morning after he and Sarah aired their differences.

"We each got a note from Cassandra," he said. "I already read mine. I made myself read her explanation because I love my daughter, and she wants me to try and understand why she cares so much for your aunt."

"You read it for Lucy…" Sarah murmured, fingering the note.

He nodded. "Reading it doesn't mean I'm disloyal to you, Sarah."

"But you gave up on me," she said in a small voice.

"No, I gave you a choice." And that amazed him. He had given someone he loved a difficult choice, and for his own good.

But she hadn't made her decision yet. The envelope lay in the sand between them. She hadn't rejected it. She hadn't accepted it, either.

He sat cross-legged and leaned closer to her. "I won't leave you. I'll stay while you read it, if you want."

"I warn you, I might get snarky and throw things."

"And you might not." He thought of what was in that note. It just made him feel sad for Cassandra. Yes, she'd made a terrible choice where Sarah was concerned. She'd chosen not to attend Sarah's parents' funeral.

"I guess the only way to know is to read it," Sarah murmured. "Though, afterward, I may rip up the pages and toss them into the ocean. Oh, wait, I can't do that," she said, answering her own thought. "It might hurt the seabirds. And I have a particular fondness for Larry, my piping plover friend."

He grinned at her. "Well, Larry and I are glad you considered that, because paper isn't completely biodegradable. It's better to put the pieces in a trash receptacle, not in the sand or in the ocean."

She actually smiled. "Spoken like a true environmental science teacher."

He chuckled, but she was already pulling Cassandra's letter from the envelope.

He froze, watching her.

Unlike that first day he'd met her, when Natalie had presented her with the note, Sarah took her time reading it. First one page, front and back, and then the second page. When she finished reading, she didn't crumple up the paper and throw it away. Instead, she read it again, more slowly this time. Emotions passed over her face. Irritation. Anger. Sadness. And something else he couldn't put his finger on. But her lips parted and she let out a long breath, staring at the sky as she did.

Wordlessly she passed the pages to him.

He assumed they told roughly the same story that his letter had told. But he read them anyway, to show Sarah that he was on her side.

Dear Sarah,

I know full well, as I write this, that I've made a decision which you will see as very hurtful and personal to you. I've struggled with it, Sarah, because I don't want to hurt you. I never have. To my grave, I will always regret that I wasn't there for you when your parents died. When you most needed me.

Sarah, I tried to talk to you about it, all those years ago when I visited your dormitory at boarding school, but I understand why you didn't wish to see me. You'd been through horrible trauma. That I wasn't there for you was a terrible thing.

But I'd like you to know that I honestly couldn't bear to attend the funeral for Samantha and John. I'd cut myself off from the world, deliberately. I was in my own time of pain and difficulty, though I don't excuse it or claim it could possibly be worse than a young person losing her parents and being left alone in the world. But please, Sarah, know that as soon as I heard you were in foster care, I did rush to find you. I did care for you. I do now. I always will.

When you contacted me about coming to stay in Wallis Point, I cannot tell you how thrilled it made me. Finally, I'd hoped to be privileged to get to know you again. I'm quite proud of the way you've managed to build your life so successfully. Samantha and John would be proud, as well. I comfort myself with that thought. I hope you remember how dearly they loved you.

But Sarah, I was faced with a terrible dilemma. I haven't been blessed in my life with a love or a family all my own. Some might say that is my fault. But the man I loved with all my heart—the great love of my life—didn't feel the same way about me that I felt about him. And I never could let that go. Sarah, we had a child together, and he brought him up as part of his own family. It was a painful decision—a deep, deep regret of mine. When his son—our son—called me to talk about his father, Claudio, I had to go to them. There were many truths that needed to be put into the light. There are many of us who need healing.

Sarah, my wish for you is that you remain happy and strong. I will return for you as soon as I can. Claudio is in a bad state. I cannot tell when I will be back, but my sense is that I will not be gone for long.

I have a neighbor, Sam Logan, whom I'd like you to meet. His daughter, Lucy, is a wonderful girl whom I think you can help very much. Please call me when you receive this letter. Natalie has the number. Lucy can help you with anything you need until I return. She is at the library waiting to meet you. Natalie is also here to help. I hope the cats—Simmonds and Becker— bring a measure of comfort. I've also left a separate note explaining their care. Lucy left a letter for you, too. You were always so good with animals and children.

I've left a box in the front closet with photographs of your mother as a young girl.

I want you to have them. Until I return,
please take care.
Your loving aunt, Cassandra

Sam put down the letter. His letter from Cassandra wasn't so detailed as to her personal issues. Mostly it was about looking out for her niece who was coming to visit from California and encouragement regarding Lucy.

He couldn't be angry with Cassandra. He tried, but he just couldn't any longer. He was biased, though, because Lucy loved her so much.

He folded the letter and passed it back to Sarah. "Are you okay?"

She nodded slowly.

She seemed different, somehow, affected by it, thoughtful, but he didn't know if Cassandra's revelations would help her or not.

Maybe she needed time to assimilate all that had happened.

"Excuse me!" a nasty voice said from behind him.

Sam jumped up. The short man who'd summoned Charlie at his lifeguard chair—and then had harangued Sam when he'd shown up on an ATV—stood at the top of the dune and glared down at Sam and Sarah.

"You're not supposed to be in there!" he insisted, his face red. "It's a violation of state law."

The last thing Sarah needed was another emotional scene. Sam stood and drew himself to his full height. "Sir, you've reported the situation, and now it's in my jurisdiction. Please leave, or I *will* issue a trespassing citation to you." Sam pointed to the rope the man had stepped over.

Fuming, the man stomped off.

He turned back to Sarah. "Sorry about that."

She was looking at him strangely. Lips slightly parted and face upturned.

"It'll be okay," he promised. But even as he spoke to her, he realized he was talking more about the letter than about the rude man.

"Ah, hold on while I make a quick call to Duke." He fished for his phone inside his gear bag and put in the call. Duke picked up on the first ring.

"Yeah, Sam?"

"Just to let you know, and not over the public radio, but a guy is complaining about Sarah and me being in the restricted dune area. We're leaving now. Please handle this for me if it escalates. I'm off duty early today, and I'm going to be clocking out, okay?"

"Yeah, sure. Hey, Sam, how is Sarah? What's going on?"

Sam glanced at her. He'd confided in Duke earlier because he'd been so miserable. "She's good." He smiled at Sarah. "We're both good. I need to go, Duke."

Sam hung up before Duke could ask him any more questions.

Sarah was smiling at him. That had to be a good sign. He hoped.

"Let's say goodbye to your bird, okay?" Sam suggested.

She nodded, standing and brushing sand off her bottom. "Would you like to go swimming with me?"

"You want to go swimming?" he asked in amazement.

"With you."

"Really?"

"I think it will be fun."

He pondered that for a moment. He couldn't remember the last time he'd gone swimming outside of work, just for the fun of it.

"Yes, Sarah, I would." He tossed his phone back in his gear bag and hoisted it to his shoulder.

"Then let's go get changed," she said.

And that's when he knew that she would be all right.

That *they* would be all right.

SARAH FELT PERFECTLY chilled out. Perfectly calm and centered and at peace with the world.

Be Zen, Sam had once told her. Sarah had thought of Larry, and Lucy and Sam before she read her aunt's letter. She hadn't wanted to—she'd resisted it with all her heart—but now that it was over, she was glad that she knew what really happened when her aunt had left. She didn't want to talk about it with anyone just yet—she just knew that she was determined to keep this newfound peace.

And to keep Sam with her—for as long as she could.

She and Sam had put on their bathing suits and were now about fifty yards out in the ocean, riding the swells together. They were beyond the breaking waves, and she couldn't touch bottom with her feet, but she didn't worry because she was with her own personal lifeguard.

He pulled her close to him. Their bodies melded together as they rode over another swell.

"I haven't felt so good—" he murmured into her ear "—in… I don't know."

She put her wet arms around his neck and kissed him. How could she not, after reading Cassandra's words? *She* wasn't alone. The cool water felt soothing against her heated body, and the movement of the waves beneath her made her feel both powerful and blessed. He closed his hands over her bottom, and she settled her legs around his waist as naturally as if she'd always been meant to be there.

They stayed in the water, floating and talking, until it was close to dinnertime.

"I want to stay over at your house tonight," he murmured in her ear. "Would you mind if I asked my brother and his wife to drive up and stay with Lucy? They offered to help whenever I need it, and they're close enough that if they're available, they can be here in an hour. With luck, they can have a sleepover or something." He smiled and moved her wet hair from her eyes. "I'll be discreet as to where I'm going tonight."

"I like that idea," she breathed.

They waded out of the surf and toweled each other off before heading, barefoot, back to their respective homes.

But Lucy met them on the sand before they got there.

"Where have you two been?" she exclaimed. "I've been up and down the beach looking everywhere for you!"

Sarah paused, her heart thumping in her chest. "What's wrong? Are you okay? Are the cats okay?"

"Are you kidding?" Lucy almost shouted. "I'm so great! Guess what, Sarah?" Lucy danced around them in a circle, her iPad clutched to her chest. It was so unlike her, all Sarah could do was stare.

"Lucy, tell us what's going on," Sam chided.

"It's the best thing ever!" Lucy's eyes were shining. "Sarah, I got an email from the Future Tech Scholars committee! They love my app design! They want me to fly out to California and present it to them immediately!" She turned to her father. "Can you believe that? Dad, we have to do it. Please! We have to go now!"

A roaring was sounding in Sarah's ears.

Her phone! She'd had her phone turned off for the past two days.

She bolted for her cottage. When she got inside and turned it on, her fingers trembling, the screen blew up with notifications. She opened the top message. It was from Richard Lee.

Be back at your desk on Monday.

He wanted her back! She was finally recalled from Wallis Point! And right when she'd just decided she never wanted to leave Sam.

But now everything had changed. She had a shot at her dream again.

And Lucy did, too.

CHAPTER FIFTEEN

SAM SAT IN a business-class seat beside his daughter on their flight from Boston to San Francisco. Lucy had arranged for all the necessary permissions from her mother, and now, here they were. He shook his head, still not quite believing what had happened. He'd spent most of the flight attempting to come to terms with the thought of his life changing so suddenly and irretrievably.

He could hear Sarah talking on her phone a few rows ahead of them. She was excited to be going home, that much was obvious. He stood and walked by her aisle seat on the way to the restroom. Sarah was feverishly typing on her computer. So engrossed was she in her work that she didn't even notice Sam. She'd mentioned something to him about how she'd been given access to the company email system and was eagerly catching up on business from her weeks away from the office.

He had doubts about this trip. Everything they'd been building might easily fall apart again.

But when he returned from the restroom, he found that Sarah was sitting in his seat, her head touching Lucy's, immersed in conversation with his daughter. Surprised, he paused, watching the two of them from his vantage point in the aisle.

For the first time, something very interesting struck him. Lucy and Sarah sat in their seats and spoke with the same animated posture. Their hairstyles were identical. Now that Sam looked more closely, he saw that Lucy, like Sarah, wore mascara on her lashes this morning, as well as a pale beige lipstick. Since they'd left Wallis Point together, it was as if Sarah had transformed herself again, maybe back to the person she needed to be to survive and thrive in her California life. What worried him was that Lucy seemed to be mimicking her persona. From the hairstyle to the mascara to the mannerisms. The tilt of her head. The practiced smile.

Sarah noticed him standing there, and she stood quickly. "Oh, Sam!" She smiled at him, seeming so genuinely happy to see him that for a moment he was caught off guard.

The old Sam would have easily replied that Sarah should stay seated, finish her conversation with Lucy and not to worry, that Sam would sit in Sarah's seat.

But he hung back. Because it had just occurred to him that Sarah needed Lucy to behave in a certain way this week in order to help bring back what Sarah had lost and desperately wanted to regain. Sam was torn. He truly wanted Sarah to be happy. But he *needed* Lucy to be happy. And at the moment, the girl was still enough of a cipher to him that he wasn't sure exactly how he could help make that happen.

He should figure that out, and soon, because the journey west was nearly over. Soon they would be meeting with the committee head for the Future Tech Scholars competition. He was also the major investor with Sarah's firm.

A flight attendant tapped Sam on the shoulder. "Sir, if you could please take your seat? We'll be landing shortly."

"Right." Sam stood firm and waited for Sarah to rise.

Sarah squeezed his arm as she moved past him. "It will all work out, Sam," she murmured. "Don't worry."

But when he sat beside his daughter and buckled himself in, he asked, "Lucy, what did Sarah say to you?"

Lucy gazed up at him with her big brown eyes. "She said it's okay to be nervous in my meeting. That you and Sarah are both supporting me, and that I should make any choice I want to, as long as it's the best choice for me, and not to worry about what you and Sarah think."

He stared. "Sarah said *that* to you?"

Lucy nodded. "Yes, Dad." She curled her hair behind her ears, and then looked seriously at him. "I'm also supposed to tell you something, too."

"Oh? What's that?"

"That Mom might be Skyping into the meeting with us tomorrow in Richard's office."

He let that realization sink in. Colleen, face-to-face with him, Lucy, Sarah and the investor-partner Sarah was trying to impress.

Lucy shoved her knapsack back under the seat in front of her as the flight attendants made announcements to prepare for landing. "It will be okay, Dad." Lucy reassured him. "We'll all decide together what to do. Like a family."

"Did Sarah say that, too?"

"Yes, Dad. Sarah sat in your seat just now and said, 'We'll all decide together.' I'm the one who used the word 'family.'"

SARAH FELT LIKE doing a little cheer. Finally, she was back on her home turf!

She led Lucy and Sam through the airport she was so familiar with and out into the cool, moisture-laden San Francisco air. With efficiency born of practice, she guided them through the maze of humanity, cars and awkward wheelie luggage bumping across their path until she found her driver, Paul, wearing his dark livery suit and standing beside his polished black sedan.

"Paul, meet Lucy and Sam," Sarah said as a greeting. "They're my friends from the East Coast. You'll be driving us all to my home this afternoon, please."

Paul blinked, as if surprised by her statement. Sarah remembered that she hadn't spoken much to Paul in her old life, never mind introduced him to the people she was traveling with.

She likely hadn't used such a kind voice with him, either.

But personal power was a tricky thing, something different than she'd originally conceived of. Now that she was part of Lucy and Sam's little family—however temporarily, depending upon Sam's final decision as to where to send Lucy to school—she was going to wield her power with kindness and as a service to them. She felt better that way. Her heart had grown during her weeks in Wallis Point. She ached to include them in her world, but she knew it had to be their decision.

Maybe I'm on my best behavior, she thought.

But it didn't feel that way. It felt like she'd finally settled into her own skin. Something comfortable that she would wear along with her business armor.

While Paul loaded their luggage into the trunk, Sarah opened the rear door and directed Lucy to get inside first and take the far window seat. Sarah climbed in next and sat in the middle—over the bump—which was really a shock to her, because that was the worst seat of all. But she wanted Lucy and Sam to feel comfortable.

I love them both, she realized with a start.

She also realized that it would be horrible for her to have to let them go, should it come to that. It would feel like having a part of her ripped away.

But from Sam, she'd learned not to think about that just yet. *One step at a time*, she told herself.

Sam climbed in beside Sarah and shut the door. They all fumbled to put on their seatbelts, and Paul slowly pulled out into airport traffic.

Sarah felt for Sam's hand and held on to it. She clasped Lucy's in her other hand.

Sam leaned close to her ear. "I appreciate what you said to Lucy back on the airplane."

Sarah nodded. She knew exactly what he was referring to. A small pain pierced her heart. "I'm aware of how difficult and emotional this change might be," she murmured back to Sam.

He applied pressure on her hand, squeezing it. "She used the word family."

"She said that to me, too."

"We'll figure it out. While we were on the plane, I reviewed the entire Future Tech Scholars program on the website. Did you know there are menus and submenus and pages of notes to read? I checked on the history of every past winner. I researched all the judges' bios. Mostly, I researched the Future Tech Scholars campus."

"We should take a ride there tomorrow," Sarah said. "Make sure Lucy is comfortable with the school, just in case she ends up winning the competition."

Lucy turned from staring out the window to look at them. Sarah was acutely aware that she was listening to their conversation.

"What if I don't like the academy?" Lucy asked in a small voice. "Then what?"

Wasn't that the question of the hour, Sarah thought.

"Did you like it when you were a student there, Sarah?" Lucy asked.

Sarah exhaled. A flood of mixed emotions poured over her. Involuntarily, she put a hand to her chest.

But Lucy's situation and hers at that age weren't similar at all. It wouldn't be fair for her to bring up her own experiences as a point of comparison for Lucy.

Sarah made sure to smile carefully at the girl. "We'll take the tour tomorrow. I'm sure the campus has changed greatly in the twenty-plus years since I last saw it."

"That long?" Lucy asked, shocked. "That's ancient history."

"I suppose so." *Ancient history, indeed.*

Perhaps it was time to let go of old feelings that had only served to block Sarah and bring her pain. She was looking forward to living with a new perspective.

"It will be interesting to see what we find."

CHAPTER SIXTEEN

"Wow, Sarah," Lucy said. "You are *rich*!"

They stood in the foyer of Sarah's large, extravagant home. Everything inside looked new, expensive and luxurious.

Sam gazed, stunned, at the high ceilings, the rich fabrics, the crystal and gold lighting.

He placed their luggage on the floor and reminded himself that all of them were just people. He hadn't thought much about Sarah's wealth when they were back in Wallis Point. It shouldn't matter to him that Sarah was obviously better off financially than he was, likely on her way toward fighting for a multimillionaire's crown. And yet, she wasn't acting any differently now than she had yesterday.

His daughter was, however. Sam watched her, growing worried. She hopped from room to room, her eyes dazzled.

"Where would you like me to put our luggage?" Sam asked Sarah quietly.

"Come upstairs," she said, equally quietly. "There are two rooms near mine that I had the housekeeper make up for you. I know we're all tired from the cross-country trip."

"It's early here, still," Lucy exclaimed, gazing at the new phone she'd never let out of her hand since she'd unwrapped it on her birthday. Her laptop was packed in the knapsack she wore on her thin back. "I'm not tired at all. Sarah, can you give me your Wi-Fi code, please?"

"Of course," Sarah replied and smiled secretly at Sam.

Sarah showed him to a guest room with a queen-sized bed, and Lucy received a similar room across the hall.

Sam went inside and flopped on the bed, his head aching. Sarah joined him.

"I know it's different from what you're used to." She kicked off her shoes and climbed up on the bed beside him, stretching out and putting her arms under her head to stare at the ceiling, as he did.

He reached out with his foot and rubbed her bare toes. "We'll figure it out." It had been his refrain for the past twenty-four hours.

She turned her surprised face to his. "You sound hopeful."

"I'm out of my element, it's true. But like Lucy said, we've formed ourselves into a family and we might as well see where it leads us."

Sarah rolled onto her side, studying him. He

noticed she wore the delicate gold chain around her newly tanned neck. The little shark charm had disappeared somewhere in the folds of her dress, while the heart charm rested inside the little hollow just above her breastbone.

He reached out and fingered the charm. Then he rubbed the pads of his fingertips across Sarah's cool, silken skin.

"I've fallen in love with you," he said quietly.

She blinked, pressing her hand to her mouth. A little sob escaped.

"What's the matter?" he asked.

"I can't imagine going back to my life without you guys," she choked out.

He gathered her tighter into his arms. *We'll figure it out*, he was inclined to say again. But, honestly, he didn't see how just yet.

Assuming Colleen agreed—a big assumption—and that Lucy did, indeed, win a scholarship to the school here, how was he going to survive this strange place? There was no beach outside the window, which didn't thrill him, even if being here meant being with Sarah and Lucy.

He'd just been dragged around to so many places as a kid, and he'd finally found the one home that made him happy.

But this decision wasn't only about him. It was about his daughter's opportunity. It was about connecting with her. And it was about Sarah's love for them making it all possible.

He *cared* what happened to them all. None of them were leaving him. He wasn't leaving them. That gave him strength.

He turned to Sarah. "Should we get dinner?"

"My fridge is cleaned out for the summer." She thought for a moment. "I have beer, though." She grinned.

He couldn't help laughing.

Hand in hand, they crept past Lucy's closed door so as not to wake her, and downstairs and into a kitchen that looked like it came straight out of an architectural magazine. "It seems wasted on you," he teased her. "You don't even cook."

"No, but *I* do," Lucy interjected. She was already downstairs, wide awake and still dressed. She skipped over to Sarah's refrigerator. "Look at this, Dad." She placed her hand on the glass, and the interior lit up. "It's so high-tech! I love it!"

Sarah pointed at the glass. "Pass your dad and me two of those beers, please. For you, Lucy, your choice is water or sparkling water."

"And I see vitamin water, too." Lucy opened the fridge and pulled out their selections.

They all sat at Sarah's island, which was four times the size of his and made of white marble, or maybe it was quartz. He hated to say it, but he could get used to living in this house. The region, he wasn't so sure yet. He doubted that California would accept his teaching license—he would probably have to go back to school or take some additional certification tests. He hadn't checked into that yet, but now he could see through to doing so.

Sarah opened his bottle with a fancy gadget and then passed the beer to him.

"This one's from New England," he said, surprised.

"Yes. I've always been partial to my home turf." She lifted her beer to her lips and drank deeply.

"So, you liked living in New England?" he asked.

"Yes," she admitted. "I did."

"Could you ever see yourself in Wallis Point? More permanently, I mean."

She was silent. She wasn't saying yes to him.

She had said her ambition was to start tech company after tech company, he remembered. She likely needed to be here, in Silicon Valley, to do that. And it probably wouldn't be great for her psyche to be so close to Cassandra back in New Hampshire.

And that was when he realized tomorrow's meeting was more important for them as a unit than he'd realized. If Lucy didn't win the contest and get accepted to the genius school, or if Colleen threw in a monkey wrench, then it would be even more difficult for the three of them to stay together.

Ultimately, though, it came down to his and Sarah's choices together. Would they choose as a unit, or would they split up?

CHAPTER SEVENTEEN

THE NEXT MORNING, Sarah sat in the back of Paul's black sedan pressing her hand to her chest. Her skin felt clammy and her head was swimming slightly. She wasn't sure, but it appeared she might be having a minor panic attack.

They were idling at the entrance to her company parking lot. The car door was open—cool air had rushed in—but Sarah couldn't feel it anymore. She just felt sick. Sam and Lucy stood outside on the sidewalk, waiting for her to get out.

Paul waited, too.

Upstairs, the senior staff awaited her. Gregory had texted her twice already this morning.

Paul swiveled in the driver's seat. "Ms. Buckley? Can I get you anything? There are water bottles in the console."

She shook her head, struggling to smile.

Why was she panicking?

Sam climbed back into the sedan, took one look at her and closed the door again. He took her hand in his. Whatever he thought about her clammy palms and shaking fingers, he didn't say.

Instead, he leaned close to her ear. "Do you want to rest your eyes with me?" he murmured.

Despite herself, she choked out a laugh. He was asking her if she wanted to *meditate*. "Oh, what I wouldn't do for Larry, my piping plover, and a swim in the ocean with you."

Sam smiled, the lines around his eyes crinkling. He really wasn't *so* young after all, she decided. He was perfect for her. Just as he was.

He kissed Sarah's cheek. "Relax with me," he murmured.

She rested her head on the leather seatback and thought of eating a peanut butter sandwich with Lucy. Or sitting out on the deck with Simmonds and Becker.

She sat up with a start, but Sam gently eased her back down with a whisper in her ear. "Just forget it all. Be here with me."

Be here with me.

That one, single line gave her so much comfort. She nestled beside Sam, breathing easily in and out with her eyes closed. The warmth of his body gave her hope and increased her strength.

It was a true strength. Not a negative power that punished and pushed back upon people, but a feeling of faith in herself that she could weather any crisis or storm.

Sarah opened her eyes. The clamminess was gone. She no longer shook.

"I'm ready," she said to Sam. "Let's go watch Lucy wow everybody with her presentation."

WHEN SAM WALKED into Sarah's office building, bringing up the rear of their little group (Sarah was in the lead with Lucy protectively sandwiched in the middle), all he could think, with awe, was that Sarah had built this place.

Her ideas, her vision, her company.

As they filed into the elevator, a man and woman joined them and noted Sarah's presence. Sam didn't think he was imagining it, but they seemed to shrink from her, fear in their eyes.

He couldn't help smiling to himself. He remembered that fierce, ball-busting Sarah, too.

This morning, she calmly nodded to the two workers as she pressed the button for the top floor. The executive suites, he supposed.

The man and the woman departed on a lower floor, and then he, Sarah and Lucy were alone on their way to the top.

Sarah seemed to be mentally girding herself. Lucy shifted her knapsack on her shoulders. Inside was her new laptop plus her presentation notes. She carried her phone in the palm of her hand.

"Turn the ringer off," Sam gently reminded her.

"Oh!" Lucy said. "Right!" She deftly flicked a button. His daughter had only possessed the new electronics for a short time, and already she'd taught herself how to use all the features and shortcuts.

The elevator doors opened, and Sam stepped out last, after Sarah and Lucy. A soaring glass ceiling let the sun shine down on them. There were real, growing trees inside the main reception area. He half expected a bird to fly by.

Lucy stopped short. "You *work* here?" she whispered to Sarah.

"Yes. My company doesn't actually own it all, though. We lease the building from a management company."

Nevertheless, Sam was blown away.

"Come on." Sarah led them to a reception desk. "Let's get you signed in. Sam, you'll need to show them your ID."

"Right." He pulled out his wallet. He was a long way from his work turf of standing before a middle school earth science class or patrolling a state beach in an all-terrain vehicle.

"Hello, Donna," Sarah said to the receptionist, who cringed from her as if on reflex. "I'd like to sign in my two guests, please. This is Sam Logan and his daughter, Lucy Logan."

The receptionist swallowed and set about her task, eyes down.

Sarah thanked her then led them down a corridor into a plusher section of the office, away from the glass rooftop.

They stopped at a smaller reception area where a middle-aged man with a closed expression and fastidious dress also checked their credentials.

"It's good to see you, Gregory," Sarah said to him. "Allow me to introduce Lucy Logan and her father, Sam Logan." Sarah turned to them. "Lucy, Sam…this is Gregory. He is Richard Lee's personal assistant, and if you ever need to reach Richard for any reason, Gregory is the man you'll want to contact."

The corners of Gregory's lips turned up. Sam wouldn't exactly call it a smile, but it was probably as close as Gregory got to one. Sam didn't extend his hand for a handshake because Gregory resolutely kept his arms at his sides. Sam noticed a bottle of hand sanitizer on the desk. That might explain it.

"You may go inside to see Mr. Lee," Gregory announced. "He is expecting you."

"Thank you, Gregory." Sarah motioned for Sam and Lucy to follow her.

Mr. Lee's office door was open. Sarah went inside first, then stopped short. Her hand went to her mouth.

Sam nudged past Lucy to get a better look inside, instinctively wanting to protect her—not only her, but Sarah, too.

Colleen faced him. Or rather, a three-foot-tall close-up of Colleen's face, as projected onto a large screen set up in Mr. Lee's office.

"Mom!" Lucy exclaimed. And like the twelve-year-old that she was, she stepped forward and waved at her mother.

Sam's veins turned to ice. Sarah had warned him, and yet he hadn't pictured it like this. He'd thought she would be a disembodied voice on the telephone, as he was used to. He remained at the threshold and pulled Sarah aside.

"Did you know about this huge screen thing?" he asked Sarah, peeved. But then he got a good look at her expression, and even through her fixed "business face," Sam could see she'd been somewhat blindsided, too. Her jaw seemed to tighten as she looked at him.

"I'm sorry, Sam. This wasn't quite what I expected."

"Have *you* ever spoken with Colleen?" he couldn't help asking. He didn't know—maybe Lucy had talked to her while Sarah was in the room.

Sarah shook her head. "No. This will be my first time."

"Then buckle up," he advised. "It's going to be a bumpy ride."

CHAPTER EIGHTEEN

SARAH LED HER little group inside the office and did her best to calmly smile at Richard Lee, sitting like an emperor behind his massive glass desk.

There was protocol to be observed. One did not sit first when it came to Richard. One did not speak first. Sarah used to ignore that protocol, but it had been to her detriment.

Now, she stood and simply gazed serenely at Richard's Zen sand garden with the little rake behind it and waited for whatever other surprise he had to dish out to them.

Beside her, Lucy was still waving at her mother on the big screen. Sarah had tried not to look too closely. She'd nodded and smiled at Colleen and had done her best to quickly assess Lucy's mom without staring at her for too long.

Colleen was pretty. She had blond hair a few shades lighter than Lucy's and the same stunning chocolate-brown eyes. She was made up like an accomplished professional entertainer, and she had a magnetic presence about her. A man stood behind her, as if he'd wandered into the call by accident—and he was quite handsome, too. Maybe the drummer Lucy had mentioned, Sarah thought. Sarah glanced at Sam, and he seemed to be adjusting to his ex's presence. Grim but resolute, Sarah supposed.

She remembered Sam saying that he'd seldom talked with Colleen in person since Lucy was a baby. That was a long time. It must be strange for him, she thought.

"Welcome." Richard Lee rose and pressed his hands lightly together, then gave them each a short, pleasant nod. Sarah knew better than to be fooled by his mild persona, however. Richard had the power to upend all their lives.

But she had power, too. She smiled and nodded back, and placed her hand lightly, protectively, on Lucy's shoulder. In turn, Lucy moved closer to Sarah, as if sheltering under her wing.

"Well, Sarah, it is pleasant to see you, indeed." Richard indicated three chairs set before his massive desk, empty of everything but a single black fountain pen and a stack of thick white paper. Richard was famous for his idiosyncrasies and was universally proclaimed a genius. Sarah, however, wasn't intimidated by his reputation anymore. Instead, she had personal experience in how best to deal with him.

Richard clasped his hands together once more. "I'd like to see Miss Logan's presentation now."

"In a moment," Sarah interjected. "First, I'd like to be introduced to the participants dialed in remotely." She turned to the screen, which was off to their right, beside Lucy's chair. "I haven't met them yet."

"That's my mom," Lucy whispered to her. "And Ringo."

Sam glanced at her. "Ringo?"

"Uh-huh." Lucy nodded. "Ringo. His real name is Randy, but because he's a drummer, my mom says that everybody in the band calls him that."

Okay...

Sam leaned back in his chair. "Hi, Colleen," he said to the screen. His voice sounded tired and on edge. "Thanks for attending the meeting. Lucy has been working hard for this opportunity."

Colleen seemed startled that he'd addressed her directly. "Hello." She leaned forward and squinted into the screen. "My connection isn't that great. I can barely see you."

"How is the cruise ship?" he asked politely.

"It's great. In fact..." Colleen glanced up at Ringo, who smiled into her eyes as if he adored her. "I'm thinking of signing on for another tour."

"Right," Sam said slowly. He glanced at Lucy,

who frankly didn't seem surprised. "You and I will talk about that later. I'm happy to keep Lucy with me for as long as she wants."

"Oh…" Colleen waved her hand. "Our lawyers will deal with that. No need for you and I to discuss it."

"Actually," Sam said, his voice carefully neutral. "I'd rather you and I deal with it." He gave her a smile. "I think we can handle it ourselves."

Colleen squinted into her webcam again. She didn't look as if she was onboard with this at all.

Sam stood, addressing the screen directly. No one was making any pretense of acting as if Richard was in charge of his own meeting anymore. "This is about Lucy's project," Sam said. "Someone needs to stay with her if she wins the scholarship and needs to go to school out here in California."

"Oh," Richard interrupted. "Didn't Ms. Logan tell you?" He gazed at the girl. Lucy squirmed and ducked her head.

"What is it Lucy?" Sam asked, turning to his daughter.

Lucy just looked uncomfortable.

Sam turned to Richard. Sarah saw a vein jumping in Sam's neck, indicating that he was angry but keeping it in check. "What's going on here?"

Richard steepled his hands and nodded to

Lucy. "I reached out to the parental email address included with the application."

"*I* emailed with Richard," Lucy said contritely.

"When?" Sam asked her.

"The day before I told you I was accepted into the competition." She squeezed her fingers together. "Richard emailed me asking me for Mom's phone number…" Here, Lucy glanced guiltily at Colleen. "And since she's not available all the time, I gave him mine, instead."

"I knew you shouldn't have given her a phone," Colleen sniped at Sam. "I didn't tell you you could do that, you know."

Sam, to his credit, didn't take the bait. He gazed steadily at Lucy. "And what happened after that?"

"Well, Richard and I talked. He asked me all about my app, and I told him." She looked helplessly at Sarah. "I kept working on it like you said. And I'm glad I did, because he wants to see what I've done!"

Sam stared Richard down. He stood and leaned over the table. "Why did you drag her into all of this? She's a twelve-year-old girl. You have no right to go around us. We're her parents."

"Agreed." Richard tilted his head to the side. "But I think you're going to like what I have to tell you. Yes, I think you're going to like it very much, indeed."

Lucy gasped and put her hand over her mouth. She bounced in her chair.

"Lucy, please show me your app," Richard instructed.

Lucy leaped up and set up her laptop on the edge of Richard's glass desk. "It's not finished, of course," she said quickly to him. "But this is what I have so far." She gazed into each of their faces, and then turned to the screen. "Mom, can you see my computer?"

"When did you get a computer?" Colleen asked. Sarah noticed that Ringo had left. Colleen glanced at her watch. "Never mind. We need to make this quicker, okay? I'm about to lose my connection."

"Okay." Lucy nodded. "Really quick, this is my app and—"

But Richard took the laptop from Lucy and turned it so that he could clearly see the screen. Lucy, bless her, walked around his desk and leaned over his shoulder, explaining to him what she'd done, as if he was simply a kindly grandfather rather than a master of the universe.

Or a master of Sarah's universe, at least.

Sam leaned close to Sarah's ear. "What's going on? Should I be ticked off? Because I am. This guy is such a jack—"

"I know," she interrupted him, whispering, before he said something that would get them all thrown out of Richard's office. "But he's an important one. Let's give it one more minute before we shut everything down, okay?"

Sarah had a funny suspicion. The way Richard was behaving with Lucy wasn't at all like the Richard Lee she knew. Something was different about him. Something she couldn't put her finger on.

Finally, Richard had seen enough of Lucy's app. He nodded at Lucy, smiled, and then shook her hand. "Well done," he told her. "It's always a pleasure to meet the next generation of talent, and you are a talent, Lucy Logan."

Lucy closed her laptop and stashed it back inside her knapsack. She seemed to be holding her breath. And Sarah was gobsmacked. She'd known Richard for years now—she'd worked closely with him for months. And yet, she didn't have the mental connection with him that Lucy seemed to. The two generally seemed to be on the same wavelength.

Richard turned to Sarah. "Thank you for bringing Miss Logan to my attention. As you know, it's part of my personal mission statement to sponsor worthy young candidates."

"Yes," Sarah said. "You've agreed to sponsor

Lucy in the Future Tech Scholars competition. We know that already."

"No." Still smiling, Richard shook his head. "Since I spoke with you last, Sarah, I've had a realignment of my personal mission and values."

Oh, no, she thought.

"What's he talking about?" Sam muttered.

"You went on a retreat, Richard," Sarah remembered. "You left your electronics at home and you spent weeks in meditation."

"I did." Richard nodded. "Much as you did, Sarah. And like you, I've had a realignment."

Sarah held her breath. This could mean anything. With a genius like Richard, no one ever knew *what* he was going to say or do.

"I no longer believe in competition," Richard announced.

She nearly choked out a laugh, but she restrained herself. *The capitalist no longer believes in competition?*

"Ah," was all she said.

"Instead, I'm offering Miss Logan and her family…" Here, Richard turned to Sam. The screen overhead was dark. Evidently, Colleen's connection had cut out. She was sailing the vast Alaskan seas again, it seemed.

"I'm offering Lucy and her family my full financial support for Lucy's education at the Future Tech Scholars Academy campus, here in San Jose."

There was a shocked silence all around.

"So, Lucy doesn't have to compete in the Future Tech Scholars competition to win the scholarship or a place in the class?" Sarah clarified.

Richard shook his head and smiled. "No. And since I am on the board of directors of Future Tech Scholars Academy, her place in the fall class has already been secured."

"What are your conditions?" Sam asked him. Sam was right; there had to be strings attached. This was *Richard* they were speaking to.

Richard lifted his hands. "None." His expression was open and beatific.

Sam gazed at Sarah as if to say, *what do you think of this?*

Sarah wasn't convinced it was legitimate, either. She shrugged at Sam.

"Perhaps Lucy would like to tour the campus," Richard suggested.

"Oh, I would!" Lucy said. And then she jumped up and down like a little kid. "This just makes me want to happy dance! I can't believe I *won*!" she said.

Richard winced at the word *won*. But Sarah understood what she was saying.

"She's achieved her goal," she explained to Richard.

"I'm a girl of substance," Lucy said. "Sarah's taught me to work hard and not let discouragement defeat me." She gazed at Richard. "So I *did* win. I didn't beat other people, I just defeated the setbacks in front of me."

"Spoken like a wise young lady," Richard praised her. And Sarah nearly laughed with relief. Who could have predicted Richard's whims? But Lucy would get all the wonderful opportunities she deserved. Sarah was sure of it.

STILL IN SHOCK over what had just transpired, Sam sat in Sarah's office just down the hall from Richard's suite.

Sarah's assistant brought Sam a cup of mint tea for calm energy. According to Gregory, Richard had taken up a new healthy habit, and as such had removed the coffeemaker from the shared wing of their two executive offices. Sarah had accepted the minor change with a beatific smile and nary a comment. Now, she directed her full attention to her telephone conversation, a conference call including herself, Lucy and a woman whose name Sam didn't catch, arranging the details for the tour of this…genius kids' school, was all Sam's stunned mind could seem to grasp of the situation.

Sam looked at the pale green liquid sloshing around in the coffee mug and pushed it aside.

His stomach felt like he was stuck in a rip current that was sucking him out to sea, and there wasn't anything he could do to stop it.

Was he losing Lucy? He didn't understand how any of this could have happened. He found that he couldn't make himself care about the money he would save by having Lucy's schooling funded by this eccentric billionaire.

Only *Lucy* was important to him.

He gazed over at them. Sarah had hung up the phone and put her hand on Lucy's shoulder. They were in a close tête-à-tête. Sarah seemed to be offering her gentle counsel.

"Sam?" Sarah beckoned him over. "I set up the tour for tomorrow morning. Is there anything else you think I should do? Questions we need to get answered?"

We. She'd said *we.* Sarah still considered them a team, and that gave him a better feeling. He joined her and Lucy in front of the computer.

"Can't think of anything at the moment." He studied Lucy. She still seemed so jazzed and happy. "What did your mom say when you called her back just now?"

"She said it's okay that I go. But she said you'd have to stay with me."

He put his hands on her shoulders. "I have to ask you, Luce. Were you bored in your old school? When you first came to Wallis Point this summer, you told me your teacher had called your mother at home the night before. Was she calling because of anything like this? Do you feel unchallenged?"

"Well…sort of. I just don't fit in there." Lucy shook her hair over her shoulders. "Okay, yeah, I'm bored," she admitted. "But I'm always bored. I just thought that's how school was supposed to be."

"It's not. It would be great if you felt excited to go to school every morning."

"Well, I don't. Maybe this place will be better for me…" Lucy actually seemed hopeful.

He sat and gazed out the window, just thinking. Sarah leaned back in her chair, but waited to speak until Lucy left to go to the bathroom.

"Sam, are you *really* okay with this?" she asked.

"Bottom line, I'm gonna do what's best for Lucy."

Sarah nodded curtly. "That's good."

"And, yes, I also want to commit to you," he said, "in case that isn't totally apparent."

She laughed, but it was with joy and not tension. And then she got up from her chair the way Lucy had done, making little hops and boogying around the room.

If he wasn't mistaken, his formerly uptight business executive love was happy dancing her way around her office. She looked so cute, he couldn't help joining her.

"SARAH! SAM! WAKE UP!" Lucy called from outside their locked bedroom door.

Sam groaned and squinted at the bedside clock. Last night, wide awake from lingering nerves and tension over the obvious upcoming move, he'd quietly stolen across the hall to Sarah's room and gotten into her bed, where unfortunately, he still lay beside her. He'd meant to get up earlier and go back to his guest room, but it seemed Lucy had beat them to it.

"We have plenty of time," he grumbled to Sarah. "I don't know why she's waking us up so early."

"I think that's just Lucy's way of letting us know that she knows we're together," Sarah remarked. "Lucy!" she called. "Chill out! Make yourself breakfast in the kitchen if you want. I ordered grocery service, so baked goods are on the counter, and there are eggs, yogurt and milk in the refrigerator."

Sarah fell back to the pillow, and Sam chuckled, brushing her hair from her face.

"I love this," she said. She stretched again and made a little noise of contentment. "I could wake up this way every day."

"And you will." He'd never known how much he could enjoy it, either.

"Want some coffee?" He stood, stretching in the dawn light. Sarah propped herself up on her elbow and gazed appreciatively at him. He had yet to put his clothes back on.

"Coffee would be nice," she remarked.

"I'll bring up two mugs." He looked around for his pajama bottoms. "Do you think this genius school will have coffee machines? Everyone seems so healthy out here."

"I'm not a fan of mint tea, myself." Sarah shuddered. "I'm sorry about that. It looked like you were drinking grass yesterday, Sam."

"I admit, I was longing for my own familiar coffeemaker at home."

She gazed at him curiously. "That reminds me. I was wondering...what are you going to do with your beach house?"

"Keep it. Why?"

She shrugged. "Because unless Colleen changes her mind, it looks like we'll be out here on the West Coast."

"Yes," he agreed, still not sure he had come to terms with everything yet. "But the house in Wallis Point will make a good vacation home for us. You have to admit that."

She smiled at him. "You're right. It'll be fantastic for us to vacation every year in your old lifeguard haunt."

He felt a sting of sadness at that thought, he couldn't lie to himself. But he quickly brushed it off. For Lucy, he was doing the right thing, he felt it in his bones. In time, he would be used to California. He hoped. Wallis Point was his true home. He was trying not to feel devastated.

He coped by helping Lucy get ready. An hour later, they were all showered and ready to go tour the genius school.

Lucy brought her knapsack and her phone with her, and she met Paul at the curb. When Paul opened the sedan door for her, she said, "I brought you a scone. They're really good. I didn't make them myself, but Sarah's delivery service is top-notch. I highly recommend them."

Paul took the scone graciously and nodded to Sam. "You have a great daughter," he remarked.

"Yes," Sam said. "I do."

But later in the morning, he didn't understand how it could have gone so wrong, so fast.

CHAPTER NINETEEN

THE CAMPUS WAS close to what Sarah remembered, only bigger. Much bigger.

What had been a tightknit, provincial community for Sarah was now a great, teeming metropolis of brilliant kids from all over the world, ages twelve through eighteen.

Sarah had won her scholarship at thirteen. Lucy was a year younger than Sarah had been, and maybe that, coupled with the school's large size, made the critical difference. Because within moments of Paul dropping them off at the curb near the admissions office, Lucy's face fell.

"What's the matter?" Sarah heard Sam ask her.

"I don't know," Lucy whispered back. "I studied the website at home, but I didn't know the school would be so...so..."

Overwhelming, Sarah silently answered for her.

Inside the main building, Sarah steered the girl away from the tour group they'd been assigned to, and found a bench for her to rest on near one of the computer labs. Sam joined them, concerned, but Lucy waved him off. "I'm okay," she said with a false smile.

She wasn't. The vibes Sarah was getting from the girl told her that Lucy might break into tears at any moment.

Sarah's plan for the perfect life was falling apart. If Lucy didn't want to live on the West Coast, then Sam certainly wouldn't, either.

Sarah got up and paced, not sure what she should do.

"Lucy and I will take the first part of the tour," Sam said quietly. "There's a break in thirty minutes, and we'll reassess then. Do you want to join us, Sarah?"

"I'll catch up with you at the break."

"Okay. Sounds good."

Sarah watched as Lucy and Sam headed over to join the small group waiting by the admissions office. Sam lightly kept his hand on Lucy's shoulder. A thread of anxiety wound through Sarah's heart.

Sarah used the half hour alone to sit on the bench, close her eyes and slow her breathing. She relaxed her shoulder muscles and rested her brain.

In her mind, she was back on their sand dune again. She and Sam and their summer by the sea. The tide crashed and rolled in the distance, and the salty breeze cleared out her cobwebs. Her brain was rested but, oh, so clear...

She "woke" again when the wheels of a cart rattled past on the corridor floor. Checking the time, Sarah gathered her purse and rose to walk the familiar route to the school cafeteria, where the second stage of the tour had been scheduled to begin.

Inside the cavernous room smelling of fresh-baked bread, Lucy and Sam sat alone in a far corner. Lucy's head was bowed. Her ragged teddy bear was in her arms—she must have carried it in her knapsack. Sam was speaking to her intently, close to her ear.

Sarah swallowed. An important part of her told her to join them, because she so longed to be part of their little family. Both Sam and Lucy would welcome her. All she had to do was walk over. All she had to do was show up, and they would accept her...

It was why she'd gone East to begin with. That was the truth that resonated inside her. Sarah had wanted Cassandra to accept her, her only family. But nothing had turned out the way Sarah expected. She'd found a new family, instead. A man and his daughter who'd made room for her in their hearts.

Knowing in her bones who she was and what she wanted, Sarah strode over to them without hesitation. Her heels clicked on the linoleum floor, and Sam lifted his head. His eyes brightened and he instinctively touched her hip when she came alongside him. "Are you feeling better?"

"Yes. I took a few moments just to breathe. It helped immensely."

"That's great." He pulled over a chair.

"And how are you?" she asked Lucy, seating herself beside him so they formed a tight circle.

"I'm just not sure. I'm really sorry." A tear rolled down Lucy's cheek. She hugged her bear harder.

"I suggested she give it a chance, take a bit more of the tour, but Lucy is adamant. She doesn't want to go to school here," Sam said quietly. "I'm telling her that you and I can help her find her another school that will be a better fit for now, and that maybe in a year or two, she can visit this place again and see if she feels any differently about it."

"That sounds like a wise plan. What do you think, Lucy?"

The girl nodded, her gaze cast downward.

Sam appealed to Sarah. "You must know some other, smaller schools nearby that we can look at?"

Her heart beat like a drum. "In California? You still want the three of us to stay in California?"

Sam seemed surprised. "I told you, we stay together." He took Sarah's hands. "There's no splitting up. We make something work for all of us, or it's a no-go."

Sarah felt boneless with relief. "*Really*?" she squeaked.

"Yes." Sam eyed her. "Why are you so surprised?"

The corners of Sarah's eyes prickled with feeling. "Because I just... I never thought..."

Sam chuckled. "You know what I think, Luce? I think I really need to take Sarah engagement-ring shopping because that's the best way I can think of to get this through her head."

He leaned over and murmured in her ear. "In case I didn't tell you, you're the one person I most want to see, along with Lucy, when I walk into a room. You're the person I most want to talk to at the end of the day. No one, *no one*, makes my day better than you do."

Sarah couldn't speak. Beside her, Lucy had both hands over her mouth and was bouncing in her seat.

"Are you happy about that?" Sarah had to ask her.

"Oh, yes!"

"We stay together," Sam said. "If you're here, Sarah, then I'm here. There's nothing you can do to make me leave. And besides..." He grinned.

"Maybe I can convince you to take your business remotely in the summers, and we can live together on Wallis Point beach."

The tears were rolling down Sarah's cheeks. And the more she lost her composure, the more Lucy did, too.

"Hey," Sam said. "Are my suggestions really that bad that you both have to cry? I don't think so."

He was the best guy *ever*. That was the problem. Sarah couldn't resist him.

"I know of a school for Lucy," Sarah said, wiping her eyes, thinking back to the academy in New Hampshire she'd impulsively stopped by earlier in the week. "It's small and pretty, and it overlooks the ocean. But what Lucy might like most is that it specializes in smaller, more inquisitive classes."

Both Sam and Lucy were gazing at her with interest.

"There are computer coding classes, yes," she continued, "but there are other courses available, too, so it's not so intense and focused on tech. Lucy could read literature and follow her other interests. I know, because I saw this school."

"I'd like that." Her cheeks suddenly red, Lucy tucked the teddy bear back into her knapsack.

"Okay," Sam said, nodding as well. "Why

don't we go ahead and schedule a tour of this place? How far away from your house is it?"

"Three thousand miles."

He looked confused. "What are you talking about, Sarah?"

"It's on the coast road from Wallis Point to Maine. I passed it during those two days we weren't speaking. Those two days when I was meditating."

"No." Sam shook his head. "If we do that, then we'll be separated. And we all know you can't run your company remotely for the long-term. For the summer, yes. If you leave California all year, then you would, in effect, be giving it up."

"Yes," she said calmly. "I understand the sacrifice."

"But that's too important. Your company makes you happy."

It had. But Sam and Lucy made her happier. "I'll give it up if that's what it takes to give Lucy what she needs."

They both stared at her, astonished. Sam, in particular. He knew what she was sacrificing.

"Your *company*," he said in a low voice. It was Sarah's baby. He knew this.

Really, it would be okay. She had woken up from her meditation realizing that wherever she lived, she could handle it. Whether she stayed here with her company, or was in Wallis Point growing a new company in one of the tech incubators near Boston or on the coast nearby, then she had the strength inside her to bloom wherever she was planted.

"Do you remember that vision I had, Sam?" she suddenly remembered, feeling even stronger now. Feeling more certain that what she was doing was *right*. "I think it's meant to be. It's time for me to start a new business—this one on the East Coast. Something completely different."

His lips parted. He obviously remembered the vision he'd guided her through that day in the sand. He knew that what she was giving up, and what she would replace it with, came from her heart.

"I love you, Sam," she said. "And I'm a woman of substance, so you can believe me when I tell you that I know exactly what I want."

EPILOGUE

One year later
Wallis Point Beach

SHE'D PLANNED THE perfect wedding.

Sarah stood on Sam's deck at dusk. The breeze drifted in from the ocean and lifted the edges of her white lace wedding dress. The scent of white roses and daisies from her bridal bouquet made her feel especially beautiful. Beside her, Lucy, her attendant, watched over the gathering crowd on the beach, most of them settling into white folding chairs on either side of a central aisle also decorated with white roses and daisies.

"It's almost time, Sarah," Lucy said.

"In a moment," she murmured. She enjoyed watching Sam, even from afar. He wore a smile that hadn't left his handsome face for weeks and weeks. Tall and athletic, dressed in a black tux, he stood above the crowd as he waited for her with the reverend. Duke stood beside him, serving as best man.

"We're all getting a happy ending," Lucy said dreamily.

Sarah smiled at the girl beside her. "Yes, we really are." Lucy was happy in her new school. She'd just finished her first year—and launched her first app. Richard Lee, surprisingly, had been mentoring Lucy even from afar. Sarah's own startup was giving her personal satisfaction, even if sometimes she still spent too many hours absorbed in the intricacies of getting it off the ground. The thrill of starting over was something she was particularly enjoying, and Sam got a kick out of helping her in the business wherever he could.

Sam...her almost husband.

She smiled dreamily to herself as Lucy checked Sarah's sprayed-into-place hairstyle one more time.

"We're all set. And I think everybody is here now," Lucy remarked.

Sarah gazed out over the seating. Sam's brother, Michael, and his family sat beside Sam's parents, who Sam was making more of an effort to patch things up with these days. His colleagues and friends were interspersed in the rows behind them.

As for Sarah's people...there weren't as many of them. Sarah frowned, the one pang of sadness that still pierced her, even on her wedding day. She and Cassandra were still working through old wounds.

Colleen, too, wasn't present—she'd signed on for another season of Alaskan cruise ship gigs, and was quite happy with both Ringo and her job. She visited Lucy between sailings. And last winter, over Christmas, Colleen and Sam had hammered out a shared custody agreement. Lucy was pleased. She was especially happy that her parents' relationship was much improved.

"I have Sam," Sarah murmured to herself. "And Lucy. I'm quite lucky, and I know it."

"What's that?" Lucy asked, fussing with the train on Sarah's dress again.

"Nothing." She smiled at the girl. "I'm ready. Although I'm still one minute early."

"Wait!" Lucy straightened. "Look! It's Natalie's family. And Cassandra is with them!"

The group of five had evidently just parked and were now hurrying down the sandy lane between the two homes. Natalie looked pretty in a pale-blue dress, and her handsome navy-recruiter husband hustled along with their toddler, James, on his shoulders.

Lucy waved to their daughter, Hannah, who

was seven. Lucy had done a bit of babysitting for the family, and they'd all grown quite close.

Natalie stepped over to the edge of the porch and waved in greeting. "Sarah, you look beautiful!"

"Thank you. And thank you for coming." She waved to Cassandra, who waved gamely back. She and Casandra might never have a very close relationship, but they were finding their way to at least being friendlier to each other.

Sarah's longing for a family had been fulfilled. Her new personal confidence was enhanced by how secure she felt in the family she was creating with Sam and Lucy.

As Cassandra came closer, she reached over to clasp Sarah's hand. "You look beautiful, Sarah." Then she smiled and patted Lucy's hand. "But we should all get going!"

With a lump in her throat, Sarah lingered for one last moment, gazing out over her new family and friends.

"Now?" asked Lucy, glancing at her phone. Then she turned the ringer off and tucked it carefully inside her rose-colored bridesmaid's purse.

"Now," Sarah said, happiness filling her heart, as she focused down the beach on Sam, who had lifted up his hand and was waving to her.

"He's calling us," she said to Lucy, who took Sarah's hand. "I think it's time we go get married."

"So do I."

* * * * *

We hope you enjoyed this story from
Harlequin® Superromance.

Harlequin® Superromance is coming to an end soon,
but heartfelt tales of family, friendship, community
and love are around the corner with
Harlequin® Special Edition
and **Harlequin® Heartwarming**!

Romance is for life, and these stories show that
every chapter in a relationship has its challenges
and delights and that love can be
renewed with each turn of the page!

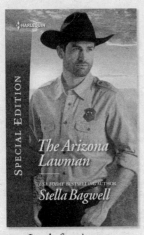

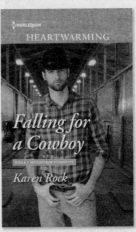

Look for six new
romances every month!

Look for four new
romances every month!

Get 2 Free Books,
Plus 2 Free Gifts -
just for trying the Reader Service!

Get 2 Free Books,
Plus 2 Free Gifts—
just for trying the Reader Service!

READERSERVICE.COM

Manage your account online!

- Review your order history
- Manage your payments
- Update your address

> ### We've designed the Reader Service website just for you.

Enjoy all the features!

- Discover new series available to you, and read excerpts from any series.
- Respond to mailings and special monthly offers.
- Browse the Bonus Bucks catalog and online-only exculsives.
- Share your feedback.

Visit us at:
ReaderService.com